# THE
# *LAST*
# *ANIMAL*

# THE
# LAST
# ANIMAL

{ STORIES }

ABBY GENI

COUNTERPOINT • BERKELEY

Library of Congress Cataloging-in-Publication Data

Geni, Abby.
[Short stories. Selections]
The last animal : stories / Abby Geni.
pages cm
"Distributed by Publishers Group West"--T.p. verso.
ISBN 978-1-61902-182-2
I. Title.

PS3607.E545L37 2013
813'.6--dc23

2013014415

ISBN 978-1-61902-182-2

Cover design by Tim Green, Faceout Studios
Interior design by Elyse Strongin, Neuwirth & Associates, Inc.

Counterpoint Press
1919 Fifth Street
Berkeley, CA 94710
www.counterpointpress.com

Printed in the United States of America
Distributed by Publishers Group West

10  9  8  7  6  5  4  3  2

*For Milo*

# CONTENTS

# TERROR BIRDS

JACK: My mother used to tell me that I was a changeling, born out of an ostrich egg. We lived then on an ostrich farm, so it was not as strange as it sounds. At the age of nine, I went through a monster phase, in which Mom indulged me. She and I would drive to the library and come home with books of real-life horrors, which she would read to me before bed, as though to guarantee I would not fall asleep until dawn. I loved them all: giant squids, alligators, and woolly mammoths, now extinct. But none could touch the majesty and strangeness of the beasts I was accustomed to.

There were nearly a hundred ostriches on our farm. The pens were arranged in a grid, bordered by strips of dusty road, and the birds stalked proudly beside the fences, booming their raucous shouts. They grew to be eight feet high. The males were black and white, the females gunmetal gray. Once I saw my mother climb on the back of a hen and—screaming with laughter—race from one end of the paddock to the other, her hands around the bird's strong neck. It was barely a stretch to imagine that I, like a dewy chick, had been found in one of those enormous eggs. My mother told me that she had tapped open the shell with a hammer and found me curled inside, blinking at the light.

⸎

SANDY: None of us really liked Arizona, out in the scrub and cacti. The heat kept Jack awake, damp in his bed, and he came to breakfast with shadows printed under his eyes. My husband, Kenneth—a young man then, no white whiskers, no paunch—worked as an architect. He had always dreamed of building the perfect Montessori school, complete with gyms, an auditorium for music and dance, and a working organic farm for the middle school students to maintain. However, in our small town, out on the fringes of Phoenix, there were no Montessori schools, and Kenneth was given his choice of office buildings, strip malls, or unemployment. I can still see him there, bent over his desk late into the night, sketching out trickier ways to hide the mall exits so that the shoppers would have to traipse back and forth past enticing store windows, searching in vain for a way out.

I spent my days tormented by ostriches. Kenneth once said to me, "So they're birds that can't sing, fly, or build nests?" They nipped my arms and legs. There was the day one of the cocks shattered a farm worker's arm with one hot blow of his beak. They scratched up their necks trying to break through the fences. When the birds were bored, they would eat the feathers right off each other's backs. Their bodies were made to run, as fast as horses. In the wild, zebras and gazelles treat the ostriches as lookouts, and when the birds flee, everyone else does too, even if no enemy has been sighted. My ostriches raced each other from one side of the paddock to the other. They shook the dust from their feathers a hundred times a day.

∾

JACK: At the age of nine, I ran away from the farm. I had my reasons, none of which had anything to do with the place itself; the ostrich farm was paradise to me, particularly on my long summer vacations, when there was nothing to do but feed the birds and chase the baby chicks.

It was June when I made my plan. I waited until the early morning, when my mother let the alarm go off four or five times in sequence, slamming the snooze button over and over and cursing to herself. My father had already left for work. I fished out my red backpack and stuffed it with water bottles, comic books, granola bars, and a compass (which would do me no good, as I had no mental image of the map of my local area—but in my adventure books, people always brought compasses along, and I felt obligated to follow tradition). I thought all this would sustain me. I thought I knew about the desert, since I had lived there all my life, but naturally there is a world of difference between spending half the morning outside—then retiring into the house for a cool glass of water, a snack, and a quick nap in the gloom of the couch—and walking through the Arizona wilderness alone. By late morning I was staggering along, half blind, parched beyond reckoning. By noon I had entered the realm of the walking dead. My throat was a grainy cavern. Every joint creaked. But it did not occur to me to go back. To be frank, very little occurred to me then. I had reached the stage where I would walk until I died.

I remember every moment of my two-day jaunt in the desert with grim clarity, regardless of the intervening years. I definitely wished to be dead, though I didn't have the language to know that death was what I was yearning for; I knew only that I wanted to become part of the dunes. I wanted to stop being a fleshy aberration in a universe that, except for me, was comprised of heat, air, and sand. But there was nothing else for it. I made my way in baby steps, inch by inch, head bowed, arms barely moving. It took forever to get anywhere, but it cost me almost nothing to move at that pace. Eventually the sun did begin to sink, but I didn't really believe it. It seemed as though I had never done anything but walk in the desert, with the sun beating down on me, until it wasn't clear if I was crossing over sand or the surface of the sun itself. At some point darkness fell, and the first tingling coolness wafted through the air. I glanced up and saw the sky netted with stars.

Of course I had no clothes to protect me from the desert's chill. I had not planned for that either. The cold felt good at first, but eventually I was shivering, and finally I buried myself in sand to keep warm. I did sleep a little—it was more like dropping in and out of consciousness—but the pain in my body was enough to wake me every time. I remember that the stars were intensely bright. The sky was painted with milky constellations. I remember a fat lizard crawling right over my belly. I remember that something howled, a long, sweet cry that hung in the air like mist.

But mostly I remember the pain. Over the next few hours, once the sun rose and I began to walk again, the pain never ceased. In the morning the sun pushed me along, blazing on my back, and at noon it hung over my head, mocking me. Then it began to sink west, dragging me after it as though it had me by the throat.

∾

SANDY: I was the one who found him, miles from the farm, on a dirt road that angled off the highway. I rounded the bend in the old pickup truck (Big Orange—Jack always liked to name inanimate objects) and saw him shimmering like a mirage against a hillside, stumbling along in a resigned sort of way. I swerved off the road, sobbing, and stumbled out of the pickup. I tackled him to the ground.

My son was covered head to foot in grime. His eyes were bloodshot, his mouth chapped to splitting, his left side bruised from a nasty fall when the parched shoulder of the highway had crumbled and sent him into a ditch. The sun had broiled his skin and blurred his features. If not for the tufts of dark hair, his gender—his very species—would have been all but indeterminate; he could have been a miniature golem or a monkey escaped from the zoo. He hit me weakly with both fists and then collapsed against my chest. In the delirium of heatstroke, he muttered about ice cubes and rain.

On my way to the hospital, I dialed Kenneth on the cell phone I had borrowed from one of the farm workers. I wept for a full minute before I could get out the words. Jack rolled in the passenger's seat and kicked the car door. As I drove, I checked him again and again with my hand—his forehead, the side of his cheek, his sweating palms—to prove to myself that he was there. He had been missing for two days. The police had found his backpack that morning, dropped carelessly beside a boulder, and everything since had been one long dark tunnel of fear.

A young social worker met us at the hospital. Until I saw Jack in a white gown, the sheet up around his waist—until I saw in the doctor's face that there was no cause for concern—I could not gather my wits enough to answer anyone's questions. The nurses put an IV in his arm, a moist towel on his forehead, and a balm on his sunburned skin, even his chest and back, which had burned right through his T-shirt. I sat beside him in the hospital room, looking up into the face of the social worker, and whispered my answers. She was kind, for which I was thankful.

I explained that there had been no quarrel, no change, no abuse. I had simply woken up and found Jack's bed empty. It took me a few hours to be sure there was a problem; he often rose before me and was a great favorite among the farm workers, so at first I had assumed he was out on the grounds somewhere. I made breakfast, which usually brought him home on his own. When he did not come, I searched the hatchery and the pens, shouting for him, annoyed at his forgetfulness. A swelling wave of maternal anxiety began to rise, cresting into a blazing peak, and suddenly breaking, tipping over—at which point I sounded the alarm. Since Jack had no earthly reason to run away, I assumed he had been taken. We called the police, and I, unable to sit still, climbed into Big Orange and went out to scour the countryside.

In the hospital bed, Jack moved in and out of sleep. Presently the social worker beckoned Kenneth and me out into the hallway. Amid the chaos of that day, her figure stands out in my mind: a tiny woman, saucer-eyed, with pale, flyaway hair. In a mild voice she explained that Jack seemed a bit "shut down." He had point-blank refused to discuss his reasons for fleeing the farm. She suggested that we try family therapy—at which point Kenneth lost his temper and stormed off down the hall.

∾

JACK: I did think about telling her. Running away had broken my spirit, and I was ready to tell someone. But I could not bear it to be my mother, with her lovely, anxious face, permanently lined by the sun. I would not dream of telling my father; I could barely meet his eye and shuddered away from his gentle touch. The social worker, however, seemed sympathetic and benign. She had asked me so sweetly, as though she really cared about the answer, as though we had been friends for a long time. You could tell she had done this sort of thing before, wheedling awful information out of children in hospital beds. I almost believed her; I felt that I *did* know her quite well, that she would fix the situation. And yet I did not give in. I pretended to myself that I was a soldier on a dangerous mission. Even then, I understood the power of the secret I was carrying. It was too big for me to cope with, but I knew that once it left me it would do horrible damage. My ability to keep the words in my mouth was all that was holding things together.

For two weeks I had been burdened by this weight. Children are supposed to sleep soundly, and my mother definitely did. (It took her half an hour each morning just to drag herself out of bed, and it was usually another hour after that before she could be civil, glowering over her coffee cup at the offensive sunlight.) That was certainly what my father had counted on. But one night I had woken up during the small hours. The full moon shone through a crack in my curtains. My mind was filled with the monsters Mom had been reading to me about—anacondas and vultures and I don't know what else. I thought I might just get up and visit my parents' room, to make sure I was adequately protected.

But as I made my way down the hall, I saw something flash past one of the windows in the living room. It looked like a human hand. I could not be sure of what I had seen—it happened so fast, a pale flicker. I held still, ready to scream. Then it happened again. A small white palm landed, *smack*, against the glass, spread open like a starfish.

Without question, it was the most terrifying moment of my life. As in a dream, I moved forward. The hand appeared to be signaling to me; I lost all thought of waking my parents and moved help-lessly down the corridor. In the distance, one of the ostriches gave its deep, rattling cry. The hand was tugged away before I got there. It slid down the glass. I reached the window, my heart pounding so hard that it was interfering with my vision—at the crescendo of each beat, the world danced a little. Two figures were lying on the patio of our house. I could see them plainly in the moonlight. One was my father, and I was instantly reassured, although he did seem to be in the process of killing the other person, a woman pinned beneath him. At first I thought it was my mother. But the figure was too tall. Her feet, kicked up beside his back, were too delicate. I watched, entranced. The girl was Megan, who worked on the farm. (Until that moment, I had nursed a bit of a crush on her, something my mother had been quick to tease me about.) Megan could usually be found in the hatchery, tending the eggs that glistened in rows in the steamy darkness. She dealt with order forms and the newborn chicks that we nurtured in the pen behind her station.

Now she lay sprawled on the ground, her arms moving as though she were making a snow angel. My father was moving too. He was dressed in his usual silken pajamas, except for his bare bottom, which swiveled around in the air. I had seen that naked orb before; I had seen all of him without clothes on, as he tow-eled off in the bathroom or changed in a hurry after work. His hairy frame held no surprises for me. But now it was different. He was pumping away like a piston. Megan's hand rose up again and clapped suddenly against the window, inches from my nose. I jumped back, screaming a little, but they didn't hear me. They were making breathy sounds of their own. My father dragged her hand down and pinned her to the patio. I backed away, shaking all over. Two weeks later, I ran away.

❧

**SANDY:** His recovery was astonishing. Jack coughed the dust out of his lungs, the sunlight glittering in his exhalations. He slept away his residual fevers in angry naps on the living room floor. At first he split the night with frustrated wails as the soft surface of the bed against his sunburned skin kept him from sleeping. Over breakfast, the seams of his T-shirt made him wriggle and sob, but after a few days the burn was gone altogether and he was drenched in a mahogany tan. His mousy hair looked blond against the brown of his cheeks. I caught him lifting away the bandages over his scabs to peer at the inflamed area. His energy returned in surges. One day he was drowsing on the couch—the next scribbling frantically with markers and butcher-block paper scattered over the kitchen floor—the next out on the farm, his cheerful shouts carried to me on the afternoon breeze.

I did not mean to check up on him constantly. Kenneth and I had imposed stricter rules, which Jack obeyed to the hilt, letting one of us know before he changed from one location to another, remaining within yelling distance of an adult at all times. Still, on my breaks, I always went hunting for him. When I was too busy, and the most I could manage was a fretful glance back toward the house, I would see Kenneth's long, thin silhouette striding out to search the barn or the hatchery on the edge of the grounds.

We found Jack in the strangest places. I came running back from the pens one morning—half crazed with worry, for no apparent reason at all—and unearthed him beside the Dumpster. He was tucked beneath a piece of plywood and had two toy diplodocuses fighting to the death across his knees; he looked up at me in surprise. Kenneth found him in the balmy hollow of the shade behind our house, half hypnotized as he catalogued the movements of a jumping spider. I found him inside the hatchery, seated with his hand against the door of the incubating room, trying to sense Megan and her eggs in the warm darkness. Kenneth found him out of bed one night. On his way to the kitchen for a glass of water, he saw Jack curled up on the couch, his eyes on the rising moon.

Soon he was back in the company of his friends. Megan had long been the subject of my son's near-worshipful adoration. She was everything I was not—delicate, pale, and still, with freckles like chips of sand caught in ice. Jack pined over her. (I had once eavesdropped, with covert glee, on a conversation between them; in an attempt to mimic what he clearly imagined to be polite adult chitchat, Jack came out sounding like a butler from a Victorian drama: "Hot today, isn't it? Simply dreadful weather.") Though I found Megan hard going—reserved and difficult to talk to—I was amused whenever I saw my son bobbing dutifully along in her wake.

At night, when Jack fell asleep across my legs on the living room couch, it was all I could do to carry him into his bedroom and leave him there, out of my sight. Sometimes Kenneth went to bed without me as Jack sweated and dreamed against my thigh. The moon rose hollow, and the stars appeared, as precise as dents in metal. Wind breathed through the screen door, carrying the earthy smell of ostriches, the sting of desert flowers. The tiny glimmering bulb over the kitchen table was the only light on, and as the wind shook the chain and set the lamp to rocking, the glow washed back and forth across the living room like sunlight breaking through the surface of water. I checked Jack's pulse, looked for the rise and fall of his breath, and tried to distinguish the whispered words he muttered through the thickness of drool. I slept that way, upright and rigid as a block of stone, with one hand on my son's back so that the slightest shift of his ribcage dislodged me from sleep. Kenneth found me there in the mornings, limp with exhaustion, my smile triumphant.

ॐ

JACK: After a while I began to get used to this new, strange mindset. It was as though I were divided in half. Part of me knew what was really happening, and the other part went along as I had always done, playing with toy cars, visiting the ostriches, chasing lizards between the cacti. Sometimes I wanted to kill Megan. Sometimes I wanted to dredge up that torrid memory—the bare bottom working up and down, her white hand reaching—and stick myself in my father's place. But on the surface, all was well. My father kissed my mother's temple as he headed out to work with his briefcase. My mother sang off-key as she did the dishes. Sometimes I actually forgot that he was having an affair. When he took me out into the yard and spent all Sunday teaching me how to cut open a cactus and find the water inside—when he absently took sips from my mother's cup of tea, as though what belonged to her was naturally his as well—when he chased me into my bed at night, playing Tickle Monster, and I hid beneath the sheets, screaming with fright and laughter—it was impossible to believe he could have betrayed us. Then I would remember.

ॐ

SANDY: Finally Kenneth and I were able to make love again. That was when I knew all our selfishness had returned; even a terrified parent cannot be expected to live on the brink of anxiety all the time. My husband was a bamboo pole of a man, slender and trim, not quite my height. He sometimes felt as insubstantial as a child to me. His smallness lent an edge to his sexuality. He did not like when I climbed on top of him, and even my sudden kisses or flirtatious glances, if timed wrong, made him tense up. Now he breathed against my neck in the dark. I ran my hands over his willowy torso, and he nudged me with his body until I faced away from him, back to belly. It felt better like that, with no eye contact or brush of hearts. He wrapped his legs around mine until there wasn't space between us. He was angry—angry at Jack, but he took it out on me—and I let him, because I was angry too. He entered me before I was ready. (Since Jack was born, we had never needed birth control. Complications during labor had left me infertile, unable to produce the brood of children my husband had always hoped for.) I cried out as he thrust, dry, as deep as he could go. He slammed against the inside of my belly and pressed his hand over my mouth to shut me up.

In the morning, as penance for having forgotten Jack, however temporarily, I beat two eggs in a bowl and had all his favorite breakfast foods laid out on the table. He came shuffling down the hallway, his pajama bottoms loose around his legs, his pouf of a stomach bare in the sunlight. I filled the kettle and put it over the flame for Kenneth, who was singing in the shower, his reedy tenor echoing around the bathroom. I handed Jack a cup of orange juice and touched his head tentatively to bring his eyes onto me for a moment. There was a quietness in the air, as though we were waiting for something.

"Where is Greenland?" Jack asked finally.

I leaned against the stove. "Far north. Iceberg north, in fact. My friend Anika—remember Anika?—was going to move there and teach English, but they told her she would have to keep a gun with her at all times, to deal with the polar bears. She went to Cuba instead."

"Do *real* Eskimos live there? In igloos?"

"We'll go to the library and get a book about it. Next time we're in town. Okay?"

His gaze slid to the window again. I glanced out at the ostrich pens and saw that one of the males had his head rocked back and was beating his black wings against the sky.

"Are there Christmas trees in Greenland?" Jack asked.

"No," I said. "It's strange, but I don't think much grows in Greenland. It's mostly ice and snow, and the name has nothing to do with what it's really like. Maybe they named it that to try to trick people into visiting there."

"Can we move there?"

A flicker of insight thrilled at the back of my head. "You want to go there?" I asked casually. Down the hall, the shower rattled to a halt. The pipes grumbled in their way, knocking inside the ceiling.

"I think *we* should go there," Jack said blithely. "As a family. It seems very safe."

I watched him through narrowed eyes, and asked, finally, with an edge in my voice, "How *long* have you wanted to go there?"

He looked at me with total innocence, and my suspicion faded away. Greenland was a whim of the moment—and even if it were not, if it had taken hold (as Madagascar had obsessed him the previous fall, until he had driven Kenneth and me mad with flags, and educational videos about the rainy season, and the unusual habits of the native lemurs, and the number of beetles unique to the region that were dying every day), Jack would not have tried to walk to Greenland. Even at the age of nine, his mind all unformed, he would surely know better than to head out, alone and unprepared, to a place he believed to be some igloo-studded Shangri-La. I bit my thumb. I had the urge to grab the boy in both my hands and shake him until he told me, in plain English, with none of the dodges or prevarications to which I had become accustomed, just what on earth he had run away for. The social worker had come up with nothing. It had been weeks and weeks, and though I had tried every trick I could think of to get it out of him—sneak attacks, games, guilt trips, straightforward questioning, throwing a book across the room and screaming—I still had no idea why he had walked into the desert. I had gone so far as to ask Megan if she had any insights; she was, after all, the object of Jack's youthful infatuation. But she had just shrugged irritably, as though the motivations of children were beneath her notice.

Jack sipped his juice. His plate was clean but for a lump of egg in the corner.

"Eat that," I said, "and we'll go check on the ostriches."

"I'm full."

Kenneth came into the kitchen, smiling.

"Hey," he said, nudging me. "I just found the phone off the hook. I wonder how long *that* was going on?"

"We run a tight ship."

He laid a hand on my shoulder as he passed by, his fingers warm and damp. His hair was slicked back from the shower. He took the kettle off the flame just as it began to rattle and spout wisps of steam. Jack's eyes were on the horizon. I could see that Greenland was still in him, probably a muddle of fantasy and fact now, Christmas trees digging their roots into the flesh of an iceberg. His mouth fell slack as he considered these wonders. Kenneth grabbed a mug from the cabinet behind me and poured himself a hissing cup. Our lovemaking had lifted a weight off him; he whistled as he gazed over my head at the ostrich pens.

"Come on, Jack," I said. "Let's get dressed and out the door before these birds figure out how to fly and get away from us."

His face lit up, and he scurried from the table. Kenneth lifted the last bite of egg from Jack's plate between two fingers and ate it. My eyes stung at the fact that my son was still young enough to believe that ostriches might fly, and old enough, already, to be filled with mysteries.

⁊

JACK: Caesar was my favorite of all the cocks. I had known him since he was a chick, small enough for me to hold him in my hands. My mother squinted behind her sunglasses, and together we leaned against the fence, watching Caesar and his two hens. The big cock strutted to and fro, tall and imposing, his eyes and knees stained red with lust. His hens were all agitation. I bounced up and down on my toes. Mom laid a hand on my back to calm me. Caesar mounted one of the hens, and they mated briskly—Caesar doing the bizarre, requisite dance, his wings flapping, his neck twisting back and forth like a python. Beneath him, the hen pecked nonchalantly at a few pebbles, gobbling them down to help crush the feed in her stomach. When they were done, both ostriches got to their feet, and the second hen fell into line behind them.

The birds pawed the ground and disarrayed their napes. Caesar kept shaking his bill, then raising himself to his full height and eyeing me sternly. I saw my mother glance around the paddock, and I knew that she was looking for rattlesnakes, strange pools of water, or fallen garbage that might be causing the birds' upset. But there was nothing. Sometimes ostriches, like cats at midnight, were gripped by an inexplicable frenzy.

Caesar threw his chest forward and let out that hoarse shout, like stones clattering at the bottom of a barrel. I jumped backward, and Mom took my hand. As we watched, Caesar skipped on his red legs and broke into a run. Like cadets at an academy, the hens dutifully followed him. Dust rose in their wake. Their heads were lifted, their wings spread to catch against the surface of the air. They thundered past us, inches away.

Abruptly, with a kind of wild elation, all three ostriches began to twirl. I had seen it before, but it never failed to delight me. The birds spun like tops, like ballerinas, their girlish eyes half-shut. They each kept one wing awkwardly aloft. Their strong legs tottered in precise circles. Mom gripped my arm and laughed, a wide-open, exultant sound I rarely heard. Caesar crowed again. One of the hens got dizzy and lost her balance, stumbling to the ground in an explosion of dust. I was overcome altogether and darted down the path in the sunlight. I too spun in rapturous leaps, all the way home.

∽

SANDY: That evening there was thunder in the air. Black clouds roiled on the horizon. Pockets of glow flickered eerily beyond the western windows. Jack went to bed early, just as the wind began to gust through the screen door. In the living room, Kenneth and I sat up, restless. I sprawled on the floor by the coffee table, price sheets and diagrams of incubators spread out before me. Kenneth lolled on the couch and frowned at his book. After a moment he sighed, shifted his weight, and turned the page back to check what he had just read. A deep boom shivered in the distance, and our silverware and glasses trembled audibly in their cupboards. Wind poured through the screen, carrying a chill and another concussion of thunder.

Kenneth set his book aside and I shuffled my papers into a heap, which I tucked beneath the leg of the coffee table so the breeze would not scatter them. Together we stepped onto the patio to watch the storm. The clouds were torn at the bottom, streaked like smeared charcoal where rain was falling. The air was as limp as tea in a cup. Occasional curls of wind, scouts before the onslaught, lifted my hair and rippled Kenneth's shirt. I had grown up in urban, crowded Detroit and never got used to the openness of Arizona. I could *see* where the front began, a cusp of rising dirt and tumbled raindrops.

"Should we wake Jack?" I asked. "To see this?"

"No, I don't think so. He's exhausted."

Lightning pulsed in blue and yellow, showing inconsistencies in the thickness of the cloud layer. Before my eyes, rain swept over the ostrich pens. The birds were huddled beneath their cinderblock shelters, their heads tucked under their wings.

Inside the house, the telephone sounded. This was a rare enough occurrence that Kenneth and I exchanged a surprised glance.

"I'll get it," I said. "It's probably my mother."

"Cheers from sunny Detroit," Kenneth said. "Don't answer it. You'll miss this."

I struggled to open the screen door against the wind. The phone jangled again. It was bound to be my mother, a jazzy, elegant lady who phoned regularly from her suburban apartment, always with spectacularly bad timing. If the phone rang when Kenneth and I were having sex, when Jack was bawling, when a coyote had gotten into the pens, it would invariably be my mother, full of polite small talk and veiled hints that I should leave the ostrich trade at high speed.

"Hello?" I said.

Someone was there. I heard a confusion of breath, and then a purposeful inhalation.

"Is this one of Jack's friends?" I asked kindly. "From school? Is this Elias?"

Thunder rumbled, and the line crackled juicily. I glanced at the caller ID, but the number was withheld.

"Hello?" I said, sticking a finger in my other ear.

"Sandy, for God's sake, you're missing this," Kenneth shouted from the porch.

The person on the other end coughed, a musical sound.

"This isn't funny," I said.

"Sandy!" Kenneth shouted. The rain hit the side of the house, drumming on the roof. Inside the kitchen, I ducked instinctively. A fine spray misted through the screen door as though cast up from the hull of a ship. I heard the gutters overflow and gush onto the patio. Kenneth whooped wetly beneath another beat of thunder.

"I'm hanging up!" I shouted into the phone. "Hello?"

"Oh *God*," said a distant voice. "I'm calling—I have to say—"

"What?" I roared. "I can't hear you!"

In my peripheral vision, I thought I saw Jack. For a moment I was sure he had crept into the doorway to peer at me. I turned sharply, but the hallway was empty.

"This is impossible," the woman said. Her cadence was oddly familiar, though she also sounded drunk. "You have to—"

The line went dead. At the same instant the lights flickered; we often lost power during a storm. I slammed down the phone, exasperated, and hurried to the front door. The desert was transfigured. The bushes were dark stains on a landscape of flashing silver. The ground could not take in so much moisture, and the water pooled in puddles and streams, its surface smashed into a mosaic by the rain. Kenneth, on the patio, stood ankle-deep and drenched to the bone. His shirt hung off his back. He turned to face me and flung out a hand, pulling me into a squelching bear hug. He was shuddering and gasping.

As abruptly as it had come, the tempest passed over. The rain melted away into a shimmering mist. Frogs were already singing in the fresh-formed sea. I heard the tentative call of an ostrich.

∽

JACK: Hidden behind my bedroom door, I watched my parents on the patio. In a stagy, quixotic move, my father took up my mother's hands and began to waltz with her in the watery light. After that I tried to go back to bed.

It was not the first time Megan had called the house. I knew because I had become a careful spy. Usually Megan opted for the afternoons, when Mom was almost guaranteed to be out on the grounds, checking the feed or the fences. My father would answer it and glance around, deliberately casual; after a moment he would head into the bedroom. (Neither of my parents had ever bothered to get a cell phone, since the service was notoriously spotty this far from the city. We had only one landline in the house—there was no privacy to be had—but by pulling the cord until it nearly snapped, my father could shut the door behind him.) I would hear his voice rising and falling, sounding angry and tired at the same time.

I knew they were fighting. I even knew what they were fighting about. My father was deceptive, but he was not cautious. The windows in our house always stayed open, allowing the breeze to wander from room to room. All I had to do was creep outside and crouch beneath the sill. From there I could hear everything. The argument was the same each time, but the two of them never seemed to get tired of it. My father was worried that I was insane. I had run away, nearly killing myself in the process—he could not leave us when I was so unsettled. Hearing that, I felt not relief but an intense pressure. Running away had been the right thing; I had preserved the family. But what was the right thing now? Enchanting my father with my skill at lizard-catching, hanging on his every word about architecture at dinner, taking the phone off the hook to keep Megan's voice out of the house—my bag of tricks was running low, and I could not hope to keep him with us much longer.

Megan would scream that he had promised, her tinny voice thick with tears, even from where I sat. My father would bang his fist on the dresser. Once or twice he had started to cry himself. Then their voices would drop to a murmur, low and soothing, tinged with sexual heat. At this point I usually absented myself, sometimes to kick rocks, sometimes to vomit into the bushes, sometimes to find my mother and cling about her legs like a much younger child.

∾

SANDY: It was late August when I woke one morning to the sound of heavy footfalls outside the bedroom window. The blinds shook with each distinct beat. I sat up and registered that the sun was half risen, the air hazy and shrouded. People were shouting in the distance. Kenneth slumbered on, his bare shoulder visible above the blanket. Something moved past the window, flicking its massive shadow against the blinds. The impact of its feet shook the whole room. With a yell I flung myself out of bed.

The ostriches were loose. At a glance I could see that *all* the ostriches were loose. Between me and the paddocks stood a scene of total chaos. The birds were everywhere, running at full tilt, trailing wakes of dust like the crisscrossing trails of airplanes. The young birds moved in groups of eight or ten. The breeders stayed in their original cliques, two gray hens with each black cock. They ran with grace, precision, and madness; they had nowhere to go and were stupefied by their sudden freedom. No one was in charge of them. I counted at least fifty ostriches at first glance, which meant that forty-odd birds were elsewhere on the grounds, scraping the flesh of their legs on the fences, crashing through the barn, trying to break into the hatchery.

Several farm workers were already on the scene. My family was the only one to live on the property—the others all went home at night, many to Phoenix, in a big cheerful huddle of a carpool. Now they were running between the pens, shrieking to one another. Next to the birds, the people seemed to be moving in slow motion. Some of the ostriches were clearing forty miles an hour. I put a hand on the doorjamb to steady myself. Ted was skidding between the cacti in his cowboy boots. I watched him lift one leg and aim a kick at a passing bird. A brood of seven ostriches bore down on Samuel and Amy, who shouted and pounded their sticks against the ground.

"Hey," I screamed, waving both arms. "Hey!"

It had no effect. No one heard me. Ted gathered up a rope and was clearly trying to implement some complicated maneuver. I squinted, but for the life of me I couldn't figure out what he was doing. Amy swatted at Caesar with her broom; he was dashing across the field with his hens in tow and did not appear to register the blow.

"Kenneth," I roared into the house.

As I watched, twenty young birds rounded the barn, running in formation. They had the air of creatures that have lost all reason, galloping along for lack of anything better to do. Amy and Samuel were holding their ground, back-to-back, waving their sticks in the air. Ted sat down in the shelter of a boulder and began picking something from the sole of his boot.

At the top of my lungs I shouted, "Hey!"

Something in my voice—the desperation, maybe—caught their attention. Everyone looked up. Samuel shielded his eyes. I waved both hands, and Ted, seated in the middle of the field, waved back.

"Get inside!" I screamed. "Get back inside! There's nothing to do now! We have to wait for them to exhaust themselves!"

No one moved. They stared at me. Amy cupped her hand over her ear.

"Inside!" I screamed. "Everyone come here! Come here! Everyone!"

I made huge signs for them to head my way. Ted got to his feet. Amy and Samuel linked arms as they walked. In the distance I watched the young birds round the barn again, running together. The dust they had kicked up on their last lap had not yet settled. As the farm workers came closer, I could see their frightened faces and heaving chests. Amy appeared to be limping. Ted had a bloody bandage over one wrist.

The morning passed in a frenzy. The first thing to do was tend to the wounded, and Kenneth and I ran around with gauze and disinfectant. Ted made tea. Samuel distributed our mismatched cups. Amy was in some sort of shock. The sun rose higher, and the ostriches continued to pound in circles outside the house. At my urging, Kenneth went to check on Jack and reported that the kid was out cold.

As we sheltered there in the living room, I was reminded forcibly of a hurricane I had once weathered with a gaggle of cousins in North Carolina. Here were the same worried faces, hushed voices. Ted sat in the corner talking solemnly with Samuel. There was nothing to do except wait. The birds would wear themselves out eventually. Most of them would return to the paddocks, out of habit, out of fear, out of thirst; there was no other water to be had on the grounds but the pools in their own pens.

I stood at the window, my cheek to the glass. Dark shapes were already beginning to settle in the dirt. The ostriches sat with their immense legs folded under their haystack bodies, their heads lifted. Behind me, everyone was asking the same question: How had the birds gotten loose? Could it have been the wind? Could a crazed ostrich—Could a burglar—Could a rustler—Could one of the farm workers—? My heart burned in my chest. I could not believe any of our employees had done this. And yet my only experience with rustlers had been a distant rumble in the darkness—a truck engine far off—and three birds missing a few days later when we had finally bothered to count them. No rustler would make a mistake of this magnitude; they slipped in and out like ninjas and survived on their work going undetected. Out in the field, I watched a group of birds making their way back into the pen, their postures curious, as though they had never been in there before.

I felt a hand on my shoulder and jumped.

"People are saying it could have been that animal rights group," Kenneth said in a low voice.

"Oh, no," I said. "This wouldn't make sense for them. They usually just picket and write letters."

"That's what Samuel told me. He thinks it must have been a prank. Teenagers from Phoenix, or something. The farm is pretty famous out there."

I shook my head wearily. "But who would take that risk? To open *all* the cages? And you know they had to shoo the birds out too, actually go inside the pens and scare them. The ostriches wouldn't *all* have left the paddocks if someone didn't make them. Whoever did it, he's just lucky he isn't dead."

And then I gasped. It was like being struck by lightning. My hand went to my mouth, and for the first time in my life I thought I would faint.

"What?" Kenneth said.

But I was already pushing past him, stumbling over the legs of the farm workers on the couch, elbowing Ted out of my way. I was crying with rage and panic before I had even flung open the door to Jack's bedroom. All morning I had been steadying myself at the sight of that door, certain that he was safe, dreaming so deeply he hadn't noticed the pandemonium outside. His curtains were drawn, and I was momentarily blinded by the darkness. I went in anyway. Kenneth had fallen for a nine-year-old's trick—a heap of blankets in the bed. I tore apart the sheets. I flung open the closet door and sent the box of toys crashing to the ground. Kenneth came into the doorway, and Amy gazed, openmouthed, over his shoulder.

Kenneth said nothing. He looked dazed. I shoved past him, wiping away the tears. Everyone in the living room had heard the commotion and looked at me with concern.

"Jack is somewhere on the grounds," I said. "I think he—" My words caught in my throat.

Amy clapped her hands over her mouth. I ignored her.

"It should be pretty safe now," I said. "The ostriches are calming down. Everyone get into groups. Kenneth will head one team, and I'll take the other. We don't have a minute to lose."

They obeyed me. The look in my eye gave them no choice. Armed with sticks, brooms, and frying pans, we walked outside, into the awful sunlight.

⚘

JACK: My favorite monster was always the Terror Bird. Mom was forced to read that one aloud to me any number of times. I liked the Loch Ness plesiosaur and the blue whale, but for my money, the Terror Bird was the most interesting. This ten-foot creature had stalked the South American plains after the demise of the dinosaurs, slaying its prey with a hooked beak. Its head was the size of a horse's. I remember the picture in the book, lovingly painted, right down to the flash of mad light in that black eye.

Monsters are endlessly comforting to a troubled boy. I was never interested in human superheroes, which offered nothing more than a pipe dream. Their powers were just a pale imitation of what already existed in the natural world. X-ray vision was an amalgamation of a dolphin's sonar and a snake's ability to see in infrared. Super-strength was possessed by the great apes; I had read about a female gorilla that bench-pressed a ton idly, without apparent effort. It was silly to imagine that human beings could ever attain the sheer power of the cheetah, the T. rex, or even the ostrich, which was equipped with claws that could rip through a car door if the birds were in the wrong mood. In the wild, I knew, an angry ostrich could dispatch a lion with one kick.

Humans might have had the brains, but animals had the brawn. I was all right with that equation. I had no interest in a superhero with a mind at work. I loved the ostriches—and all the other monsters—for what they were: sheer brute force, untempered by either conscience or consciousness.

∾

SANDY: By evening, Ted and I were circling the outer fence together. I had bitten his head off more than once, and he was now trailing deferentially behind me, trying not to make too much noise. I was filled with a primal rage, a need to defend my son. I half wanted an ostrich to dare to threaten me; I would have broken its neck with one blow of my staff. But the birds were worn out, dotting the grounds with their white necks. Their feathery bodies changed the landscape. The farm had become an orchard of ragged bulbs, a thicket of gleaming trees.

Then Kenneth began to scream. He was standing by the house, Samuel and Amy with him. I peered across the field and saw my husband dash up the steps, into the living room. I ran—I fairly flew—leaping over boulders and bushes. I skirted dangerously close to a pack of resting birds, all of whom swiveled their imperious faces to watch me. Samuel and Amy stood together by the shed. Amy was already sobbing. There was blood on the ground. I could see it staining the soil, and I staggered against the wall. Someone was lying there, a mass of red pulp.

But it was not Jack. Eventually I was able to make sense of the figure, to see that it was too big to be my son. It was a woman's form, complete with long, slender legs. Her hat had fallen off. One sunburned hand was curled around a stone. She was stirring weakly.

I knelt over the prone figure. Megan did not look like herself, the flower-faced waif Jack had trailed around the farm. There was a bruise on her temple. Her arm was visibly broken beneath the lacy blouse she wore. Her stomach was slashed—I had lived with ostriches long enough to recognize the work of those vicious claws.

"Kenneth's calling an ambulance," Samuel said softly.

I felt Megan's pulse through the mat of her hair. She did not appear to register my touch. She had been lying there for some time, hours maybe, bleeding into the dirt. Tucked behind the house, she had escaped everyone's attention. There were a few moments of dreamlike unreality. Ted and Samuel debated the pros and cons of moving her inside. Amy was led away to have hysterics somewhere else. The whole day had slipped through my fingers; the sun hung low above the horizon, and darkness was gathering in the east. The moon was a chunk of hot stone. I saw Kenneth inside the house, pacing back and forth, clutching the telephone. My head was swimming.

Kenneth emerged again, running across the patio. As I watched, he collapsed at Megan's side. The expression on his face was familiar—so much so that it took me a moment to recognize it in this context. He had looked at me like that perhaps once or twice in my life, as though I were his whole world encapsulated in human form, as though I were made of something finer than flesh and bone. It was almost an out-of-body experience, observing Kenneth's raised eyebrows, his open mouth, so much care and compassion directed at someone else. At his touch, Megan's eyelids flickered. She was not remotely beautiful now, disfigured by dust and blood. But my husband did not appear to see that. He stroked her forehead, murmuring. For the first time, I noticed that Megan's outfit was inappropriate for wandering an ostrich farm, even on her day off. She was wearing a pretty little skirt, just right for hitting the bars, beneath which—even in her bedraggled state—I perceived some very nice, expensive underwear. There was a sudden movement beside me, and Samuel stood up and moved discreetly away, failing to catch my eye.

⁓

JACK: I huddled in the ditch, gazing through the bars of the gate. I had fallen there in the early morning, twisting an ankle, and ever since had lain in the shadow of the fence, observing the mess I had made. My plan had been a simple one: release the birds, then get to the front gate and stay safely outside the grounds until it was all over. But I had been outfoxed. Several ostriches had trailed me as I made my escape. These fierce, foolish birds—who would eat themselves to death if their feed wasn't regulated, who would twirl like ice dancers when they felt elated—understood perfectly the meaning of an open gate. It had been all I could do to get out of their way, diving into the gutter as several ostriches pelted past me. Helplessly I had watched them careening down the road.

I was now prepared to tell my mother the truth. I had been lining up the words in my mind, trying to figure out the best arrangement of sentences. Perhaps there was a way of phrasing it that would make it easier for her to bear. Evening was falling, and I could see the house between the slats of the fence. There was my father, running to and fro like a chicken with its head cut off. There was limp little Amy—I had never liked her—sobbing into her hands. My father appeared to fall to his knees, and I realized that it must be Megan he had found. The birds had done their work after all.

But I had eyes only for my mother, who was observing the scene, standing a little way apart. I watched her lift one leg in a characteristic stance, holding on to her walking stick. She stood absolutely still. My father moved, and Amy moved, but my mother was frozen. In that moment I knew that she had understood everything. I did not have to be the one to tell her. And indeed, I never had to say a word.

☙

SANDY: I noticed it at sunset—I should have caught it hours earlier, but only in the gloaming did that metallic glint catch my attention. The gate was not locked. It was swinging slightly on its hinges, gleaming in the failing light.

Everything else left my mind at once. Stumbling a little over the dark terrain, I hurried between the clumps of bushes. In the distance, an ostrich called out sleepily. I pushed the gate open and stepped outside.

"Jack?" I said. "Baby? You out here?"

On the ground by my foot was a mark in the dirt. I knelt to touch it: the gouged claw-print of an ostrich.

"Jack?" I whispered.

There was a rustling from the ditch beside me. A wet gurgle in the gloom. Jack was sitting in the culvert, one leg bent awkwardly beneath him. I could see his eyes—I could almost taste them— dark as a coyote's, thoughtful as a man's. He was too proud to speak, too stubborn. He was evidently afraid to believe I was real, in case I turned out to be a trick of his weary mind and left him lonelier and more frightened than before.

"Hey, kid," I said.

"Mom," he said throatily. "Over here."

"I know. I see you."

He began to cry. That was what woke me up. In a heartbeat I had him cradled against my chest, his head cupped in my palm, his weight in my lap. I got as close to him as I could without breaking bones. We sat like that for a while, testing the reality of each other. Jack wept quietly, almost calmly.

His mouth worked silently for a moment.

"I have bad news," I said gently.

Jack took a shuddering breath.

"It's about your friend Megan," I said. "She was kicked by one of the ostriches. We're calling an ambulance now, but—"

"Will she die?" Jack asked.

"Maybe," I said helplessly.

At once, his whole body relaxed. He began to fall asleep, right there in my arms. The adrenaline had finally shaken out of his system. Beyond the fence, the house glowed, peppered with golden windows. I saw a small procession moving carefully across the patio. My husband and the farm workers were carrying Megan's limp form indoors.

∞

JACK: In the years that followed the events of that summer— after my parents divorced, and my mother and I moved away—I would meet with a social worker. There, for the first time, I was able to talk about how it had been. I came to understand that for a nine-year-old, family can be a matter of life and death.

It was natural, I suppose, that my father should leave us. After all, Megan had suffered terrible injuries, and her need was now greater than mine. It was natural, too, that my mother should lose her job. The people who owned the farm—I had always thought it was my mother who owned it, but apparently she was just the manager—asked her to resign. But she would have left anyway. She could not bear to be pitied, for people to see her shamed and abandoned. She could not bear for anyone to think that she had been taken in by her own husband, as innocent and trusting as a wild bird.

Six ostriches escaped the farm that night. One broke his leg in the desert and was found dead, days later, by a cattle rancher in his pickup truck. Two birds made it nearly thirty-five miles to the home of an old man and his bedridden wife, who were astonished to see these vivid apparitions of Africa drinking greedily from the well in the backyard. One traveled in a bewildered circle straight back to the farm, where Samuel found her standing at the front gate and let her in. But the last two birds—both females, young and strong—were never found. The police hypothesized that the pair of them wandered beyond human knowledge, died of thirst and exposure, and left the rich farmland of their bodies stretched out on Arizona stone to feed the grubs and rodents. But my mother and I have a different theory.

Settled in our new apartment, we kept our eyes on the Phoenix newspapers. Dinosaur footprints were found in one schoolyard. There were multiple reports of an incoherent homeless man who could never be found in the park at night, though he was shouting at the top of his lungs. Several confused citizens called in to ask about a minor earthquake that had woken them at dawn; their blinds and ceiling fans had trembled at what sounded like the beat of thundering hooves. An honest drunkard, in the hospital with a broken arm, could not begin to explain how the towering shadow he had seen in an alley had wounded him so badly—and so *fast*. My mother would read each tidbit aloud to me. I cut the articles out of the paper and pinned them to the fridge. I knew just what it must have been like: twin birds, eight feet tall, skimming across the desert. They topped a red, parched hill and looked down at the shimmering buildings and smog, the rumble of trains and car engines, the chattering crowds. And without fear, without thought, they plunged together down the slope, into this new beginning.

# DHARMA AT THE GATE

Lucy wakes up with his smell on her clothes. Before school she packs herself a lunch, putting in extra food for him—he will not bring anything from home, and she can't abide his habit of getting by on nothing but sodas and candy bars from the vending machines. It is not yet dawn when she hurries to her car, the frost crackling beneath her feet. She has to leave early and detour south along the highway to pick him up. Xavier is already waiting outside the house when Lucy gets there. Despite the cold, he has no coat; he leans against a tree, posing for her, his ears and nose charred red by the chill. He climbs into the car and kisses her wildly, as though he has been drowning without her presence in the long hours of the morning.

On the way to school they fight. It is the same argument as usual—Lucy has been applying to colleges, and Xavier needs to be reassured, over and over, that she will not go far, that she will not forget him. He himself has no use for higher education. He will go into his father's garage and work as a mechanic, make a good living. By the time she pulls into the high school parking lot, Lucy is exhausted. The weight on her shoulders is exquisitely familiar, bearing down on her as they walk together across the sweeping lawns. Xavier holds her hand, fondling her fingers. He murmurs that she is beautiful, his little porcelain doll.

As always, Lucy meets him before second period, after third period, before fifth period. He is present for her even during her classes. They pass back and forth their own private notebook—an ordinary-looking spiral-bound thing, into which they can scribble letters to each other while appearing to take notes on trigonometry or Aristotle. In the hallways, they exchange wet kisses. Xavier often grabs her in a muffling embrace, going on long beyond the bounds of what is normal, as people dart around them like water streaming around a stone. They eat lunch together on the scrubbed, windswept grass in front of the school. Xavier takes what Lucy has brought him, thanking her absently, as he might thank a benevolent mother for doing exactly what is expected of her. They take sips from her juice box, share bites of the same apple. During recess, whatever the weather, the high school empties onto the grounds, students picnicking wherever they can find room. Xavier likes to observe his peers in the manner of an anthropologist, droning on about the social forces that cause the cheerleaders to laugh almost spontaneously, or the stoners to gather in front of the gas station across the street, marking their separation from the rest of the herd.

Lucy eats quietly. She can predict how Xavier will respond at any given moment. She knows when he's in a prideful mood and might be offended if she offered him her scarf, though the sky is an icy slate and snow has begun to fall in downy tufts. She knows when he will curl up and doze off in her lap, weary from a long night of video games in his house with no curfew. She knows that when lunch is over, he will insist on throwing away their garbage alone, chivalrously braving the stink of the cans and the presence of the pigeons and squirrels that hover possessively around what they perceive to be their own territory.

On the way to her next class, Lucy tugs their special notebook out of her backpack, wondering what on earth she will find to write in response to the letter he has scrawled there. Xavier will be waiting for the notebook after seventh period, with his haunted, adoring face. She is no longer amazed at how he can consume her entire day, though they do not have one class in common. People often ask about him, how he's been lately, what the two of them did last weekend. Lucy and Xavier have been a couple so long—four years now, since they were freshmen—that no one can imagine them apart. No one knows anything about her except that she belongs to Xavier. Once, in health class, as the teacher rolled a condom onto a banana and explained its function, Lucy got the giggles, imagining Xavier as her own personal condom, a barrier that surrounds her completely, keeping the rest of the world at a distance. She has no particular friends anymore. Nobody would know to ask about her dog, about the trails she has been blazing in the woods on the edge of town, about her father, now permanently in a wheelchair. Instead they ask about her boyfriend, and Lucy smiles brightly and says that all is well. People glance at the back of her hand, where Xavier has inked a heart, or at her jeans, where he penned his name along the seam, and she sees them roll their eyes, smirking.

After school she drives him home. Snow has begun to fall in earnest, the whirling flakes blurring the horizon line. Xavier dozes in the passenger's seat, now and then coming to and remarking that she really ought to get the car cleaned—every seat is coated in golden fur, the back windows smeared with dog snot. Lucy acquiesces mildly, though like most dog owners she knows there isn't much point in cleaning a space that will be dirtied again the second the animal returns to it. She watches Xavier slouch up the walk to his house. The place has a distinctly unloved air, the bushes half dead, the screens caked with dirt. Lucy has never been allowed inside, not once—the father is a dangerous drunk, the mother a cipher. The house has the same ramshackle, uncared-for aspect as Xavier himself, with his falling-apart jeans and his hair in an unwashed tousle. Lucy waves him inside, wishing, not for the first time, that he would be mowed down by a bus. A car accident. A plane crash. Something sudden, painless, and unexpected, as though God himself had reached down and rubbed her boyfriend out of existence with a big pink eraser. What a blessing it would be, after four long years—her entire high school career—to have Xavier out of her life, gone entirely, and to know that it was not her fault.

∾

The blizzard continues into the evening, and by morning all of Ohio is swallowed up in white. Lucy bounces with anxiety before the radio until they announce that school is canceled. Her parents are already gone—they navigated the snowy roads early that morning to take her father for a checkup. Lucy wraps herself up in sweaters and gloves. Her dog is planted by the front door, beating his tail against the hatstand and moaning with anticipation. Lucy takes him to the arboretum. The walk is over a mile long, and soon she is loosening her coat, sweating beneath her layers. During the storm last night, sleet fell and froze, so the surface of the snow is crusted and cracking. Lucy leaves cavernous footprints. Dharma

• 40 •

skids and slips over the uneven surface, falling through with a startled yip. At the arboretum she lets him off leash, and he pelts away between the trees, kicking up a sparkling wake. Lucy follows him down the slope and scrambles over the frozen stream, making her way to her favorite log, where she can sit and let the stillness settle over her. Branches droop, their weight doubled by a coating of ice. Here and there, snow topples off a twig, landing in a floury explosion. In the distance, the dog is barking. Every so often he appears at the top of the hill, his tongue hanging ecstatically out of the side of his mouth. When Lucy smiles at him, he takes off again, whimpering with joy.

Dharma came to her six years ago. He was technically a birthday present—she had always begged for a dog—but even then, at eleven years old, Lucy knew better. For the first time, the doctors were certain that her father would have to spend at least some of his days in a wheelchair. The house was in an uproar: ramps to be built, the bedroom moved downstairs, the kitchen remodeled so that coffee cups and plates would be easily accessible. Lucy learned to lock the bathroom door when she showered, so that the workmen would not barge in on her accidentally. She learned to do her homework at the library, where it was quiet, no hammering, no phone ringing off the hook. She learned not to ask her mother for anything—there was too much going on for Lucy to have a new backpack or a friend over, thank you very much. Even the dog was more a present for her father than herself. Her father was querulous, nervous, ashamed; he did not meet Lucy's eye for months, struggling around in his wheelchair, hollering for help from the bathroom, where he was stuck between the tub and the sink again. He no longer felt himself to be the head of the household, the protector. Lucy was not told any of this, of course. She was told that the dog was her own gift, a combination birthday present and a thank-you for her patience and understanding. But she saw how her father nodded approvingly when Dharma barked at the mailman—how her mother smiled, watching her father— and she knew who was really being appeased.

None of that mattered, however, after the first few days. It was love from the beginning. Dharma followed her from room to room, laying his head on her knee. He clambered into the empty space beside her in bed, his body burning like a coal. He whined when she left for school. When she wasn't paying attention, he would rush up behind her, a chew toy in his mouth, and bash into the back of her knees, hooking one paw around her ankle. Dharma was a font of unintentional humor. He howled along with distant sirens. He charged around the house at top speed and, unaccustomed to the hardwood floors, skidded full tilt into walls. Lucy was almost embarrassed by how fond she was of him. She had never been one of those girls, cooing with delight over kittens or sketching deformed horses in the margins of her homework. This was something else. Every day after school, she linked a leash around his neck and walked for hours. In the rain he would dance in the brimming gutters. In the spring they made tracks together across deserted parks. Eventually Lucy discovered the arboretum, and the two of them tried in vain to map the network of trails that wound among the trees, Dharma ducking under twining creepers, chasing the moths that hovered in the watery light.

At last the dog bounds down the hill, panting and shuddering. He has worn himself out. Lucy scratches his head, and within minutes he is curled up in the snow, a red-gold bundle of fur, his nose tucked beneath his tail, in what Lucy likes to call his Dead Dog Impression—so deeply asleep that he can scarcely be bothered to breathe. She plans to stay in the arboretum as long as she can stand the cold. Already her feet are numb. Clouds loom in the western sky, dark and smoky. The pine trees shake snow off their branches. The boulders are spangled with icicles. Dharma snores quietly, and Lucy's mind empties out as though someone has pulled the plug from a drain. For a while she is able to contain the easy silence of the forest. One of her history teachers—a man who quite clearly regretted never chucking his career and heading off to be a yogi in India—once spent a lesson on the rudiments of meditation. Lucy never mastered it; her mind is always crowded with Xavier, so that sometimes she feels as though she has a double brain, her own thoughts bouncing around in a sea of his. She carries him with her. But in this place, if she sits still long enough, she can finally let him go. The sun emerges from between the clouds, and the snow gleams painfully. Bright whorls dance across the forest floor—and yet the light gives no warmth. Lucy is freezing. Her calves are buried in snow. Still, she can bear it a little longer. She takes a deep breath and closes her eyes.

∾

Back at the house, her cell phone is waiting. As a rule, Lucy does not bring it with her to the woods. The trees block any semblance of service, giving her an excuse to render herself, while there, temporarily untethered. Three voice-mails have accumulated in her absence. She glares at the tiny screen as she towels off the dog's feet. Dharma flings himself gratefully into his kennel, where he will sleep for the rest of the afternoon. Lucy putters around, opening the fridge and arranging the leaves of the plants on the countertop. She refreshes the water in Dharma's bowl and stares out the window, waiting in vain for her parents to come home.

At last she can put it off no longer. All three messages are from Xavier, of course. The first is a cheerful hello, isn't it awesome about school being canceled, so sad that he won't see her today. He misses her. Give him a call when she climbs out of bed. Lucy sighs and skips to the next message, which contains a note of anxiety. Xavier's voice spools out, filling the sunlit kitchen. Is she still in bed? She must really need her sleep, hah hah. He's a little worried though—could she call, just so he knows that she's all right, that her house didn't lose power or anything? Lucy rolls her eyes. She is accustomed to that particular plea, the *are-you-okay?* gambit. By the third message, Xavier's tone is annoyed. Lucy lays her head in her hands. The implication is clear: *He* celebrated their day off by telephoning her immediately, whereas *she* has left him in a state of bewildered abandonment. He says in a crisp voice that they need to talk about the college thing again. Where exactly is she thinking of applying? He's been doing some research. Call him as soon as possible, please. He sounds like a guidance counselor reprimanding a wayward student.

Helplessly, Lucy dials his number. She bites her lip as she listens to it ring.

∾

Xavier has tried to kill himself three times. This is the secret that she keeps for him. His first attempt happened early in their relationship; he went into his garage and endeavored to hang himself from the rafters. He told Lucy afterward that he did it because his father smacked him around and broke his computer. Xavier spent that night lying awake in his bedroom, gazing at the ceiling, and by morning he was nearly out of his mind. The rope was there in the corner of the garage, flung carelessly across a heap of tools. Xavier got it over the beam on the third try. He wound the knot with precise care and climbed onto the sagging hood of his father's old Ford. Then he stepped into space. But the rope was ancient and rotten. Xavier felt a blinding pain in his throat—there was an explosion of dust—and with a groan the noose snapped clean through. He landed on the floor in a daze, perfectly intact; but Lucy knew something was wrong as soon as she saw him the following morning. He was as pale as a vampire, his brow clammy, his voice a faltering whisper. After burying himself in her arms, he tugged his collar back to show her the scar, a livid red rope burn that has since dimmed to papery brown.

The second time was different. Xavier took all the pills from his mother's medicine chest and swallowed them ceremoniously, one by one. He and Lucy had been dating for over a year, but she was out of town at the time; her parents took her to Canada for the Christmas holiday, to visit old family friends and wander the quaint little tourist-trap shops. Lucy did not find out what had happened until she returned. Xavier went to bed, delirious from all the medicine in his bloodstream. But after a few hours he woke with his belly on fire. He spent the rest of the night vomiting into the toilet, shuddering on the bathroom tile, and trying not to wake his father. By dawn he had thrown up everything. He took the next few days to convalesce, and by the time Lucy came back he was marginally better—he looked as though he'd aged a few years, but he was well enough to gobble down the soup and crackers she brought for him.

The third incident, according to Xavier, was more of an accident than anything else. Lucy privately disagrees, believing that accidents involve things like misplacing your wallet or tripping on the stairs, rather than self-mutilation. One day in chemistry class, Xavier lost his temper and punched a hole through the window. The story is famous now around the school. His experiment wasn't working right. One of the chemicals they'd been given was labeled incorrectly. The teacher, pausing at Xavier's desk on her way around the room, chided him for not following directions. Xavier responded by shouting that no one else was doing any better and he was tired of being picked on. When she threatened to keep him after class, he stormed to the window and glared out. (Though she wasn't there, Lucy can picture it vividly: Xavier eyeing his own reflection, a caged bird challenging the rival that flickers in and out of the mirror.) He breathed through his teeth. His cheeks flamed. The classroom grew still around him, everyone riveted in gruesome anticipation. At last, almost as an afterthought, Xavier hauled off and socked the glass. Blood dripped onto the pavement three stories below. His forearm was studded with icy shards. People screamed and bolted. One of the girls fainted dead away.

Lucy picked Xavier up at the hospital that evening, his arm swathed in a wad of bandages. On the way back to his house, she pulled into the deserted parking lot of a strip mall, and they sat for hours in the shadowy darkness, Xavier crying, Lucy insisting that it was time for her to tell someone; she had been aching to tell someone. But Xavier begged her not to. If anyone knew—Lucy's parents, the guidance counselors—he would be removed from his home and placed in the foster care system. There had been a scare, apparently, back in elementary school, when he had to stay away from the house for a few nights, all his things packed in a plastic garbage bag. He did not wish to repeat the experience. He could be taken out of their school permanently, away from Lucy herself—just saying it aloud made him look terrified and desperate. Lucy was in over her head. She promised not to tell. She promised and promised again, Xavier pulling the words out of her like a mantra, like a magical incantation.

During the long months of the winter, Lucy works on her college essays. Downstairs the fire crackles, and periodically she hears her father grunt at the newspaper. The smell of wood-smoke drifts up the stairs. The dog lies by her feet, drooling into her socks.

*His name,* Lucy writes, *had already been given to him when we got him from the animal shelter. I remember I tried to change it to something dumb and girly, like Socks or Fido, but now I'm glad my dog wouldn't let me. Many parts of his personality were already there at the beginning. It is difficult to explain what it means to me to have a dog . . .*

Lucy has been lying to Xavier. They agreed that she would look at colleges only in their immediate area. She knows his litany so well that she could say it with him, word for word: He will visit on weekends, on holidays, and if one of them gets a crush on somebody else, he will uproot himself and move to be with her. But Lucy has requested applications for schools in California, Alaska, and Maine—as far from Ohio as possible. She has been thumbing through pictures of ocean vistas, half concealed in mist. She imagines walking with her dog beneath redwood trees so tall that the canopy might as well be another planet. She will buy a pair of hiking boots. She will let Dharma chase seals down the rocky coastline, climb over glaciers, charge through swamps. It is all a dream, of course. She throws these enticing applications away as soon as they arrive, hiding the evidence—it is enough of a rebellion just to have looked at them.

Seated before the computer, she chews her fingernails, and Dharma glances up hopefully at the cessation of clatter from the keyboard. Lucy reaches down absently and scratches his ears. What she wants to say about him drifts tantalizingly at the back of her mind. There is something important here. In her anthropology class, she once read that dogs and humans coevolved, creating a relationship that stands in stark opposition to the normal pattern of domestication. In every other case, as people brought animals into their sphere (to use them as workers, food, protection, or transportation), the animals' brains would gradually change. Over the millennia, horses lost a significant portion of their frontal lobe—the decision-making sector—as this side of things was relegated to their masters.

But in the case of dogs, the situation is different. Humans and canines *both* changed. In their domestication, dogs became permanent puppies, never fully maturing as they would in the wild. They did not need to mature; their owners would tell them what to do and would care for them. People, however, also lost a portion of their brains—a section that had to do with the emotional experience. Part of the human capacity to have feelings disappeared, surrendered to their canine companions.

Lucy sits up straight again, and Dharma, recognizing the signs, gloomily retires to the corner beneath the desk.

*Without my dog*, Lucy writes, *I would not know how to feel certain things. Without him, I do not believe that I would ever feel joy.*

∾

She tumbled into her relationship with Xavier almost accidentally. At the age of fourteen, she liked a boy in her Spanish class, kissed him once or twice behind the bleachers, and before she knew it, Xavier was head-over-heels in love, planning already to marry her, picking out baby names. It happened so fast that it made her head spin. Lucy was flattered; she could not get her bearings. She had never expected to be adored so entirely. Xavier gazed into her small, freckled face as though he had been blind before the sight of her. He treated her like his own personal gift, something he had always waited for and deserved, now finally delivered to him.

At first Lucy had been proud to have a real boyfriend, holding hands in the movie theatre, falling down the rabbit hole of delirious make-out sessions, her friends cornering her in the hallways to demand all the details. She spent hours chatting with Xavier, sprawled across her parents' bed, the phone crooked between her shoulder and chin, one ear slowly going numb. She listened to tales of his alcoholic father, of beatings and neglect. She told him about her own father, his many surgeries. Her father was in and out of the hospital then, her mother half mad with worry, ferrying him to and fro, on the phone with specialists day and night. Xavier said it made them more alike. They were both abandoned children, nearly orphaned—and though Lucy knew, even then, that their situations were not at all analogous, she agreed just to please him. But she did not love him—had never loved him—had never yet loved anyone.

Soon he began to want to have sex. Lucy refused, surprising both of them with her firmness. It is the only place (she sometimes thinks, in particularly low moments) where she has been able to hold her own. Xavier whined and pleaded. After a year of dating, in a burst of annoyance, he even told his buddies that they had done it. Lucy was relieved by this, rather than angry, since it took some of the pressure off. At least he would be able to brag and swagger. At least he would not be able to complain about her to anyone. Every now and then, as the months passed, he would try again to win her over with his powers of persuasion, and Lucy would disingenuously agree to it all without once changing her mind. Yes, they had done everything else, so this last barrier scarcely mattered. Yes, where love was involved, it probably wasn't a sin. His genitalia struck her as faintly floral, the bi-lobed bud at the top, the strong pink stem, the bulb of the scrotum, all matted with rooty hairs. Lucy was able to please him well enough. Sometimes she even wanted to go ahead and cross that final threshold. But still she held her ground. It was the one blessing of those ubiquitous health classes: The phrase "I'm not ready" had become a powerful weapon, three words that were not to be argued with or comprehended, only obeyed. Lucy was not ready; every so often she would say it again, and Xavier would have to acquiesce.

∾

Over the winter holidays, Lucy and her family load their gear into the car and spend a weekend touring the state, scoping out colleges. The trip is hard on all of them. Her mother is a nervous driver, her knuckles white on the steering wheel as she negotiates around trucks and copes with potholes. Her father fidgets and grumbles in the passenger's seat. Dharma, who generally loves a good long ride in the car, becomes nauseated after so many days of travel, and sits moaning with his head in Lucy's lap, occasionally passing gas so foul that the whole family has to roll down the windows, despite the drizzle outside.

On each campus, Lucy gazes up at the ivy-covered dorms and the imposing pillars of English halls and theatre buildings. She watches the students hurrying by her, wearing ripped hoodies and hand-knitted scarves, their hair still mussed from sleep. She sits in on a few classes, her eyes lowered to her desk, expecting at any moment to be called out as a fraud. She makes sure to telephone Xavier every night, aware that he will be waiting anxiously. Her parents, on this trip, seem to fade almost into shadows. Her father's difficulties worsen in unfamiliar settings. The car makes his back ache, and he has trouble getting any rest on the cots the colleges provide for their prospective students. Her mother is in constant attendance upon him, her usual solicitousness increasing to almost saintlike proportions. When they return home at last, Lucy watches her mother lean over the passenger's seat, her face filled with gracious consideration, every particle of her being alive to her husband's discomfort—and Lucy feels an odd shiver, as though she herself is in danger. Something in her mother's posture reminds her of her own way of moving. That delicate sway of the neck. The shoulders bent in sympathy and concern.

Spring comes in with a thunderclap, bringing days of lashing rain. Undaunted, Lucy and the dog take longer walks than before, crossing to the very edge of the arboretum, where the woods open unexpectedly into a genteel golf course. Lucy gets the sniffles from tramping around in a downpour. Dharma shakes himself dry in the living room, sending out silvery cascades of water. Crocuses shove their determined heads through the soil. Mist curdles out of the gutters. Lucy walks along the highway into unfamiliar neighborhoods. Sometimes she feels as if she is disappearing, a sensation that is reinforced when she and the dog reach the very outskirts of her hometown, staring together down a dirt road that caps a hill and vanishes from sight. Sometimes she loses her way, wandering helplessly down side streets, unable to navigate in the hazy evening. Street lamps shine between the trees, the glow echoing off the branches in concentric circles, so that the bulbs appear to be wreathed in haloes. Lucy rarely makes it home before dark.

She and Xavier have been fighting worse than ever. First he accused her of scoring too well on her SATs; then he accused her of looking down on him because he had no desire for a college degree. How will it be, he shouted, when they are married and have kids who watch and learn from their parents' attitudes? Will she continue her snobbish, self-absorbed behavior then, or will she be able to consider the greater good? Sometimes, during these squabbles, Lucy will literally begin to pass out, so wearied by his circular logic that her eyes grow heavy. Xavier's "accidents" have become more frequent as well. He kicked the wall at his father's shop and busted his toe, limping around for the next few weeks. (Lucy took it upon herself to drive him everywhere he needed to go.) He bruised his elbow in gym class, falling against the mirror and leaving a flower-shaped series of cracks in the glass, the petals expanding outward in a glittering ring.

One day, while he and Lucy are on their way outside for lunch, Xavier pauses by the vending machine. As Lucy watches, he grows increasingly frustrated. The mechanism spits his money out, then jams, so that his treat dangles tantalizingly over the void. Xavier shakes the machine and swears at it. Finally he punches the plating, hard enough to leave a dent. Lucy looks wildly around for a security guard, but as a rule there is never one nearby in a crisis. Xavier leads her outside to a sheltered spot beneath a tree, waving his candy triumphantly, as though he has just pulled Excalibur from the anvil. Before long, however, his hand begins to swell. The knuckle blooms into a taut purple grape.

At the hospital, the doctors tell him that he broke the vein, not the bone. As long as he is careful not to hit anything else, it will heal on its own. For weeks, Xavier walks around with his knuckle swollen, unable to hold a pencil or make a fist. Even after the vein returns to a normal size, the bruise remains, like a splotch of violet paint on the back of his hand.

ↀ

At last Lucy's acceptance letters begin to arrive—big, fat packets from schools all over Ohio. Her parents are overjoyed. Lucy is a little startled by their enthusiasm, unaccustomed to having their full attention. Her father claps her on the back, his weary eyes watering. Her mother pulls her into an impromptu waltz around the living room, keeping time in a jubilant hum. Even Xavier gets into the swing of things. He is proud of his brilliant girlfriend. He is gentle with her, forgiving. He comes over whenever he can get away from the garage, poring through her letters and playing with the dog. (Xavier once had a dog himself and likes to wax poetic about how close they were. "When we're married, we'll have a whole bunch," he says, and Lucy's mother, overhearing, smiles indulgently.) At school, no one can talk about anything else. People throw their arms around each other in the hallways, squealing with delight, or burst into tears in the student lounge because they were rejected from their first choice.

Lucy finds herself somewhat numb. Her hopes for college were modest all along: the chance to take a few classes Xavier might not approve of; the chance, perhaps, to make a friend. It has been a light for her at the end of a long, dim tunnel. But now she can picture herself there in earnest: Xavier walking her to class and back again, lurking outside her dorm, and sharing her bed whenever her roommate is away. "Yes, that's me and my bodyguard," she will say to her teachers, to her new classmates, who will give her the pitying, bewildered look she is accustomed to and turn away.

ↀ

In the last week of school, Xavier disappears. Lucy picks him up in the morning, as always, but when she goes to their usual rendez-vous spot before second period, he never shows up. She does not think much of it at the time. The hallways are in an uproar. Banners are hung every few feet, celebrating school spirit, only occasionally vandalized or torn down out of spite. Classes are canceled for graduation rehearsals. Xavier could be anywhere, now that the routines have changed. After third period, Lucy hurries into the courtyard to meet him in back of the Art Wing. But again, he does not appear. She waits for a while, confused. By fifth period she knows something is wrong—she checks her cell phone, but there is no message from him. She goes to his locker and stands there idiotically, as though waiting for him to throw open the metal door and climb out.

At lunchtime, Lucy is alone for the first time in her memory. She is baffled by her strange new freedom. She can sit anywhere she likes. She can eat the contents of her lunch all out of order, without comment—she can throw her food away, opting not to eat at all. She wanders across the grassy lawn, kicking up twigs and leaves. Eventually she climbs halfway up an apple tree and swings her feet in the breeze. The day is unseasonably warm, and students are set-tled around the grounds in knots, like flocks of migrating birds at rest. Every so often, as Lucy watches, someone will suddenly leap to his or her feet and begin to do the Bee Dance—darting away from the invisible assailant with arms flailing. Hidden among the branches, Lucy contemplates what it would be like to join one of these groups. She could do it; she remembers how. She could plunk down with her bright smile, pushing her hair out of her face, and say, "God, it's hot. Hey, did you understand that part about cloud formation in fourth period?" She does not do any such thing, of course—it would be a kind of betrayal—but still, she *could*.

After eighth period she pauses at the drinking fountain and splashes water on her face. There is still no message from Xavier, though she has been checking her cell phone obsessively, earning herself a reprimand from her English teacher. A group of boys is gathered nearby, and Lucy hesitates, wondering whether she ought to ask if they've seen him. They stand with their heads close together, their jeans slung low around their hips, tossing a ball of tinfoil back and forth. They are discussing the various pranks they might play for graduation—hilarious tricks like going without pants beneath their robes and thereby obtaining their diplomas while wearing boxer briefs, or else taking a hit of acid before the ceremony and hallucinating all the way up to the podium. Lucy rolls her eyes, smirking. Reflexively, she hears Xavier speaking in her mind, his sputtering strictures on their stupidity and inferiority. Then one of the boys lowers his voice, asking whether anyone else heard about that thing in the locker room.

Lucy holds still, her heart beginning to pound. No one seems to know quite what took place, but apparently there was a lot of blood on the floor, a crimson spray across the wall. The boys laugh, deciding that probably someone was murdered. Lucy gasps for breath. In that instant she knows exactly what happened. She has been expecting this moment for years.

The bell rings, and the boys jump and begin to scatter. Gathering her wits, Lucy reaches out and plucks one of them by the sleeve—she knows him by sight, but is not sure of his name.

"Which locker room?" she asks. "I heard you talking."

"What?"

"Which locker room did—"

"Oh. It was the one by the small gym, out in the East Wing." He leans in curiously, his eyebrows raised. "Why? You think Xavier had something to do with it?"

Lucy flushes—she may not know the boy from Adam, but of course he knows who she is dating.

"No, no," she says quickly. "Just curious. It's nothing."

She ditches her last period, slinking quietly through the halls. When classes are in session, the high school changes. The hallways darken perceptively, empty except for the occasional scuffling footstep, a janitor or teacher heading off for a coffee break. Sounds drift, muffled, through the heavy doors. Lucy catches the monotonous drone of a teacher lecturing on free market economy as she slips into one of the stairwells. She will avoid the security guards, if she can—though they are easy enough to deceive; all she has to do is blush shamefacedly and say that she needs to see the school nurse, and they will back away without asking too many questions.

She finds the gym deserted. The wood floor gleams. The windows show a cloudy sky, and dust motes twirl in the uncertain light. Lucy crosses the basketball court, clutching the straps of her backpack. The door to the boys' locker room stands ajar, outlined by a sharp fluorescent glimmer. Lucy can see a stain of red on the floor. Someone evidently began to clean up the mess but stopped in the middle of the task; a mop stands abandoned against the doorjamb. The blood is still there. A pool beneath the sinks. A smear heading out into the gym. The bristles of the mop caked in it. Lucy stands in the doorway, shaking. She can see how he did it—the razor blade is sitting where he dropped it beside the garbage can. There is a spatter across two of the mirrors. The moldy green towels that the school has reused for years are heaped against the wall, and Lucy can see that they are soiled as well, speckled with dark blotches. She knows that the blood is Xavier's, as surely as though she can smell his own distinctive musk in the crimson puddle on the tile. He might as well have signed his name.

She does not sleep at all that night. Her bed is hot, then cold, and the dog is restless as well, clambering around on her calves and trying to cram his furry body in between Lucy and the wall. Eventually she gives up and goes downstairs, wrapped in her blanket. The windows are open, letting in the spring air, a wet wind smelling of freshly cut grass. Her parents are sound asleep in their bedroom at the back. She does not have to worry about waking her father—his pain medicine knocks him unconscious, sometimes zonking him out during the daytime as well if he sits still for too long—but her mother, if aroused by any small sound, has a nasty habit of marching around for hours, neurotically checking that the oven is off, the toaster unplugged. Lucy does not wish to talk to anyone. Xavier called earlier, just briefly, from the hospital, sounding thoroughly drugged. In a slurred voice he explained that they were keeping him overnight. The gym teacher had found him. He told her he was sorry; he might have been crying. He told her not to try to visit, as she would not be allowed to see him. Only family were allowed in. Lucy promised to come by in the morning and got off the phone as fast as possible.

She knows the routine by now, exactly how it will unfold. She and Xavier have it down to a science. Once he is discharged, she will wait outside the emergency room, in the hollow of the driveway, squinting through the glass doors. She will bring the dog in the back seat, for company and to make Xavier smile. He will show her his wounds. It is her job to wince, and shudder, and shriek with dismay as he explains exactly what the doctors did to him. Xavier will be pale and noble. He will describe some quarrel with his father, some apathetic jibe on the part of his mother. He will explain how he lost control. For the next few weeks, the two of them will be closer than ever. Xavier will need help with unexpected things, ordinary things—tying his shoes, turning a doorknob. Lucy will leap to answer the phone when it rings. She will check on him five or six times a day. She will sing him to sleep, cut up his meat for him, rub his back gently to relieve the tension. For a while, it will be as though she gave birth to him herself.

By 3:00 AM, she has given up any hope of sleep. She suits up, putting on her walking shoes and her jean jacket, muffling Dharma's enthusiastic whining by feeding him a lump of peanut butter to stick his jaws shut. The neighborhood is absolutely still. Most of the houses are dark, each pane a black and shuttered eye; occasionally one upper window burns with a muted glow, a fellow insomniac whiling away the witching hour with a book or a pornographic website. Lucy sniffs the air. The dog seems unusually sober, marching importantly ahead of her as though they are on a mission together, his tail waving in a plumed salute.

Above the treetops, the sky is a great bowl of stars. The moon, as thin as a fingernail clipping, hangs low in the west. Lucy takes the shortest route to the arboretum, walking along the highway. A few trucks lumber past her. Now and then Dharma growls threateningly into a bush or ditch—unusual behavior for him—and Lucy wonders if, because of the strange hour and her own black mood, he feels a burgeoning need to protect her from danger.

At last they reach the woods. Lucy blunders around for a while, unable to locate the trail. In the gloom, everything looks different. Light comes in shifting patches between the trees, so that the underbrush is as shadowy and chaotic as the deep ocean. Lucy skids down an unfamiliar hill, catching her feet in brambles and mud. When she laughs in helpless amusement, the dog pants approvingly. She keeps him on the leash, and he manifests no desire to leave her, though usually by this point he would be bounding around like a rubber ball, mouthing the rope. Together they find the stream. The water rushes like black ink between the boulders—an occasional flash of silver indicates foamy rapids. Lucy settles on a cold, flat stone. Dharma leans against her shoulder, sniffing maniacally and following each new sound with a lift of his ears. As soon as they are done crashing around, the forest returns to business as usual. An owl cries. A fish jumps clear of the water. The trees surge overhead, moving in unison like kelp in a current. Lucy shivers, tugging her coat more securely around her shoulders. The dog lies down, gazing into her eyes.

When the sun rises, they are still there. Something is happening to Lucy. She feels like her mind is trying to clear—as though she has been in a fog for a long while. For the first time, she wonders if Xavier has always known that she does not love him. She has tried to give him the benefit of the doubt; the only way her sacrifice would be worthwhile was if Xavier never knew what she was giving up for him. But perhaps her instincts have been right all along. Perhaps there has been a silent conversation taking place between them: She has told Xavier that she wishes she could leave, and he has answered that he will kill himself if she tries. His ostensible reason for hurting himself has always been something different, of course. But each injury has been a shot across the bows for her. A warning of what might happen if he were ever left alone. She has felt the terrible weight of his life in her hands.

The sun crests the horizon, and the dog rises to his feet, stretching elaborately. The birds begin their riotous chorus. Lucy passes a hand over her eyes. There is an image in her mind of flesh on a table, glistening pinkly in the light. She can name every wound on Xavier's body, each broken finger and bloodied knee. Each one was a piece of himself he threw away, only to claim a piece of Lucy instead. Her fingers. Her knees. More than once, he has nearly disposed of his own life, just to hang on to hers. It is like being devoured slowly; every so often she will turn around, only to find that another part of her has been consumed. Her sense of humor. Her laughing acquaintances. Her capacity for unadulterated happiness. Xavier's hunger for her is unending. Each bite he takes leaves her weaker and dumber, and he has come at last to her vital organs. Of course Lucy has never wanted to sleep with him. In some deep and quiet place, where they are not friends and lovers but combatants engaged in a long and bloody war, she has been fighting for possession of something dear to her—her identity, maybe, or her own soul—and if she gave in at this last hurdle, she would have given in completely. She would have nothing left of her own.

~

In her first semester at college, Lucy moves around the campus like a ghost. She dresses unobtrusively in secondhand hoodies and jeans. She does not bother to decorate her dorm room beyond a few posters of dogs. Her roommate, she is sure, finds her to be quiet, innocuous, a bit dull—unwilling, for example, to gate-crash one of the keggers at the frat house down the street, unwilling to stay up late discussing the cute T.A. in the Literature 101 class the two of them share. Lucy goes to bed early every night. She does not explore the town beyond the insular campus, wandering, as so many freshmen do, into the theatre district or the shopping malls. The phone rings frequently for her roommate, but Lucy does not get many calls—just her mother, now and again, gently checking in, or her father reminding her fretfully to get the oil changed in that car of hers. Between classes, she spends her time at the library, an immense stone building whose interior is as segmented as a hive, packed with shadowed corners. Lucy sits there by the hour, flipping dreamily through her textbooks beneath the drone of the fluorescent lights.

She feels empty. She finds herself without the words to answer the cheerful burble of her roommate, the calm questions of her professors. She feels like a barely-there person, sketched lightly on the air. As she has instructed, her parents do not mention Xavier when they call. They are both baffled by the whole thing, accepting without comprehension Lucy's decision to disappear so absolutely from her long-term boyfriend's life: changing her phone number and her e-mail address, asking them not to pass on any messages he might leave with them. Her mother tries, once or twice, to broach the subject in a cozy, all-girls-together sort of way. Lucy responds by hanging up and turning off her cell phone. She has brought nothing of his with her. Her photographs, his letters, their special notebooks, are at home in her childhood bedroom, to be destroyed at some later date. Lucy has not told her new acquaintances about him. She broke down and cried only once, when her roommate, eyeing the posters of dogs above Lucy's bed with some distaste, asked casually if Lucy herself had a pet. To her own horror, Lucy burst into tears, sobbing with such violence that her roommate backed away, stammering apologies. Eventually, she knows, she will talk about it to someone. But for the moment the wound is still too raw.

It was not easy, in the end, to leave him. At first, of course, she couldn't even think of it—Xavier was a broken bird, more dependent on her than ever before. He was unable to attend the last few days of high school. Lucy flew solo at the homecoming dance and class picnic, slices of watermelon and greasy cake on offer. The rumor mill ran rampant, but only a few people dared to approach her directly and ask her just what had happened in that locker room. Xavier did eventually tell her the story: "Some idiot left his razor on the sink. I was in there by myself for some reason; I guess I wanted to pick up my gym clothes. Then I started to think about graduation and everything. How everybody would be leaving. I picked up one of the blades, and before I knew it—" Listening to him, Lucy could not keep from trembling.

His forearms were heavily bandaged for a while, as though in preparation for a martial arts class. When the stitches were removed, Xavier was fitted with splints; even now, if he were to bend his wrists, the cuts could reopen. A slew of psychiatrists had fixed their beady eyes on him. Though it seemed that he would not, as he had feared, be removed from his parents' custody, there were still mandatory therapy sessions to attend, some of them lasting for hours. The summer moved along in a blur of bland, airy weather. All over town, there were celebratory parties. Lucy didn't make her way to any of them—though her imagination did linger on backyards filled with music, an illicit keg in the bushes, hot dogs turning above a bonfire. Xavier would wait for her on his porch each day, gazing down the road for her car. Despite the heat, he wore long sleeves to hide the splints, his body perfuming the day with captured sweat. Both wrists were marked by bright red lines. The doctors had told him he would have scars forever.

One day in July, Lucy drove across town with Dharma, who hung his head out the window, barking at his counterparts on the sidewalk. Xavier met her at his front door, and together they strolled down the hill to the park. He told her how his only fond memories from childhood were in this place, his father pushing him on the tire swing, his mother giving him a few bucks for the ice cream truck. They settled in the grass. The dog rampaged around them, chasing bumblebees. Lucy chatted nonchalantly enough, though she was nervous, her palms sweating, her attention wandering far from whatever Xavier was saying about the latest superhero-themed blockbuster.

She was determined to break up with him at last. Her first, tentative attempts to do so had proved futile. She had tried communicating through hints ("When I go to college, things will be *different*"), but Xavier had proved immune to this brand of subtlety—he only smiled and concurred. Then she began to induce small separations between them, hoping this fledgling space would widen and widen: She spent the evenings cooking with her mother or researching courses online and did not return Xavier's calls until morning. And yet it never worked out as she had planned. He was so eager to see her again, so ardent in his affection, that he perceived any estrangement as a simple inconvenience, rather than an act of will. In desperation, Lucy had texted *I do not love you, it's all over* into her cell phone, and then erased the message, ashamed of her cowardice. She was running out of time. In a few short weeks she would leave for college—fifteen days, to be precise. She was already packing her things, organizing her books and T-shirts, and still she had not found a way to end things with Xavier. If she wasn't careful, she would end up married to him yet, walking down the aisle in a big white dress like an automaton, her mind still churning in vain over her carefully phrased but never-voiced words of farewell.

And yet she could not do it, there in that idyllic spot, on that mild summer day. Anyone watching them from the street would have seen young love at work. Xavier tipped his head back, closing his eyes in the sunshine. At the edge of the park, the dog bounded after a bunny, dashing through a clump of bushes. The rabbit froze instinctively, and Dharma was fooled, barreling right past it. Xavier was enchanted by the fact that he, as a human being, could see through the guises that animals used to hide from one another.

It was that night that the idea came to her. Fireflies flickered beyond her window as Lucy sat on the bed, packing her sweaters and coats. Dharma panted his swampy breath into her face. The notion came suddenly, blooming with icy precision, full-formed, as though some secret part of her had been working on it for quite a while. Lucy tried to push the thought away, but it returned at once, blotting out everything else. In order for her to leave Xavier— to really leave him, to end the relationship once and for all—she would have to give him something that would sustain him in her absence. Only in this way could she be free of her burden, her acute sense of maternal responsibility. Only in this way could she guarantee that he would be safe. The plan was a vicious one, as bitter and painful as a slap across the face. But that, too, was all to the good. It was necessary that Lucy herself should suffer in the process. She had known that all along. She would need to be punished, and punished severely, for her desertion. That way nobody, not Xavier, or even Lucy herself, could fault her for it afterward. It would have to hurt like hell.

In the morning, she was ready. She took Dharma for such a long walk that her legs grew sore. She let him linger beside each enticing smell; she let him roll in garbage, and afterward, she washed him tenderly (which, unlike the rest of his species, he adored, splashing around and trying to bite the stream of water coming out of the faucet). Lucy clipped his toenails. She took a packet of chicken out of the fridge—its presence there had been causing him a certain amount of angst—and served it up for him on a bed of dog food and rice. Her parents were out for the day, visiting friends from her father's hospital support group, and Lucy was glad. She tried to think of what she would say to them later on—that Dharma had run away, that she had left him with friends for the duration of her first few semesters at school, that he had been killed, maybe. It was best that she did not have to face them just yet. In the car, on the way to Xavier's, she touched the dog's crumpled ears, the broken tooth at the front of his jaw, the black patch at the end of his tail.

But there her memory stops—the day burns away into a humming blank. Lucy is aware of what she did and said, standing in the sunshine outside Xavier's house. She knows that she handed over the dog's food bowl and chew toys. She had even printed out a sheet of directions for Dharma's care, just as she would for a house sitter, detailing how to brush his fur and cope with his dental hygiene. Perhaps she and Xavier fought. Perhaps she gave in and cried. She doesn't remember; the afternoon is broken into shards, and she has retained only flickers of the moment. Dharma darting after a butterfly. Her own heart pounding determinedly. A gleam of sunlight reflecting from an upper window. She knows that when she gave Xavier the leash, he took it quizzically, and the dog shifted obediently, plopping down beside Xavier's feet, gazing up at Lucy with his eyebrows raised. This simple act caused her to moan a little. She knows that at one point she saw Xavier's expression change, as at last he began to grasp her intention. But for once she was more absorbed in her own pain than his. She knows that she patted Dharma's head, and he looked up at her with his customary expression, hopeful, adoring. There was simply no way to say goodbye to a dog. She knows that, in the end, she drove away.

☙

In autumn the campus grows rainy and dark, the flagstones glimmering with wet. Lucy crosses the quad wrapped up in a scarf and hat. She buys a college sweater. Now and then she lets her roommate drag her out for coffee. She goes to see a few movies in the evenings. She begins to take long walks again, striding past the library, down the hill, and into the rose garden, which opens into a quiet wood and a slow, winding river, weighted down with mud.

One day she is seated in her Indian History course, her desk catching the last rays of waning sun through the window. With a jolt, she comes across Dharma's name in the footnotes of her textbook. The classroom fades away, the teacher's voice receding. Turning avidly to the right page, a lump in her throat, Lucy reads for the first time about the origin of her dog's honorific. (She does not think of him, does not let her mind dwell on whether Xavier is letting him sleep in the bed, whether Xavier remembers the way to rub him just so behind his sore left ear. She does not wonder whether Dharma has forgotten her by now, or whether he still waits, languidly in the morning, anxiously in the afternoon, his ears perking up at the whine of a car engine like hers, his golden head turning to follow the smell of her lavender shampoo when it drifts from another woman's hair.) Lucy hoists the book up off the desk. She reads that in the Epics, the great stories of Indian lore, it is written that King Yudhisthira and a party of cohorts climbed the Himalayas. This group braved ice, snow, and the thinning air, but one by one they capitulated and fell away, so that by the time the king reached the home of the gods, all his companions had succumbed to weakness and deserted him—except for his faithful dog.

Lucy sits up straight, tucking her hair back from her face. Her nose nearly touches the printed page. She reads how the gods welcomed the weary king, asking him to come in and join them. But he refused to enter if it meant abandoning his dog there on the mountaintop. This turned out to be the right choice. The gods allowed the dog in as well, and when the two of them had passed through the gates together, the animal's shape suddenly changed. He transformed before the king's eyes into the god Dharma. Blinking away the tears, Lucy trails her finger down the list of his divine attributes. *The principle of cosmic order. Righteous duty and virtue. One of the fundamental elements that make up the world.*

# CAPTIVITY

At the age of thirty-one, I moved in with my mother. This was not entirely my fault. My apartment building was about to go condo, and I could no longer afford the rent. My lanky, bookish boyfriend took a job in Florida and unexpectedly moved away. My pet octopus caught a mysterious virus and died; I came home from work and found her bobbing sadly on the surface of her tank, her skin washed clean of color. The combination of all these factors left me listless. I could not cope with the hassle of moving, much less finding a new apartment within my price range, in a good neighborhood, within a matter of weeks. It was much easier to pack everything I owned into boxes and ship it all into storage instead. I liked the feeling of shedding my belongings; it seemed as though the objects that had pinned me to the ground were lifted one by one, rendering me weightless. It seemed as though my own personality could similarly be purged of excess baggage and rendered new.

And so I moved in with my mother, half a mile away in northern Chicago. She put me in my childhood bedroom and didn't have to ask why I began to spend all my time at work. During the first week of living with her, I managed to stay at the aquarium for three days straight. It became a joke in the cephalopod wing. I tested the water samples, cleaned the tank of algae, and donned scuba gear to feed the big *Octopus vulgaris* before a crowd. I had never needed much sleep and now subsisted on next to none—a few minutes with my head down on the desk, and I was good for a couple more hours. Even my boss told me to go home, though I thought the octopuses and cuttlefish seemed comforted by the constancy of my presence. When I could no longer focus on my own work, I visited the dolphin boys. They were young, strange men, unfazed by broken femurs and smashed hands, a set of top teeth knocked clean out by a playful flick of the tail. I talked with the sea horse behaviorist, who was concerned about a fungus killing the algae and plants; it was either caused by the animals or else was dangerous to them instead. I wandered down to take my break with the sea otter crew, who all trooped outside every hour on the hour to smoke cigarettes and discuss exactly *how* Mickey the sea otter had got hold of Charley the trainer's hat. And then I went home and found photographs of my brother Jordan scattered all around my mother's house, and she and I looked at one another with a terrible politeness.

There was even a photograph of him in my bedroom, though I quickly moved it into the living room, where Mom must have noticed its sudden appearance on the end table. It showed Jordan at the age of five, wearing a purple baseball cap and making his picture smile, a grin so wide it hurt his cheeks and nearly closed his eyes with squinting. In the photo his feet were blurred; he was drumming his heels on the legs of his chair, as though the energy required in so fierce a smile had to shoot out of his body in other ways. It was not my favorite photograph. He looked manic and distressed.

I missed my mother more, living under her roof, than I had when we were on opposite ends of the same city. I knew her so well that I could predict, as she sat in the evenings flipping through the paper, when she would crack her knuckles or tilt her head back in a yawn. She was a fascinating woman, her hair silky and shot through with white, her eyes crackling with energy. She dressed like a gypsy: bright shawls, swingy skirts, and hoop earrings. At the age of sixty she still worked at the bookstore down the street from her house and loved to rattle off Einstein's reasons for supporting the creation of Israel or to calmly drop the fact that Maurice Sendak had once claimed all his books were written about the Holocaust. She often returned home with a resigned smile and a grocery bag full of brand-new books, saying, "Well, I just lost it." It broke my heart that two such interesting women found silence easier than speech, standing side by side in the kitchen as she grated cheese into the pasta and I chopped the vegetables, or watching television together with our heads cocked at the same angle.

～

Seven years earlier, my brother Jordan had disappeared. One day he was living in his trailer on the California coastline, and the next day he was gone. I flew out to San Francisco, frantic, unshowered, and mumbling to myself, while my mother stayed in Chicago and called everyone from the FBI to Jordan's ninth-grade girlfriend. The sun was dazzling in my brother's trailer park. I had visited him there before, but in my panic, my navigational skills deserted me, and I quickly grew bewildered. The trailers themselves were numbered according to no particular system. Jordan's neighbors had mischievous faces and sent me down several sweeping tracks that did not lead to my brother. At last I found the right trailer. The door swung open on a faulty hinge.

The interior space was absolutely still. The bedclothes were tumbled in a heap, revealing bare mattress. Jordan's surfboard stood in the shower, half hidden by the plastic curtain, and startled me out of my wits. His clothes were crammed cheerfully into his tiny set of drawers. His smell hung about the room. A more thorough search yielded his toothbrush in the medicine cabinet, his wallet in the back pocket of a crumpled pair of jeans on the floor, and his diary buried in the tangle of sheets. A quick flip through its pages told me only the daily weather, with the height and strength of the waves mentioned particularly. I stepped out into the brilliant sunshine, sweaty, bleary-eyed, and still wearing the coat I had needed in rainy Chicago.

Over the next few days I interviewed anyone Jordan had ever mentioned in a letter, anyone who claimed to know him, and everyone told me a different story. Rudy and Mike, his shaggy, furtive surfing buddies, said he had been with them on the water the day he disappeared. His next-door neighbors could tell me nothing except that he'd begun to frighten them—they had heard screaming from his trailer in recent weeks, a woman sobbing, furniture overturned, and the splash of broken glass. The lifeguards at his favorite beach told me Jordan was something of a menace; he tackled the highest waves, without regard for life or limb, and the young boys followed him. The man at the beachside surf shop spat on the ground and said Jordan was never without his slut of a girlfriend, an outrage against everything that was decent and moral. An elderly woman, bedecked by crystals and lace, said she had dreamed he was drowned, gone under while surfing. When I mentioned finding the surfboard in his shower stall, she crossed herself.

At the end of the week I had nothing but questions. My journal was packed with notes like *Girlfriend? What girlfriend?* My mother would be frenzied; I had not even called to say I'd landed safely, and now I had nothing to tell her. I walked slowly back from the beach. The sky was a hazy orange above me, the wind cool and mild. The rows of trailers gleamed in the setting sun. My mind was full of Jordan's stripped bed in the shadows, the sweet relief of sleep. But when I reached the trailer, there was a girl on the stoop. She wore a pink bikini and nothing else. She was so thin she looked almost ill. Her hair was as heavy as seaweed.

When she saw me coming she stood up, and warily I extended my hand. She shook it with a hot, damp palm.

"Mara?" she said. "I'm Cynthia. You're looking for Jordan."

I nodded dumbly and sat on the trailer stoop, the metal warm from the sun. Cynthia stood over me, printed dark against the sky. There was a peach-colored bruise on her right shoulder, from which I averted my eyes. She waggled a plastic ring under my nose.

"We're engaged," she said. "So when he comes back, he'll call me first."

❧

I had been living with my mother for almost a month when the postcard arrived. I was not expecting any mail; I was standing in the living room in my stocking feet, flicking through bills as the sun rose behind the trees. *I AM ALIVE*, said the postcard, in fat block letters. No signature, addressed to me. I yelled for Mom. She was in the shower, though, warbling a little tune over the hiss of the water. The front of the postcard showed only the familiar image of Lake Michigan, dark beneath a scattering of sailboats. My heart began to hammer reproachfully on the inside of my chest. "Mom!" I hollered, and I heard her bellow, "What?" from inside the bathroom. The handwriting in the address was unfamiliar—no distant bells went off. But Jordan's handwriting might have changed in seven years.

"What?" Mom yelled again. "Mara? Are you calling me?"

She switched off the shower. I folded the postcard in half and put it in my pocket, where it burned. My hands now seemed very empty. There was a clatter in the bathroom, shampoo bottles landing in the tub, and Mom muttered, "Oh, *hell.*" I remembered I'd made tea, and I hurried into the kitchen to clutch the warm cup in hands that trembled. Mom stomped into the room in her bathrobe, her hair swathed unevenly in a towel.

"What?" she asked, exasperated. "What were you hollering about?"

"You're going deaf," I said mildly. "Do you want any tea?"

She narrowed her eyes. "I am *not* going deaf. You were howling about something."

"Your turban is coming off."

"You're obnoxious." She adjusted her towel where it had fallen like bangs over her eyes. "I recorded a show for you on eels, did you see it?"

"Eels eat octopuses," I said. The postcard in my pocket was beating its wings. "I'm going to work."

I paused in the doorway. She looked up at me expectantly.

"I won't be home late," I said.

Mom batted this away with her hand.

At work I unfolded the postcard again. It continued to say *I AM ALIVE*, now with a crease down the middle. I was late to feed the big *Octopus vulgaris*, but I took the time to smooth the postcard out and pin it safely to the bulletin board. I could not take it with me into the tank. I could hardly bear to leave it, and I actually considered climbing the ladder to Falco's pool and just dropping the food in from above, but the thought of demeaning my favorite octopus to the level of a common goldfish got me out of my office and into my flippers and mask.

Falco was the aquarium's largest octopus, and the most friendly. But today, at the sight of me coming into his tank, he turned first pale, then a dark and furious red. When I reached for him, he sped to the other side of the tank and roughened his mantle to the consistency of coral. At first I didn't understand, and then I realized he must have been sensing the strangeness of the morning on me. His suckers would pick up a change in my body chemistry. It was possible he didn't recognize me at all. When I held out a bit of crabmeat, he washed the red from his skin, but there were still black circles painted around his eyes, indicating anxiety. Through the condensation-clouded viewing window of the tank, a small child was watching, his nose smushed against the glass. While I was distracted, Falco stole the crabmeat out of my bag.

All day long, the postcard clanged like a bell in my brain. Cleaning algae from the tank, feeding the morose cuttlefish, sitting in an all-cephalopod meeting, I found myself lost in time, mouth open. It was as though I walked around with the postcard an inch from my eyes. Why an image of Chicago? The one private detective who had claimed to have word on my brother (the others eventually told us all clues pointed to dead) had placed him in northern Italy—and that was three years ago. I imagined my brother seated on the shores of Lago di Como, bearded, shaggy-haired, and alone, pulling from his pocket the one dusty picture he had kept all this time: a postcard of the old skyline. The postmark, however, was local. Perhaps Jordan had crept into the city in the dark of night, chuckling to himself as he attached the stamp and fumbled with the latch of a mailbox. Perhaps he was in the neighborhood even now.

The postcard had to be from Jordan. I had been fooled a thousand times before, by letters from friends with handwriting like my brother's, countless wrong numbers from men with similar voices, a note left by accident on my doorstep, intended for some other woman, people waving from cars, too far off to be identified—and even by a heart someone had sky-written above the Sears Tower. But this was the real thing. It had to be. It had my name on it.

By evening my head was aching, my eyes burned, and I could not work or rest. The time had come to talk to someone. I reached for the phone, dialed Mom's number, and hung up promptly. Then I called her again and let it ring.

"It's me," I said.

"I had a feeling. Something wrong?"

"Shit," I said. "I don't know."

"I see." She took a sip of something. "Well, *I* had an awful day."

Her voice was tired and sad. It was the wrong time to hit her with this particular surprise, especially over the phone.

"Me too," I said cheerfully. "I forgot to eat lunch. Then I forgot to eat dinner."

"Jesus, Mara. Isn't there a food court right there in the aquarium?"

"Really? Since when?"

She took another sip of her drink. A little silence formed and I said, "I've got to go."

"Fine."

I took a deep breath. "Why did *you* have an awful day?"

She laughed. "Never mind, babe. It's nothing."

Night had fallen when at last I left my office and wandered down to the dolphin pool. The enormous room was dark except for one small lamp on a corner table. Through the windows, the skyline appeared, glittering and pristine. One of the dolphin boys knelt by the water. For a mind-numbing instant I thought it was my brother. But when he glanced up, I saw it was Roger with his narrow face and strong, square jaw. He would be fighting with his girlfriend again; nothing else kept him at the aquarium so late. When he saw me coming he laughed and said, "You look like hell."

I knelt beside him. The dolphin tank always seemed to expand and deepen when the lights were off. The black water was very still. The dolphins were hiding. Roger and I peered into the depths, and after a moment I made out the underwater silhouette of the fake stone cliffs that had been built to mimic the dolphins' original coastline. As my eyes adjusted to the gloom, I saw the pale curve of the bottom. Then a shadow flicked across it.

"They're mating," Roger said. "For a change. That's all they do. Apes, humans, and dolphins are the only animals that mate for pleasure, did you know that?"

I shook my head.

"True," he said. "Just think if you locked seven people in a house together for the rest of their lives. What would they do all day? I'm amazed that the viewers don't notice it. The big alpha will zip right by the window with an enormous boner, and they all just go, 'Aww! How *cute*!'"

I laid my hands on the cold surface of the pool. Up close, the smell of saltwater filled the air.

"You fighting with the little woman?" I asked.

He glanced at me. "Yeah, what's your excuse?"

"Make them do a trick. Show off for me."

Roger grinned and slapped his hand three times on the surface of the water. The skyline was reflected in patchy cubes of light; the ripples from his splash broke the image into shimmering snow. Before my eyes, one of the dolphins glided upward, ominous and sentient. Roger sounded two beats, and the dolphin kicked its tail and crested the water with just its dorsal fin. Roger hit the water with the flat of both hands and the dolphin leapt as though he had knocked it clean out of the pool. It didn't jump far, not nearly as high as it could; it hung for a moment, streaming water as thick as blood, and then landed on its side with a rolling splash.

"Ah, the little meathead," Roger said. "We've got to do something about him. He's getting aggressive. Bonking the aquarists on the head when we're cleaning the algae off."

"Bummer," I said.

He raised an eyebrow. "What's funny is trying to make people believe it. *Dolphins*? Never. These guys save shipwrecked sailors, man. It's like you're talking about an attack of killer bunnies."

"Has anybody been hurt?"

"No," Roger said, but his face clouded over. "Well, bumps and bruises. But I've been doing some reading. Certain dolphins will get aggressive in captivity after a few years. Usually the smartest ones. I don't want to think about what'll happen if he starts to get really violent."

He reached into a bucket beside him, lifted out a silver fish, and tossed it into the water. At the splash, a black nose broke the surface and snorked down the tiny meal.

"My brother," I began, and paused. "When I started working here, he was furious with me. Mostly because of the dolphins. *Unconscionable*, he said. We had a big fight about it. I told him that at least they were *alive* in here. Out in the wild, they could be tuna."

Roger cocked his head at me. "Something on your mind?"

"Tell me to go home."

"Mara, go home." He rubbed his nose and added, "For Christ's sake."

"I don't want to," I said.

"Tell me about it," he said wearily.

∽

On the El I sat curled in the handicapped seat and knocked my head gently against the window. The sky was still soaked with colors from the sunset, and I struggled to glimpse Lake Michigan between the buildings. I had the postcard with me, just in case the janitor somehow mistook it for garbage, removed it from the bulletin board, and burned it otherwise.

There was no right way to bring it up with Mom. The last time she and I had talked about my brother—almost two years ago—it had been a train wreck. The conversation began when I mentioned an article I'd read about amnesia and wondered aloud if that could be what happened to Jordan. Unexpectedly, Mom had thrown a plate at the wall. She screamed that he was dead. She screamed that she was living out her greatest nightmare, that of losing a child and having to go on, perpetually stunned that a human being could survive such an injury. And now, she had bellowed, looking crazier by the second, her remaining child appeared to be laboring under some fairytale expectation of a miraculous resurrection. I had never heard her shout like that. Finally I lost my temper and hollered back. I told her that my brother was alive. Perhaps we would never see him again; I was resigned to that, as much as anyone could ever be. But he was not *dead*. He could not have passed out of this world without my knowing it. Then I gathered up my coat, scuttled from her house, and shipped to Seattle for six weeks of field research.

There were giant octopuses in the cold Pacific sea. I spent my time chasing them along the ocean floor, watching their huge bodies outpace their undersized lungs; they would zoom ahead of me for a while on a cloud of looping tentacles, but gradually they would run out of breath and stop, eyeing me anxiously. I could not get used to their thirty-foot wingspans. I could not get warm. I returned home without having called my mother once, and she and I took up a tacit truce of strained good manners and careful conversations. We had not spoken of Jordan since.

∾

Mom was still awake when I let myself into her house. She was sitting at the countertop with a glass of wine beside her, apparently waiting for me. I found I couldn't meet her eyes. I knelt in front of the fridge and began rummaging.

"I can't sleep for shit," she said. "They tell you this about getting old, but I never really believed it."

"I can't sleep either these days," I said, sniffing a pack of cheese.

"You never slept, though." She sipped her wine. "I couldn't make you take a nap to save my life. These other mothers would tell me how their kids slept eight, twelve hours a night, and I wanted to throttle them all."

I found a promising container in the crisper and sniffed its contents. "How old is this pasta?"

"Listen," she said. "Something happened today."

"Tastes fine," I said with my mouth full. "You look troubled."

"I *am* troubled," she said. She was avoiding my eyes too. "Cynthia called me this afternoon."

"Who?" I asked, opening the fridge again.

There was a long, icy pause, during which I looked up and saw anguish on my mother's face. The feeling hit me before the realization—a sinking sensation, as of hope deflating. I set the pasta carefully on the countertop.

"Cynthia," I echoed. "You mean—?"

She nodded. Neither of us spoke his name. Flooded by memory, I sank onto the kitchen floor. The girl in the pink bikini, with waves of greasy hair. Just the thought of her made me wince.

"My God," I said. "What did she want?"

Mom was fidgeting with the hem of her dress. "I'm not certain. She's quite an odd woman."

"Yes," I said. "She was."

"I believe—" Mom cleared her throat. "She wanted to take me out to lunch. She lives here now. I got the sense that she's one of these young imitation hippies, you know, with the all-too-peaceful demeanor, who thinks that clarity of speech is a construct of the Man."

I laughed and brushed a hand across my face. After my one and only meeting with Cynthia—in the sleepless days and weeks that had followed, as it became clear that Jordan was well and truly gone—I had occasionally brooded over his dizzy girlfriend and her ludicrous, plastic, little girl's engagement ring. I had stayed up nights glowering and dreaming up a list of cutting retorts I should have given her. (My mother, when I told her the story, had grown almost apoplectic with rage at the silly girl's presumption and cruelty.) Eventually, though, I came around to pitying Cynthia. She had clearly been a fling, one of many thin, neurotic women to pass in and out of Jordan's life, but however transitory her relationship with him had been, she had lost him too. In the end, the only thing that kept her stamped in my consciousness at all was her proximity to his disappearance—the way the face of a bystander might linger in the brain of a witness at the scene of an accident.

And then I thought of the postcard. A spasm of pain went through me. It was still tucked in my pocket; I laid a hand on the place without thinking. My mother was watching me with concern.

"Oh God," I said. "This was today? She called you today?"

Mom nodded. "Yes."

"And she wanted to see you?" I struggled to my feet. "She wanted to take you to lunch, to be a part of our lives? That's why she got in touch?"

"Yes, that's right," Mom said. "But I made it clear that contact with her would not be welcome. I don't think she'd dare to call me again, and I can't imagine she'd go so far as to bother you. I just thought I should warn you—" She broke off, staring at me.

"Jesus," I said quickly. "It's just too strange. Her getting in touch like that after all these years."

"Mara," she began, but I wiped the tears away on the back of my hand.

"I'm just exhausted," I said. "I'd better hit the hay."

I hurried from the kitchen and up the stairs.

◈

In the morning, there was another postcard. I stood in Mom's hallway, one sock on, the other foot bare, sorting the mail. The postcard lay beneath a layer of bills, catalogues, and fliers, so well buried that it might have been intentionally hidden. Its front showed a photograph of a pizzeria, an arty shot of the rain-spattered awning and glowing interior. I picked it up and turned it over. There, in block printing, were the words *FIND ME AT AUDINO'S PIZZA*. That was all. My heart set off a firework inside my chest. I recognized the handwriting from the previous postcard; I had studied it often enough to be well acquainted with those crisp, stalwart *A*'s.

Mom was not awake yet. For the moment, I was alone and had time to think. The sun had barely risen, though the eastern sky was humming with a blue glow. I ran for my bag, dug out the old postcard, and held it up beside the new one. They were written with the same black pen; I could still smell the sting of marker. *I AM ALIVE. FIND ME AT AUDINO'S PIZZA*. The second message was mysterious: Would Cynthia be there, eating pizza, until such time as I chose to arrive? Was she sleeping in the doorway? Did she have a friend there to shelter her? I sat down at the kitchen table, holding the two postcards side by side.

It was now time to involve my mother. I couldn't face her, though. I didn't dare to shake her out of sleep, only to wave the postcards in her face. She might kill me. I left them both on the kitchen table instead. I attached a sticky note and, after some thought, wrote only the words *These came for me. Call when you can.*

❧

On the El I thought of the last time I had seen my brother. He was nineteen then, and would not go to college; he had moved to San Francisco with the money our grandmother left us to further our education. My mother sent me to California as an emissary of the civilized world. I found Jordan sitting on the stoop of a trailer with a fat red flower painted beside the door. He was wearing a swimsuit, reading a magazine, and did not notice me standing over him, out of breath, my duffel cutting into my shoulder. His hair was flecked white from the sun. There were freckles on his back the size of pebbles. Finally he glanced up at me, and he smiled all over his face. His eyes were as empty as the sky. He got to his feet, and sand showered from his legs and swimsuit. I set down my duffel and swayed from the sudden lightness. Jordan hugged me, rich with the smell of sunblock and salt. His torso was a hard knife of muscle in my arms.

But there the memory stopped—I could not now recall if we had talked for hours, if we had walked together down the sandy beach, if I had done as my mother asked and urged him to reconsider academia, or if I had envied him his freedom. I could not even precisely recall the sound of his voice anymore—was it rough, like brown sugar, or high-pitched, like a violin? These days I was left with an empty space in the shape of my brother. His absence had opened up a hole in the world, into which my own memories of him slipped and did not return. The nickname he had had for me as a toddler, the make-believe games we had once created, the kind of sandwich he ate every day for lunch, the color of his first car—one by one, over time, these things fell into the hole. Every few months I woke up and realized I had lost something else. The size of his hands. The name of that blond kid he used to bring around for dinner sometimes. His favorite kind of music. All of it gone.

෬

At work I sat for a long time with my office door locked and the lights off. I heard footsteps in the hall, voices murmuring, but I kept still. I could almost see Mom in the kitchen, bent over the postcards, her hair still wild from the shower, her mouth open. I stared at the phone, and when it rang I leapt to answer it, but the line was dead before I'd even brought it to my ear. I forced myself to check my e-mail instead. There was an update from the giant squid mailing list, in huge red letters: *The Search Continues!* Another membrane had been found off the coast of Africa. This one was three feet by five feet, floating just beneath the surface, deep red and coated with pearly eggs. It had been hoisted aboard a fishing boat whose crew mistook it for evidence of a shipwreck—a sail, a tangle of clothing, a body—and they had kept it on board, in direct sunlight, so that it was rubbery and half melted by the time it was brought to shore and identified by the harbormaster. The discussion raged online: It had to be giant squids, there was no *proof* it was giant squids. I wanted to call my mother and hang up after one ring, but instead I signed off the computer and turned on the lights in my office.

Immediately someone rapped on the door, and I jumped halfway out of my skin. I imagined my mother in the hallway, in her bathrobe, circles under her eyes, brandishing the postcards. I peered through the little window in the door and saw my boss's face elongated by the glass.

"Mara!" she said as I let her in. "What's going on with Falco?"

"Pardon?"

She made an impatient gesture. "Falco. The *octopus*. You didn't stay here all night again, did you?"

"Falco's fine," I said. "I fed him yesterday. He stole all my crabmeat."

She stepped farther into the room, crossing her arms over her chest. She was wearing a complex green outfit that appeared to be made of several layers.

"He nearly bit someone today," she said. "Didn't you read the memo?"

"Octopuses don't bite."

She rolled her eyes. "They have beaks. That's how they eat."

"They bite their prey," I said. "I've never been bitten. I don't know of any divers who've been bitten."

"They're *poisonous*," she said. I had the feeling she'd just learned this. She had degrees in marine biology, and I had field experience, so friendship was impossible between us. This discrepancy was common among the members of the administration and staff at the aquarium. The managers grouped together at lunch, no doubt grumbling about our stubbornness and absence of hard data, while we, the aquarists and underlings, bonded after hours at the dolphin pool to complain about our bosses' lack of common sense.

"Why is Falco attacking people?" she insisted.

"They really don't bite people," I said. "They posture, like cats do. They'll flash their beaks to scare off an intruder. Sometimes they attack with their arms." I remembered that Falco had turned blood red at my arrival yesterday. That was unlike him.

"What about the giants off Seattle?" she asked, leaning against the doorjamb and examining her nails. "You were there for that. The reports said they were attacking divers."

I smiled wearily. "Yes," I said. "They tried to take my mask off. They figured out that was how I was breathing. But they didn't *bite* me. They could see I was too big to be prey."

"Mm," she said. "So you think Falco's just playing around?"

I hesitated. "He's probably bored, honestly. They don't like to stay in one place. They're nomadic."

"Well, we're having a meeting," she said, stepping back into the hall. "Read the memo."

I went down to visit Falco. My phone had yet to ring, and I was beginning to hear a faint buzzing sound in the silence of my office, imaginary but persistent. Falco turned red again at the sight of me descending into the tank. When I reached for him, heavy black rings grew around each eye, and he anchored himself firmly to one of the plaster rocks in his tank. He did, however, send a tentacle out to search both my empty hands. As always, his touch hurt slightly—the suckers were not smooth, like a suction cup, but rather covered in hundreds of tiny feelers that gripped and penetrated my skin with their miniscule tips. I moved to stroke his mantle, but he reared up, opening his arms to make himself larger. I actually thought he might be about to squirt me with ink. Instead he darted into the hole they'd carved for him in the floor. His body disappeared, the flesh contracting into what looked like a heavy paste, with a baleful eye in it that watched me keenly.

His behavior was oddly familiar, and after a moment of floating in the chilly water, I remembered the time I had brought a hand mirror into his tank, on a whim. He had approached it cautiously, observing it with one lifted eye, then the other. He'd wrapped the curl of an arm around its handle where my fingers were, though he didn't try to take it away from me. Slowly he lifted a second arm and passed the suckers over the surface of the mirror as though seeking to remove the image. There was a pause, during which he regarded me with unmistakable concern. He wiped the mirror again, and even raised his arm as though intending to do so a third time. But then he leapt away and poured his body wildly into his cave, and wouldn't come out, not even for crabmeat. No one else had taken this as a sign of intelligence, though I was astounded and considered repeating the experiment, until it occurred to me that I might break his brain.

Today I had no crabmeat to tempt him out. I climbed from the tank and watched through the surface of the water until I saw two tentacles emerge, camouflaged with the muck-colored floor. I wondered what he had discovered this time to make him run.

There was a voice-mail waiting for me when I got back to my office. I flopped into the chair and took a deep breath. Mom's voice was clouded with the chatter of the bookstore: "You brat! I brought your goddamn postcards to work with me. And now you aren't there!" There was a silence on the line, as though she were debating whether to continue, and then the message clattered to a halt.

I called her back immediately and she answered, breathless.

"For God's sake," she said. "Where were you?"

"Playing with the octopuses," I said. "Is it your lunch break?"

"No, it's not my goddamn lunch break," she said. "Why did you *leave* these things with me?"

"I brought them to work with me too," I said.

"Shit." She took a heavy breath. "It's Cynthia, isn't it? The imposition, the carelessness . . ."

"Maybe so," I said cautiously. "But one of us should go down there anyway, right?"

She snorted. I imagined her tugging a hand through her hair, the way she always did when she was frantic, then furiously shaking off the strands that collected between her fingers.

"Let me go," I said. "I'll deal with it."

"You do that," she snapped. "I'm hiring an assassin."

"*Mom.*"

"Mara, this is the end."

I kicked my chair so that it rolled heavily across the carpet. For a moment I spun suspended in the middle of the room. "You're sure—" I leaned over and flicked off the lights. "You're *sure* it's Cynthia? I mean, there's no way the postcards could possibly be—? I know it's unlikely, but—"

There was a little, breathy silence. "Oh, shut up," she said finally. "Are you going down there?"

"Yes," I said quickly. "Yes, I'll go right now."

"Mara, this can't continue. There ought to be a law against it." She made a tiny sob. "I mean, honestly. Haven't we been through enough?"

"I'll talk to her," I said. "I'll let you know."

"*Fuck*." Something clattered on her end of the phone. "I'm going to have to leave work."

"Do you want to come here?"

"No," she said. "Why did you *leave* these things with me?"

"Why don't you come here?" I said. "You haven't been here in ages. I can show you the dolphins."

"I am not going"—there was another clatter, like a stack of books falling—"to the *goddamn* aquarium," she said.

"*Fine*," I shouted. We both hung up at the same time. I flipped the lights on again in my office. The fluorescents were dazzling.

I could picture my mother flying out of the bookstore, her purse unzipped, shedding scraps of notepaper and Kleenex as she flagged down a cab and slammed the car door on the hem of her skirt. In similar disarray, I fled the aquarium. First I forgot my bag, then my jacket, and then I had to run back just long enough to tell my boss I'd been taken ill. Finally I stood at the train station in a wind that was heavy with the smell of rain. Autumn had entered in full force, and the platform was scattered with wet leaves, the concrete stained red with their shapes. I caught glimpses of the lake between the buildings, a broken mass of gray and white. It never failed to trip me up, seeing that vast body of water after I'd just left Falco in his tiny pool.

I rode the train north. I found listings for two Audino's Pizzas, but one was in the distant suburbs, the other right off the Morse stop. The sky darkened measurably outside. By the time I was making my way down the slippery steps to the street, a light rain had begun to fall. I was unfamiliar with this particular neighborhood. The sidewalk was crammed with fruit stands, pubs, and dingy convenience stores, all with awnings too faded to reveal their names. My fingers soon grew numb from the cold. I stumbled up and down the block, in too much of a fevered whirl to notice at first that I was on the wrong side of the street.

The restaurant's interior was lit up, stadium-bright. I hovered outside for a moment, irresolute, clutching the scrap of paper on which I had scrawled the address. There was a window in the back wall that showed the kitchen—a row of gleaming pots, a metal countertop. A few hanging plants spilled over their containers and trickled like kelp toward the floor. The place was deserted. When I stepped inside, a bell jingled, and a young waiter hurried out to greet me.

"One?" he asked.

"What?"

"Lunch for one?" he repeated. He tried to hand me a shiny menu, but I waved it away.

"No, no," I said. "I'm not here to eat. I'm looking for someone."

The boy frowned. "Excuse me?"

"Cynthia," I said. "Or possibly—"

I had been going to say, *Or possibly Jordan, my brother.* But I kept that thought firmly in my mouth. The boy glanced around the place and crinkled his pale brow.

"We're empty, ma'am," he said. "It's the middle of the afternoon."

"Yes," I said. Beneath the waist I was all air and mist. "But you see, she told me to come here. She has long dark hair—at least, she used to have. Her name is Cynthia."

The boy was now watching me with apprehension. "Ma'am, there's nobody else here."

"So I see," I said. "Well, thank you anyway."

The boy scurried back into the distant kitchen as though he had some urgent business there. I stepped out into the wind and felt my eyes beginning to well with hot tears. I never cried, and now, twice in one week, I was on the verge of hysteria. The drizzle had grown more intense, soaking the air with a gleaming chill, and I knew I should leave, but I could not manage it. I laid a hand on the glass of the front window, and for a moment I had the impression that I was back at the aquarium, staring into the tank of an alien species. Through the pane in the restaurant's back wall, I saw the boy pass, his cheeks red from the sudden heat of the kitchens. He was laughing. A cook appeared beside him, ducking her head and laughing too. Her body was swathed in white, and as she hefted a silver pot, I saw a splatter of grease on one shoulder. Then she turned toward me. It was Cynthia.

My mouth opened, and one arm shot into the air, almost of its own accord. Cynthia saw me. Before I could move or plan a strategy, she had burst through the kitchen door and was hurrying across the restaurant toward me.

"Mara," she cried, stepping into the wind. I staggered backward, and red leaves whirled about me, dusting my jacket with their gleaming folds. Cynthia brought a rush of aroma with her: spices and meat from the kitchen, and her own patchouli and incense. I saw that her hair had gone gray in funny patches, as though someone had shaken a paintbrush over her head.

"The boy said you weren't there," I said idiotically.

"Oh." She laughed. "I go by a different name now. Rowan. It's a spirit name, you know? But you can still call me Cynthia."

"Ah," I said.

"Come inside," she said. "Come, come."

I let her take me by the arm and guide me back into the restaurant, where she settled me at a table by the window.

"God, it's amazing to see you," she said, sinking into a chair opposite me. "I'm sure you hear this all the time, but you look just like him. Just like Jordan. Except he was blonder, of course, and your eyes—"

"I wonder," I said quickly, "could I have something to drink?"

"Oh, of course," she said, smacking her forehead. I watched as she hurried around the restaurant, fetching glasses and ice as though she owned the place. I had to fight the urge to get to my feet and bolt. The first time I had met her, I had formed an intense, almost visceral aversion to her. That much had not changed.

She sat down again, and I gulped the ice water she offered me.

"All right," I said. "All right."

Cynthia leaned her cheek on her hand. "Your hair is longer," she said. "You know, I don't cut mine anymore. The Chinese believe the body is"—she carved a circle in midair with her forefingers—"meant to stay whole."

I was beginning to get a handle on the moment. It was the strangest thing to see her, as though she were radiating waves of dangerous memory. I kept catching the faint smell of seawater and sunblock.

"So, the postcards," I said finally, setting my glass down.

"Yes!" she cried, grinning. "You got them. You figured out it was me."

"Can I ask," I said, "what you were thinking when you sent them?"

"Beg pardon?"

"When I first got them, I thought . . ." I found I could not say what I had thought. "You called my mother. If you wanted to see me, why didn't you just call me, too?"

"I thought the postcards were funny," she said uncertainly. "You know, kind of like a treasure hunt."

Her big sea eyes were drinking me in. I took another sip of ice water.

"But why did you get in touch at all?" I asked.

"Well!" Cynthia clapped her hands. "When I moved here I wasn't sure how to find you. I spent awhile, you know, looking around online. And the city is so big! It took me forever."

"Uh-huh," I said impatiently. She was smiling at me, apparently done with her story. At last I said, "But *why*, Cynthia?"

She took a deep breath, looking down. After a moment she said softly, "You're just like your mother."

I gripped my glass in both hands.

"I wanted to talk to you," she said. "I *miss* him, you know. Even after all this time. I thought maybe we could"—she made a hesitant back-and-forth gesture—"tell stories. Remember him together."

"No," I said, louder than I meant to.

She cocked her head.

"It doesn't help," I said. "We've got to let the dead—" I broke off. "To let sleeping dogs lie. Whatever the expression is."

"He's not dead," she said at once.

I stared at her.

"Of *course* he's not dead," she said. "Mara, please."

I held up one finger. "The police." I held up another finger. "Any number of private detectives." A third finger. "My mother. Cynthia, *everyone* thinks he's dead."

She laughed, a foreign sound, joyful and burbling.

"Oh, Mara, your mother doesn't think that." She put a hand over her mouth. "Come on. What mother would think that?"

"At any rate," I said, gathering my wits. "None of this is why I came. I came to tell you to leave us alone. You did a great deal of damage . . ." I paused, shaking my head. "A lot of damage just by getting in touch. You need to leave us alone now."

"Really?"

"Yes." I almost laughed at the absurdity of it—she was watching me like a pupil awaiting a failing grade. "My mother said she already told you that. Didn't she?"

"Yes, but—" Cynthia knotted her fingers together. She was never still; every emotion seemed to require its own specific movement. "I thought maybe you would be different," she said. "We're more the same age, and I hoped that—"

"No," I said gently. "It's no. There's nothing more to say."

I got to my feet, eager to be out of the warm restaurant, away from Cynthia's overpowering musk and sweet, shining face.

She followed me to the door. Her whole demeanor had changed; her shoulders slumped, and she fidgeted with the cuff of her sleeve. I opened the door and felt the slap of a cold breeze against my cheek.

"Goodbye," I said, extending an arm politely.

She took my hand in both of hers, but she did not shake it. She just held on, gazing at me longingly.

"Are you sure?" she asked. "It might be good for you too, to talk about him. You could tell me stories. I'd love to hear stories from you."

There was an odd comfort in the pressure of her hands. I realized it had been a long time since anyone had touched me. Her black eyes were fixed on my face, and for a moment I felt the urge to open the Jordan file, to pull out the memories I had left and spill them on the table, to let Cynthia pick through them, holding them up to the light.

"No," I said at last.

I withdrew my hand and stepped into the rain.

∽

In the late afternoon I found myself back at the aquarium. I didn't want to go home; I had the vague suspicion that Mom would see the taint of Cynthia on me. I went to see Falco instead.

The aquarium was dark, though I heard the occasional scuff of footsteps, and in a distant room someone was laughing. On my way to the tank I ducked into the janitor's closet and grabbed a broom with a nice, shiny metal handle. At Falco's pool, I dipped this into the water and waved it back and forth, tracing a figure eight in the gloom. The octopus didn't have time to turn red; he came flying out of his hole and took hold of the broom with as many arms as would fit. When I began to draw him up, out of the water, he released the handle but did not return to his hiding place, floating curiously in the middle of the tank, his body an ambivalent brown. I dipped the broom in again, and again Falco threw himself on it, grappling with it so furiously I thought he meant to wrestle it from my grasp. It took me three tries to finally draw him into the air. Water streamed from his body, and his skin changed, no longer taut and bulbous but slightly flaccid under the sudden weight of gravity. I was surprised at how heavy he was; I found myself levering him against the tank wall.

Once he was in the air, I held out an arm and stayed still. He tested my palm and forearm with a few wet, delicate suckers. He had never touched a human outside of scuba gear, and I knew he wouldn't recognize me as the same creature. It did not take him long to decide I was harmless, though, and he climbed from the bright metal into my arms.

He was dark red now, puffed up, his tentacles coiling wildly at their tips, one fumbling with the collar of my sweater, one still fingering the broom like a lifeline. His eyes were wide and eager as I carried him around the aquarium. I let him put his suckers on the flat of a table, a computer screen, even the clacking keyboard. Out in the hallway his attention was thoroughly absorbed by a fire alarm box, its plastic surface, the handle he couldn't reach through the glass. I allowed him to trail one tentacle over the dusty carpet. He would not let go of me, and the red didn't entirely leave his skin, but his eyes didn't stop roving for a moment and his tentacles were hungry for every new surface. His curiosity seemed to buoy him up, so that he grew lighter as we walked. After half an hour, when I knew he was running out of oxygen, I brought him back to his tank. He went joyfully into the water but did not retreat from view, still watching me with both eyes raised up from his mantle. His tentacles wound around the interior walls, checking to be sure it was all the same.

On my way out of the building I met Roger, about to climb onto his bicycle. He wore his backpack and had changed into jeans with a hole in the knee. At the sight of me he started and looked sheepish. I must have made the same face because suddenly he grinned.

"What were *you* up to?" he asked.

"Nothing."

"Well, then I wasn't up to anything either." He took a pack of cigarettes from his breast pocket, squinting against the sunlight.

"I took the big octopus for a walk," I said. It made me feel fierce and strange just to say it out loud. Roger laughed, and I realized he had probably been making out with one of the behaviorists—or some other normal indiscretion.

"Where did you take him?" he asked.

"Just around the hallway," I said, though I had a sudden vision of showing him trees, benches, insects. "I let him touch my computer. They're smart, you know. I used to have a pet octopus, and she would break out of my tank all the time."

"I didn't know that," Roger said. "You had a pet octopus?"

"Oh yeah. She got all over my apartment. I couldn't figure out why the carpet was wet, so I set up a video camera and saw her break out. She was a madman. I got to watch her reading my books—just flipping through the pages, like she saw me do from inside the tank. I saw her climbing around on the couch. Once I actually came home and caught her. I found her in the bathtub, trying to pull out the plug and go down the drain."

"Seriously?"

I tapped my temple. "Smart. She figured that where water went, she would be able to find the ocean."

Roger lit a cigarette skillfully in the wind, half closing his eyes against the smoke. "*I* was wrestling with Manny."

He offered me a drag. The smoke was warm and itchy, very familiar.

"Who?" I said.

"The little dolphin." I must have looked blank because he added, "The one that keeps beating us up."

"He attacked you?"

Roger laughed. "No, it was my idea. My boss was talking about moving him into a smaller tank, away from the other dolphins, so they won't watch old Manny and pick up the behavior." He shuddered a little. "The guy has a PhD and all. I can't argue with him. But I couldn't stand to watch Manny going under. He loves a good fight, so I just went in and tackled him. We wrestled all over the pool. Nearly dislocated my shoulder. He's *bored*, that's all."

We stood for a moment and the wind grew stronger, battering

my hair into my eyes and whipping Roger's coat open. The smoke went tumbling away from us, heading for the lake.

"What a couple of loons," Roger said. "I won't tell if you don't."

"I showed Falco the fire alarm," I said.

"Beautiful!" He kicked one leg over the bike, saluted me, and wheeled away into the wind.

I looked back at the aquarium, full of sea creatures, circling in their tanks, watching the world with their inhuman eyes. Sooner or later, they would figure it out. I wondered if Falco had not already made the connection between who fed and cared for him, and who kept him in captivity. The dolphins were even more intelligent. We were going to come to the aquarium someday and find the wall broken open, the jagged edge still oozing saltwater, and all the cages empty. Already Falco could be tapping in Morse code on the wall of his tank to the electric eels on the other side. The smarter fish would make arrangements for the simple ones who knew only that the ocean had evidently betrayed them and all their food was dead. Falco could carry whole armfuls of dull-eyed mackerel into the safety of the lake. His tentacles would catch the faintest traces of salt, and the dolphins would follow him, herding the others with the help of nurse sharks and ancient sea turtles. They would migrate in the belly of the Great Lakes, stirring up clouds of sand to hide themselves. I trusted Falco to lead them to the distant sea.

Mom was sitting in the grass outside her house. She'd laid down a blanket over the mess of fallen leaves and had a shawl wrapped around her shoulders. There were four books scattered about her in various stages of reading—book-marked, splayed facedown, held open with the edge of the blanket. She saw me coming and searched the quilt vaguely with her fingers as though she had something to give me. I sat beside her in the cold grass. She looked tired and calm. I had the sense that something vast had been taken out of her, leaving an empty space and a sudden lightness.

"I came by the aquarium," she said.

"Oh, shit."

"It's fine." She shook her head. "It's a nice museum, you know, much better than Science and Industry."

I touched the hem of her blanket and the cover of one of her books. "What are you reading?"

"Oh—" She looked surprised. "I wasn't, really."

I took a deep breath. "I went and saw Cynthia," I said. "That's why I wasn't at work."

Mom smiled. "I know. I went and saw her too. She told me you had been there."

"Oh, no."

A cloud came over the sun and we blinked at the haze of shadow. Mom palmed her hair out of her face.

"Are you all right?" I asked.

"Oh, yes. I just explained it to her. She's not my daughter. She has nothing to do with me. And if she ever contacts me again, I'm calling the police." Mom rolled her hair slowly into a fat gray bun. "I'm never going to love her. And I told her that."

"Jesus Christ."

Mom nodded. "She told me that she came here partly because we were here. Can you believe it? She has no family, apparently. I said she had better leave Chicago, if that was how she really felt."

The cloud passed, and suddenly everything glowed—the edges of grass, the flat of Mom's book, the checked yellow and blue of her blouse.

"And do you know what she told me?" Mom said. "She told me I was the one that should leave."

"What?"

"She said I had better go look for him, because nobody else is ever going to find him."

I flinched. If she had said his name I might have cried out. Her face showed nothing but calm, a quiet deadness.

"Cynthia won't contact us again," Mom said, but it sounded as if she was asking.

"I told her not to, either," I said.

She nodded. "So that's done."

The sunlight flicked to shadow again. Her hair went the sleepy color of snow.

"Mom?" I said finally. She reached out to touch my arm, and her fingers were cold but familiar, as though she had once touched me like this in a dream, as though we had been family a long time ago.

∞

A month later she was gone. I settled in a new apartment, with a new pet octopus in an even larger cage, and Mom sent me letters from Greece, Spain, the Czech Republic. She soaked the envelopes in purple ink, or traced green loops all over their backs. She sent me strange, rough leaves from tropical plants. She sent me golden earth from Italy that retained its smell when I poured it onto the tabletop. I couldn't write back to her; she didn't know from week to week where she would be. Occasionally she called, and we spoke for a few minutes over a line that crackled with static and echoed with other voices. She still didn't speak Jordan's name aloud. I didn't tell her I missed her. She sent me a photograph of herself on a boat deck, waving to me, wearing maroon sunglasses I'd never seen. In the picture she was holding a blue flower and wearing a crimson scarf that had slipped from one shoulder. I pinned the photo to my bulletin board at work. It made my heart ache. Her smile said she wasn't coming back.

I didn't hear from Cynthia again, but I knew what I had to do. I waited for the spring, when the snow turned to slush and crocuses pushed stubbornly up through the dark earth. The birds sang with exhausted voices, and the wind came wet off the lake with ice in its stomach. One day in March, I left my apartment wearing a coat I'd stolen from my mother's closet. A truck turned the corner, rattling and squealing. A dog ran by me with its mouth open. The air smelled of mud, and I walked on the grass, not the sidewalk, crushing the snow to melting beneath my boots. At the mailbox I took the postcard from my pocket and checked it over. I had addressed it to Cynthia at the restaurant. I had not signed it. In fat block letters I had printed the words: *I AM ALIVE TOO.*

# SILENCE

On the morning of the first frost of winter, Jesse walks to the barn with the ground crackling beneath his feet. In one hand he holds a spokeshave, in the other a bucket of varnish. His breath glazes the air. The sun has barely risen, outlining the high clouds in gold. Jesse can hear that the neighbors' children are awake. They live down the long hill, but their flutelike voices carry on the breeze. He hears them arguing and slamming the car door; presumably they are getting ready for school. Jesse has rarely seen them in person, but he knows the tones of each member of the family. They speak in English and some foreign tongue, maybe Russian. This bothers him. The great wave of immigrants has crashed against American shores and washed inland, casting its dross into every crevice, even here, in rural Maine. People ought to stay put. They ought to stay where their ancestors are planted like bulbs in the dark ground.

Jesse tugs open the door to the barn and stands for a while, looking at his creation in the half-light. The airplane is a glorious thing, almost finished, lurking beneath the rafters like an insectoid relic from the dinosaur age. It smells of sawdust and oil. One long amber wing nearly brushes the wall; the other sags slightly, since Jesse has not yet put in the struts to support it. For a year he has been building his own version of the Wright brothers' plane, the first ever to complete a successful flight. He is making it from scratch, with hand tools and a series of diagrams laid out on the worktable. The sun pokes its fingers through one window, catching the dusty beams of the ceiling. Jesse picks up a brush and begins to varnish the exposed flank of a propeller. One of the angles in the fuselage needs to be realigned. He checks the rudders too, which will allow him to change the yaw while airborne.

Presently the sun rises high, and the room brims with light like the interior of a wood stove. Jesse works until his right hand goes numb, and he drops the spokeshave he is holding. This is the cue to break for lunch.

❧

Around noon the doctor calls. Jesse is eating cold beans from a can in the kitchen. He knows how to cook—women taught him long ago—but he rarely bothers. It seems pointless to cook for one, especially when the one in question has lost his sense of taste completely and never cared much for fancy food to begin with. Besides, in a house like this, where frost decorates the windows, where Jesse has had to break the ice on his bath now and then, washing dishes would be tricky—waiting for the water to get hot, trying to thaw out the liquid soap. The telephone rings beneath a heap of newspapers and Jesse eyes it for a while, deciding whether he ought to answer.

It turns out to be his neurologist, just as he expected. That ripe, genial voice, slightly clinical. Jesse sets his can of beans aside, wiping his mouth on his sleeve. The doctor is worried about him. Jesse missed his appointment this morning, though the MRI was all ready for him. Is Jesse all right? Has he been suffering from mental confusion? Seizures? Any more weakness in that right hand? He needs to come in right away. He must have his blood, electrolytes, liver function, and coagulation tested. All these things were lined up for him hours ago.

"I plumb forgot," Jesse says untruthfully. "I'm sorry, doc."

"That's all right, Mr. Miller," says the neurologist. "But you've got to come in this week. How about tomorrow?"

"Well, now." Jesse scratches his cheek with one dirty fingernail. "I'm just not sure. How about I take a look at my schedule and call you back?"

"That's fine. That'll be fine."

Jesse spends the afternoon in the barn, adjusting the tensile strength of the cables. He measures out the pieces of wood he will need for the elevators at the front of the plane. The motor will arrive by airmail one of these days. From the house, across the cold, pine-scented air, he hears the telephone ringing again. The doctor, no doubt, or one of his nurses, dispatched to nail Jesse down for another appointment.

There is a tumor as big as a lemon in his brain. It makes him smile, the way they think of some nice, friendly object to give you a sense of the size—he now pictures a yellow piece of fruit nestled in the meat of his head. Too deep in for surgery. All they can do now is watch it and try to palliate some of the symptoms. Jesse knows how it will progress. The doctor laid it all out for him. The weakness in his hand will spread. He will have clumsiness, maybe difficulty walking. His ability to taste has been taken from him—he may lose more, smell, touch. The headaches have already begun, with occasional bouts of vomiting. Eventually he will be unable to concentrate. His memory will go, his alertness. He will become stupid, or "numb," as his father, a Maine native, used to say. Then he will die.

⁂

There was a time when Jesse had family. He was born in this place, but after his mother passed away—a car accident, black ice on the roads—he was sent for a while to stay with her people, a million miles away in Alabama. Jesse was just a boy then, a tiny thing with flakes of white-blond hair. That period of his childhood sits at a remove from him now, as though he can look down at it only through a pane of glass.

Most of what he remembers is the noise. There were so many people living in one sprawling home—aunts, cousins, and grandparents. Jesse was not always clear on how everyone was related. At the time, the family seemed like an unbreakable thing, a many-headed, many-armed creature that could not be separated into its component parts. You were never alone in that house. Jesse would sit beneath the table and watch the feet of his aunts, listening to the chaotic song of their voices, the thousand-and-one topics they seemed to discuss simultaneously. He shared a room with his four male cousins. He suffered through hours of shopping with his grandmother, passing through stall after stall in the market, overwhelmed by the vast catalogue of necessary items she seemed to have stored in her mind. He watched television in the lap of his grandfather, hearing the watery rumble of the old man's breath, which at the time seemed like an engine of comfort.

After a while Jesse grew accustomed to their brand of close-ness—he learned to accept it, if not quite to reciprocate in kind. His aunts hugged him and wept over the loss of his mother. His uncle obligingly took him aside and taught him to draw. The boys included him in all their games, so that he spent hours outside in the wealth of the Alabama sunlight, boundless and golden. To-gether they threw stones at crows, set up traps for the vampire that lived in the pear tree, and stalked snakes in the corn. At mealtimes everyone would talk at once, passing dishes of food willy-nilly and shouting about the local football games or the behavior of the teenagers at the church social. Jesse watched it all with open eyes, drinking it in, as though trying to understand the behavior of some foreign species.

He has not seen any of those people since he was a child. Even-tually his father came and took him back home. Though Jesse knows they have moved on, growing up, some of them having babies, some of them dying, in his mind they are frozen in time, unchanging, like a photograph.

～

The next morning is palpably colder. Jesse stokes up the wood-stove, blowing on the embers and feeding twigs into the roaring red maw. He has taken to sleeping on the living room couch, near the fire, where the big picture window lets in the first bare glow of dawn. He hates to waste any time at all in sleeping. He has only so many hours left.

During the early part of the day, he works on the airplane. He places struts beneath the wing and varnishes the propellers. The cables hover between the planks like the waiting strands of a spider web. Now and then, Jesse will clamber up and take his place in the pilot's seat, lying down, his hands in the correct position, his feet dangling in space. He imagines what it will be like to fly, closing his eyes and trying to feel the wind. He cannot wait to be done, and yet there is something wonderful in the agonized slowness of the process itself. He knows that he could expedite matters with a nail gun and electric saw, but that is not his way. He wants each piece to be birthed painstakingly from his own two hands. He likes cutting the wood, making inevitable mistakes, tossing the scrap out back. He likes taking endless trips to the hardware store to buy pliers, screws, and clamps.

Today he climbs into his pickup truck and drives the bumpy road into town. At the store, he strolls through the aisles, examining packets of brads, testing lengths of wire beneath his fingertips, checking the notebook in his pocket for measurements. The clerk is always pleasantly incurious about what Jesse may be building for himself. When approached at the cash register, the man glances up blearily from beneath his baseball cap and folds away the sports page of the paper.

"Back again?" he says.

"A-yup," Jesse replies.

The clerk nods and hands him his change. This is the only conversation Jesse has with anyone all day.

❧

He knows that a life in this place is not for everyone. Though he has few memories of his mother—he was a toddler when she passed away, and his prevailing impression is one of gaudy red hair and a weary, lilting voice—he has been told certain things about her. She laughed easily. She played the piano well. She was a social sort of person, and she used to complain that she had lived in

Maine for ten years and was still treated as an interloper. No one invited her to the quilting bees. No one saw fit to buy her cupcakes at the library bake sale. Even at her funeral, Jesse was aware that the people who attended, dressed soberly in black, were there more for his father's sake than anything else. His father had been born in the small town. For this reason, though Jesse himself lived away for a few years, he too has always been accepted as a part of the community.

After his return from Alabama, Jesse remembers driving down the winding roads with his father. He was still a little disoriented from the suddenness of his transition, the loss of the constant presence of his southern cousins, the chill in the fog-soaked air. Now and then, his father's pickup truck would pass another car on the road. Toby Miller knew each face and explained who each person was.

"That's Amy Johnson. Decent woman. That there is Billy Hogg. Don't *never* go hunting with him."

"Why don't they wave?" Jesse asked eventually.

His father looked amused.

"They are waving," he said.

And then Jesse noticed it. The next car approached, and he saw the flat, bearded face, both hands on the steering wheel. The man recognized his father and lifted one forefinger slightly. Toby did the same.

"That's George Wilson," he said. "Known him for years."

◦◦

A week later the doctor calls again. Jesse is annoyed. He does not intend to go back to the hospital, not ever. He is uninterested in monitoring the progress of his tumor. He believes in spirits. When he dies, he wants his ghost to end up here, on the hillside, wandering among the pines, visiting the old house, witnessing the ice storms that come in midwinter and coat the trees in light. He does not want to die in a hospital. It makes his flesh crawl to think of his spirit trapped indoors forever, shuffling through rooms of sick people with IVs strapped into their arms.

He didn't really expect the doctor to understand this—but he had hoped the man would have enough sense to let the matter drop when Jesse did not call for another appointment. Now it seems they will have to talk the thing out.

"Mr. Miller," the doctor says. "We're all quite concerned. You understand that the cancer can progress very rapidly. We need to get a handle on what's happening in your brain."

Jesse leans wearily against the wall. For an instant he weakens. There have been a few scares—yesterday morning he vomited blood into the sink, and then there was the moment when he forgot how to lace up his boots and sat staring at them dully for the longest time. The headaches, too, have grown increasingly un-bearable. They come on like a supernova exploding behind his eyes, too severe to be checked by a little thing like aspirin from a bottle. Jesse knows that he may not have very long.

"You want to run some tests on me?" he asks.

"Yes, exactly," the doctor says, relieved. "The tests we discussed earlier, on your blood and liver. In addition, we have to get an MRI. As the tumor grows, the inflammation will begin to press on the surrounding tissue. Then, of course, you have to know that—"

Jesse's mind wanders a long way from the conversation. His father, too, had died of cancer. Toby Miller had hated doctors; he was worse than Jesse, almost phobic. Jesse had been a teen-ager then, living under his father's roof, watching the symptoms coming on. Pain in the stomach. Inability to keep anything down. As it got worse—as the cancer spread, Jesse learned later, carried

in the blood, organ to organ, like dandelion seeds on the wind—
Toby's breathing became labored. A lump swelled in his neck. He
fell ill too often. First the pain affected his moods, and then he
began to suffer lapses of memory. Jesse would find him trying to
feed wood into the cushions of the couch, rather than the stove.
He got a few calls from neighbors saying that Toby had been seen
wandering in his bare feet down the road. Still the old man refused
to go to the hospital. Once Jesse actually drove him there in the
pickup, but his father would not get out of the car, sitting hunched
in the passenger's seat as Jesse glared at him in frustration through
the window.

The doctor is still talking, explaining why it will take a few days or
even weeks to get results back on all the tests. Jesse interrupts him.

"Doc, I plan to die at home," he says. "I think you know from
my file that I have a bit of experience with this disease. My dad
passed out one night at the bar and ended up in the E.R., stuck
full of tubes. I don't want to be kept on a respirator. That won't
work for me."

The doctor begins to speak, but Jesse continues, talking over him.

"You've done your bit for me, and I appreciate it. But you
don't need to call again. We're square. There's nothing else you
can do here."

After hanging up, he regrets having confessed so much to a
virtual stranger. His father could have done it with half as many
words.

On Sunday he goes to church. The preacher drones on, gesturing
with his big flabby hands. Jesse sits in the back pew, gazing up at
the stained-glass window, tree branches just visible through the

tinted panes. He is thinking about the soul. The first time he knew he had a soul of his own was when his father came to Alabama to bring him home again.

It happened quite suddenly. Toby Miller was not one to announce his plans. Jesse had been living with the family for five years when his father stepped out of a taxi in front of the house, looking small and stooped and out of place. An hour later, Jesse was packing his bags. Through the floor he could hear the argument brewing in the kitchen, his aunts fighting to keep him, his father's firm voice drifting on the air. Jesse, folding up his shirts, had been quite sure how that quarrel would play out.

Evening found him on the sidewalk, his duffel bag slung over one shoulder. His father was already climbing into the taxi. The family collected in the front yard, the cousins looking embarrassed, the aunts bravely brushing away their tears. His grandmother darted forward to hug him, her feathery arms closing around him like a blanket, and as she pulled away, Jesse felt something rip out of his chest. He gasped at the sensation. Then his grandfather, wheezing but determined, limped forward and embraced him. When their bodies separated, Jesse felt another small piece of himself rip free. The feeling was not painful, but it was entirely alien—he was losing a thing he had not known could be lost.

The aunts came toward him, one by one, and Jesse stood like a statue under the weight of their meaty arms. He did not understand what was happening. When each woman straightened up, smiling sadly, a fragment of Jesse went with her. He put a hand to his chest, half expecting his heart to go out like a candle.

At last only the young boys were left. Their faces wore bewildered grins. Jesse stared at them dumbly.

"Say goodbye," one of the aunts prompted in a whisper, and the boys flung themselves at him, their hot hands gripping his back.

Then they raced away. Together they ripped out such a big piece of him that Jesse lost his balance. He stumbled against the door of the taxi. He did not cry, but his breath came in shuddering waves.

In the airplane, Jesse and his father sat without speaking. Toby was flipping through a magazine, quite at his ease. The plane coasted down the runway, and Jesse pressed his cheek to the window. He felt he had been halved, and halved again, until he was in such a state of shock that if his father had told him that it was time to walk over a cliff and, by falling, come to Maine, he would have done it without complaint. When the plane took off, Jesse did not feel amazed to watch the houses grow small, to see the land fall away like a carpet. As he gazed at the familiar black forests and the cloudy river, the last piece tore out of his body. He felt it go, and as the plane lifted higher, he became an empty bowl.

<br>

One day there are deer in the backyard. Winter has arrived in earnest, the ground perpetually dusted with arabesques of snow. The earth has hardened painfully. Sipping his coffee, Jesse watches through the kitchen curtains as the buck steps gracefully over a fallen log, rotating his latticework of antlers. His doe follows him. Timid animals they may be, but their faces are curiously impassive. The doe nibbles at the last spare shoots of grass that thrust up through the snow.

Jesse's cancer has taken a turn for the worse. He has begun to have seizures—or so he thinks, since they manifest as gaps in his memory. The first time it happened, he was hurrying through the front door, his saw in one hand, and then he was lying on the floor, gazing at the ceiling fan. For an instant he was sure that he had crashed his beloved airplane—launched it and landed badly.

It took awhile to understand that he had lost consciousness. A few days afterward, he was preparing his lunch at the kitchen sink and a moment later found himself on the tile, with an entirely different quality of light in the room. Maybe an hour had passed. There was a spattering of vomit on the floor, and a bloody wound on the back of his head where he had smacked the table.

He has been thinking about his father's battle with cancer. He remembers how they cut open Toby's body, so many years ago, and found him fairly riddled with it. The tumors had begun in the gut and traveled to the lungs, the liver, the base of the skull. Something about all this had made sense to Jesse. His father had been tight-lipped by nature, never admitting that he missed his wife, that he had loved her, that he was lonely. He had never once spoken of his reasons for sending Jesse away, much less for bringing him back. Jesse, remembering the openness of his Alabama kin, had wondered if Toby's illness could have come from a certain repression. In the old days, people used to check the dead to see if they had "purged"—if a froth had gathered around the corners of their mouths, indicating that they had unspoken things to share, bubbling up in the wake of their demise. After his father had finally succumbed, lying in that hospital bed, Jesse had checked the mouth, but of course Toby hadn't purged. Even in death, he had kept his thoughts to himself.

Jesse's own diagnosis—cancer again, coming on in middle age—had not really surprised him either. Over the years, he has become such a carbon copy of Toby Miller that now and then, catching sight in the bathroom mirror of a lean shoulder and stubbled cheek, Jesse will turn around and glance behind him, looking for his father.

At last the plane is ready. Jesse finishes it one evening and stands in awe, staring through the haze of waning sunlight. He is as proud as though he had invented it himself, brought it fully formed from his own head, rather than following somebody else's plan. The plane is beautiful, airy and light. Its appearance is deceptive. It looks kite-like, as though Jesse could heft it up on one shoulder and carry it—as though it could trick the wind itself. Jesse has always been a little disappointed in modern airplanes. They have nothing to do with man's age-old dream of flight. For thousands of years the human species has looked to the heavens, and yet this is what they have been able to come up with: a metal tube, carpeted aisles, stinking bathrooms, and a scratched, three-inch-thick window that gives no greater impression of the vastness of the sky than a television set.

Jesse does not know what first made him dream of building his own plane. His Alabama uncle, so many years ago, used to show him picture books about Orville and Wilbur Wright. He was pleased to have a new audience in Jesse; his own children were sick of hearing about his obsession with the Wright brothers' bicycle shop, the endless experiments with models and mock-ups, and the way that Orville had answered, whenever someone asked how he had concocted his marvelous invention: "Like a bird." After Jesse's exile, the notion of flight had stayed in his mind. Perhaps it had something to do with the geese. Every autumn they would wing above the house in Maine, straggling across the sky in delicate *V*'s. Jesse often woke at night to their melancholy calls. They soared across the miles to their dwelling places, their warm southern nests, as Jesse himself could never do.

It is too late to launch tonight. He heads into the house, stumbling in his weariness. One of his headaches is coming on. He can feel it gathering strength, pooling upward from the base of the neck. Today he lost sensation in his right arm completely. He can still use the appendage well enough, but he feels nothing—it is like watching somebody else's fingers at work. To test it, he laid his palm on a hot kettle and watched the flesh sear as though from a great distance. He could smell his blistering skin, but he didn't feel a thing.

He does not want to sleep. After a chilly bath, he curls up on the couch like a boy, gazing out the window. The stars are fiery tonight. The moon wafts between the branches like a shaving of ice. Jesse wonders whether he ever grew a new soul—after his old one was torn out in Alabama. Maybe he did not. Maybe it was just this place that filled that empty gap. He has come to love the land here as he has never loved anyone, not his aunts and cousins, not his father. He knows every corner of the hillside, the stream that churns frantically in the summer and freezes in the winter, the tiny white flowers that bloom like mist for a few days in the fall. Sometimes he will hear a wolf give an aching cry. Sometimes an owl takes up residence in the barn. Jesse has learned to determine the day's weather by sniffing the wind. He can tell whether a morning rain will burn off or settle in for the duration. In the spring he has walked over the melting ground, feeling the frost loosen and give way beneath his feet.

~

The sun rises slowly, fighting through a bank of cloud. Jesse is uncertain for a while whether he is really awake. For an instant he even wonders if he has died during the night. There is a strange thickness in the air. He rises, feeling almost weightless. When was the last time he ate? He does not remember. He fumbles with the buttons of his jeans and kicks on his boots.

Today is the day. The plane is finished. He built the track ages ago, leading down a steep hill and opening onto a wide, flat field, now patterned with ice. The rails are firmly embedded in the frost. The plane will ride the wheeled tray, which will catch at the bottom and launch the thing airborne. Jesse has gamed it out hundreds of times. He has had to make a few adjustments—the Wright brothers had a crew, not to mention each other, whereas Jesse has only himself. He is not afraid of failure. He finds his coat on the floor and wraps some gauze around the injured palm of his hand.

Snow has begun to fall as he hurries to the barn; the air is hung with fat, downy flakes, snagging in his eyelashes and landing cold on his tongue. Jesse throws open both doors and begins to elbow his creation out into the daylight. The plane grinds forward, its wings bouncing. In the distance, a crow makes its raucous call. One wheel catches in a hollow, and by the time Jesse gets it loose, he is damp with sweat, his heart hammering. He pushes the plane across the hilltop, conscious of the sheer spectacle of it—his golden achievement, the cables twanging, the propeller rotating by tiny increments. At last he has it poised on the top of the hill.

There is a moment of silence. With a childlike glee, Jesse lifts both hands to placate an imaginary audience. He used to toboggan on this hillside as a boy, in one of his few memories of being cupped in his father's lap and hearing Toby's unfettered laughter. From this angle, the track appears steep and uneven, dipping sharply downward. Jesse guns the motor, which rattles into life with a puff of smoke. The propeller begins to spin. He gives the plane a shove, and it lurches away from him, faster than he had anticipated; he flings out a hand and barely catches hold, dragging himself on board. The trees slip by in a rolling blur. The passage is rough, the wind icy—Jesse wishes he had thought to bring goggles. Jolting and groaning, the plane plummets down the slope. The cables shudder in his hands. Unable to restrain himself, he lets out a whoop of pure delight. At the bottom of the hill the plane pauses for a moment, as though taking one last look at its mundane, earthly surroundings. Then the powerful wings catch against the air, and Jesse takes flight.

# THE GIRLS OF APACHE BRYN MAWR

There were eight of us in the cabin, all Jews from the north side of Chicago. A few girls had been to Camp Reeds before and spoke knowingly and loftily about what the rest could expect, the campfire songs, canoe races, and marathon games of Capture the Flag. There was the usual scuffle over who would get the bunks closest to the window and the counselor's room. One or two girls had never been to sleep-away camp at all and were full of anxious questions about the latrines. Within an hour of our arrival, the cabin looked as though we had lived there forever. The contents of our duffel bags had exploded across the floor, and the bunks were draped with lanyards, training bras, rainbow sweatshirts, stray socks, and stuffed animals. We were already nicknaming one another, swapping *Archie Comics* and tubes of flavored ChapStick. The rough wooden planks of the walls had been vandalized by decades of campers. The window screens were festooned with holes.

From the lake came the sound of splashing and screams, and already we felt that we were moving into a different world, the sluggish, golden daze of honeyed summer.

Our cabin was called Apache Bryn Mawr, which the new girls found funny. It was the rule at camp that each cabin had the name of an Indian tribe *and* a prestigious college. At lunchtime we would hear the other kids singing about their dedication to Navajo Harvard or watch them tattooing Chippewa Princeton onto their forearms in ballpoint pen. As twelve-year-olds, we were the oldest campers there—except for Sasha Rosen, who had already had her bat mitzvah back at the end of April. (She liked to shake out the golden locket around her throat, showing off the Star of David she'd received as a gift, and occasionally she would hum her Torah portion in a low, throaty voice, almost absently, just to make sure we knew she still had it memorized.) Chaya Stein, whose mother was an anthropologist, treated us to a little spiel about the history of false Indianness and the random use of tribal names at summer camps, how this had begun only one generation after Custer's last stand, with the Boy Scouts. None of us were particularly interested. We giggled a little, standing around the wooden sign into which *Apache Bryn Mawr* had been elaborately carved. But by the end of the first week, we were all fiercely loyal to our name. There was only one other cabin of twelve-year-old girls, the Sioux Vassar group, and none of us could stand them. They were sleek, black-haired little minxes, and at lunchtime we sang the Apache Bryn Mawr fight song loud and clear, just to make sure they got the message.

◌

That was the summer Camp Reeds ended up in the newspapers. For a few days, the place was splashed over local television shows and featured unflatteringly in op-ed pieces. The girls of Apache Bryn Mawr were front and center, since it was our counselor who had disappeared. Some of us—with our parents' permission—appeared tearfully on camera. We were quoted in black and white. There was one picture in particular that seemed to crop up everywhere: all eight of us beaming gawkily at the camera, waving and giving each other bunny ears, and Danielle right in the middle of the huddle, flashing her easy smile.

Before she went missing, Danielle had been a bit of a legend at Camp Reeds. To begin with, she was a shiksa, which put her outside the norm. The camp was largely a Zionist organization, which more or less explained the odd cabin names: The administrators had found it prudent to feature education, even here, among the Hula-Hoop and pie-eating competitions, as this would theoretically make Jewish parents more comfortable sending their children off for six weeks of aimless amusement. For better or worse, education was our central creed. (Naomi Cohen, one of the girls in our cabin, told us that her *zadie* had been a rabbi and used to announce, in his rumbling voice and imperfect English, "If you have moneys only for building a temple or a school, you build the school. This is more important.") Gentiles were theoretically welcome at Camp Reeds, but almost everyone there looked rather like we did, pale and dark, with intelligent brown eyes.

Danielle, however, was tall and golden. Her limbs were long and tanned, and she moved with a casual athleticism around the mess hall, dressed in khaki shorts, blithely unaware of the havoc she was playing with the hearts of the male counselors and campers alike. Many of us in Apache Bryn Mawr had been in awe of her for years; we would return each summer only to find Danielle's glory undiminished, her hair still brassy and burnished, her tennis serve unparalleled. And now, at last, we were old enough to be her campers ourselves. It was Danielle who banged on our wall in the morning, shouting to get us out of bed. It was Danielle who led us in sack races and taught us swimming—making sure to stay near Rachael Schwartz, who was afraid of the water, now and then supporting her under the belly with one delicate hand. It was Danielle who strummed the guitar at the bonfire in the evenings, her flint-gray eyes sliding dreamily to the side. Elisheva Levy, the youngest in our cabin, could do a spot-on imitation of her, the hips slung one way, the shake of her hair behind one shoulder. Danielle was the best counselor there, and she was ours.

Our days began early. We were terrified of the bathrooms—cavernous holes in the dirt, reeking in wet weather, and always hung with a spider or two. We never went there at night, and our mornings generally began with a collective sprint down the gravel path. Breakfast took place right after dawn, when the air was still cool and laden with mist. The counselors would huddle together near the buffet tables, sipping their coffee and glowering at the younger kids, who could not eat without shrieking. Then we walked down to the archery field, where Sasha Rosen was the queen, standing erect, her posture perfect, as sanguine and self-assured as Artemis. We learned canoeing, which took us into the gray-green middle of the lake. The water was loaded with sand and silt. These lessons were generally a fiasco, mostly consisting of us trying to get close enough to the Sioux Vassar girls to poke them with our oars, and always ending abruptly when Rachael Schwartz spotted seaweed, or a minnow, or a half-submerged soda can, and went into a conniption.

Sometimes, in the afternoons, we would hike into the hills, following Danielle's lithe form, that swaying flaxen ponytail. The air was steamy, choked with the rising moisture from the lake. Mushrooms sprouted obscenely from fallen logs. The trees were draped with curtains of kudzu, which made the Midwestern hillsides look like a tropical wilderness; in some cases the vines were heavy enough to drag smaller saplings to the side, jutting out of the ground at an odd, punch-drunk angle. Julia Goldblatt, the klutz of our group, was always turning her ankle on loose stones and bringing the parade to a nervous halt. Hannah Breckenridge, who had been on nature hikes all her life, would point out signs of animal life, some of which were clearly imaginary—the print of a deer hoof, the droppings of a rabbit, the scratch of mountain lion claws in a nearby tree. At the crest of the hill, we would stop and look down on the cabins like gods, taking in the shiny roofs, the smoke rising from the mess hall, the tiny figures crashing around in the foamy lake. Danielle would sigh and tell us that the camp was her favorite place in the world.

During our breaks we lazed around the cabin, whistling the Apache Bryn Mawr fight song and munching on handfuls of trail mix. Danielle would teach us to weave friendship bracelets from thread. We might chat about whether it was logical or pretentious for Chaya Stein to insist that gentiles should pronounce her name correctly, sounding the rough *Ch* at the back of their throats. We would argue about whether scripture allowed us to drink juice during the fasting of the high holidays. We would ransack one another's makeup and sunblock; our careful mothers had weighted us down with tubes of SPF 75, mostly organic brands that also made skin-care products, but we were all convinced the other girls had a better kind—nicer-smelling, less likely to give rise to acne. Eventually Danielle would ask us which boys we liked. None of us had secrets now, not after the long nights of whispering in the cabin, hour after hour, in a kind of trance, shielded by the darkness and the unreality of the setting. We all knew that Tal Klein was moony over a boy in Ojibwa Yale. We all knew that Elisheva Levy had a crush on one of the male counselors.

In the evenings the whole camp would gather around the bonfire, the younger boys slathered with face paint, the girls bedecked
with braids and beads. The counselors would act out silly scenes for
us, tossing logs carelessly on the fire, the sparks cascading upward
in spirals. Sometimes we would all sing together, fearlessly, the way
we could never do in school, no matter how much our teachers
prodded us. Sometimes we would have what was called a powwow,
a session in which we were asked to share anecdotes from the day—
but to make the whole thing more Indian, the counselors taught us
to speak in a fake pidgin: "We-um like Camp Reeds-um." Hannah
Breckenridge, who had a political streak, found this offensive and
refused to participate. Chaya Stein humored her, and the two of
them crept off to one side, debating in whispers the letter they
were planning to write to the camp's board of directors. The rest of
us, however, had never met a real Indian and couldn't have cared
less. Sometimes, at the end of the evening, Danielle would dance,
spinning and leaping to the rhythm of the guitar. She would throw
back her head and give a laugh of sheer happiness.

❧

And then one morning we woke late, bewildered by the bright
sunlight and the loud roar of the kids at the lake. We had missed
breakfast—there was no Danielle to herd us down the path to
the mess hall. Tal Klein knocked timidly on the counselor's door
and got no reply. We went in, calling Danielle's name in uncertain
voices. The bed was tossed in its usual uproarious heap. Her guitar
sat in the corner as though waiting for one of us to pick it up and
give it a strum. "Maybe she's at the bathroom," someone ventured.
There was nothing to do but wait. We were lost without her guidance. We spent the morning lounging awkwardly on our bunks,

flipping through books, braiding Julia Goldblatt's thick, inky hair, and glancing out the window every few seconds, like victims of a quarantine. Danielle never came. Around lunchtime, Rachael Schwartz, who was prone to melodrama, burst into tears. At this point Sasha Rosen took charge and led us authoritatively to the administrator's office.

Mr. Benson, who ran Camp Reeds, seemed completely unruffled by the whole thing. Apparently it was not unheard-of for a counselor to prove unreliable—not Danielle, of course, who was a staple of the camp, but Mr. Benson assured us that there was bound to be some logical explanation. He got on the phone and barked a few orders through his thick red goatee. To our horror, our new counselor would be the lifeguard, whom we had never seen and could not picture outside of her ridiculously small bikini. We knew her as the woman who blew her whistle ferociously and gestured to prevent us swimming out too far. Indeed, she had been rather unkind when Tal Klein had got her first period and did not want to participate one day. Her name was Ilse, but among ourselves we always called her Itsy-Bitsy, because of her tiny swimsuits. Mr. Benson summoned her to his office, and she appeared, looking nettled, now clad in denim shorts and pigtails.

Itsy-Bitsy led us competently enough through our day's activities. She slept in our cabin that night, and the next night too, but she did not participate with us as Danielle had done. During archery lessons, she sat around examining her fingernails. During our session at the crafts table, she abandoned us to our own valiant but doomed attempts to stamp precise letters into leather pouches. Even her appearance was an affront to us. She was not tawny like Danielle, with a smile as bright as sunlight caught in a sprinkler. Instead, Itsy-Bitsy was pale, and her fishy skin was scattered with freckles the size of ladybugs.

By the third day of Danielle's absence, we began to worry in earnest. We had believed Mr. Benson's assurances that she would pop back very soon. We were hurt by her desertion, of course, but were fully prepared to forgive her as long as she offered us the juicy details of whatever family crisis or love-affair-gone-wrong had taken her away so unexpectedly. Each time the screen door of our cabin bumped in the wind, we all looked up hopefully. When we were out on the tennis courts and caught a glimpse of someone's blond hair in the distance, our hearts leapt. But there was no sign of her. We were not the only ones to be concerned; at mealtimes, the counselors left their tables and gathered together in the corner, talking in urgent voices. Mr. Benson, despite his pretense at insouciance, was spotted yammering away on the telephone at all hours, gesturing fervently to the air around him. The information that something was amiss percolated down to the younger campers, who began to generate fantastic theories of their own—Danielle had been kidnapped, Danielle was a Russian spy in disguise, Danielle had swum into the lake the night she disappeared.

We would learn later on that Danielle had been a foster child. Bounced from house to house in her youth, she had no central family unit to act on her behalf. Since she was a college sophomore now, and no longer a minor, the state would not intervene either. It was up to the camp to decide whether she should be declared missing. Day by day, Mr. Benson put it off, knowing the media storm that would ensue, waiting, as we were waiting, for Danielle to come strolling down the path again, swinging her bronzed arms and humming some popular medley softly to herself.

Camp Reeds had its own ghost story. At night, around the fire, one of the counselors could always be coaxed into telling it, though most of us knew it by heart anyway. Many years ago—so the story went—a cruel counselor had beaten his charges, torturing them and making them sleep on the concrete floor. But his deserts had come: One night he had fallen—or was pushed?—into the bonfire and, burning furiously, had dashed into the forest. The story held that on moonless nights he dragged his mangled body out from the underbrush and lurched around the grounds, looking for stray campers on whom he could exact his revenge. There was some dissension among the girls of Apache Bryn Mawr about whether this story was true. At ten o'clock, when we climbed into our bunks and lay whispering together, as the distant voices from other cabins were carried to us on the breeze, the story was certainly false. But around 3:00 AM, if one of us woke up on her own, listening to the unfamiliar whine of the ceaseless crickets, it suddenly became very real indeed. We got used to hearing each other whimpering in the darkness. We got used to waking suddenly to Elisheva Levy's panicked fingers clutching our shoulders, shaking us awake as she hissed, "Oh, thank God! I thought you'd been murdered."

One night none of us could get to sleep. It was bright outside, the trees bathed in unearthly blue, the moon glowing like a searchlight. On past evenings we had played word games or gathered around for Light as a Feather, Stiff as a Board. We had listened for the mossy footsteps of the camp ghost and painted our fingernails inexpertly in the gloom. Tonight we were jittery, uncertain.

At last Sasha Rosen reached under her bunk and dragged out her Ouija Board. We sat ourselves importantly in a circle, and a few girls put their fingertips delicately on the pointer, ready for channeling.

"What should we ask it?" Hannah Breckenridge whispered. It was not the sort of night to bother the spirits with nonsense, wondering whether our crushes liked us back or which of us would be next to get her first period.

"We need to know about Danielle," Sasha said.

"Right! Danielle."

"Are there spirits in the room?" Sasha asked, each word distinct. "Is there someone who can answer us?"

*Yes*, said the Ouija Board, right away. A few girls shivered.

"Good," Sasha said firmly. "Now tell us, please. Is Danielle alive?"

*No*, said the Ouija Board.

Chaya Stein moaned. Rachael Schwartz rose awkwardly to her feet, and then, hovering over us all, glanced around and sat quickly down again.

"Did somebody murder Danielle?" Sasha asked.

The pointer of the Ouija Board began to move. It glided erratically over the board.

"I don't think—" Naomi Cohen began, her voice higher than normal.

"We have to know," Sasha said.

*Yes*, said the Ouija Board, finally.

At that moment, Itsy-Bitsy, evidently annoyed by the ruckus we were making, kicked the wall between her bedroom and ours. It had happened before—she had hollered at us to be quiet, knocked with her fist, even hurled a shoe. But this time we all screamed in a paroxysm of terror. We scattered away from the Ouija Board like leaves in a strong wind.

⁂

The media descended on Camp Reeds in a frenzy. They were not allowed on the grounds, of course, but it lent a certain strangeness to the proceedings when we glimpsed their vans parked in the far lot, their flashbulbs glittering as we hiked down the path to the beach. Sasha Rosen dolled herself up and let herself be interviewed, pointing to a photograph of Danielle and begging anyone who had information to *please* come forward. Elisheva Levy, too, appeared on TV, arm in arm with Naomi Cohen. We watched them on the flickering set in the lobby, one rainy evening. Sasha clasped her hands together, looking breathless and distressed. Elisheva was unusually eloquent, though we had not realized how often her speech was peppered with *you know* and *like* until we saw her looming larger than life on the screen. Noami, abashed by the perfectly groomed interviewer, said nothing at all. She just hovered there like a deer in the headlights, her eyes wide.

There is a way that, at the age of twelve, you can love an older girl, somewhere between the child's worship of a fairytale princess and the adult's idolization of a reigning beauty. A few of us were genuinely heartbroken by our loss. The camp was a sheltered sphere, and each day there felt like the equivalent of a few weeks in the normal world. The letters from our parents and postcards from our friends came in from another planet, a realm we had relinquished long ago. It seemed that we had always lived in the rickety cabin with the screen door that slammed. It seemed that we had always subsisted on beans, pizza, and scrambled eggs. We felt that we had known Danielle for a long time—we had trusted her, telling our secrets to her, taking her advice about clothes, letting her experiment by putting makeup on our faces. It hurt to think that she could have detached herself from us without a word, a note, a backward glance. Perhaps that was why we took it upon ourselves to find some more sinister agent that might have caused her disappearance.

Tal Klein, who had read a lot of detective novels, said that our first job was to find out as much about the victim as possible. There wasn't a lot to go on, however. We knew that Danielle had a boyfriend at Camp Reeds. His name was Kyle, and he played the guitar around the bonfire each night with a rock star's bravado, the lenses of his cosmopolitan glasses glinting in the light. We had spotted him holding hands with Danielle, and they often sang duets together—but of course, that was not enough evidence, since Danielle was a happy-go-lucky, amiable sort of girl, tangibly affectionate with all her friends. But then, Rachael Schwartz had once glimpsed what she *thought* was Danielle, backed up against the side of the nurse's station with her arms around Kyle's neck. Rachael had told us about it afterward: how she had hesitated, unsure whether she ought to dash off and summon the rest of us, and so had missed her chance to verify if they had been kissing with tongue.

In recent days, Kyle had been particularly vocal about wanting Danielle found, even shouting at Mr. Benson once, from inside the office, in tones that could be heard all over the grounds. Kyle was looking haggard, just as he should, just as Romeo might have done when exiled to Mantua. He no longer grinned mischievously in the mess hall, flicking strands of noodles at his friends. More than once, he had hefted his guitar into his lap, plucked haphazardly at the strings, and then set the instrument aside, as though he just couldn't bear to play alone.

❧

After a week or so the storm passed over. There was still no news of Danielle, and the media moved on to fresher stories. A few of the younger children were withdrawn from camp by parents who wanted to be on the safe side. Several of our mothers made similar noises, offering to drive up early too, but we quickly put a stop to that. Sasha Rosen told us proudly that she had wept for ten minutes at the very mention of it, until her mother actually apologized over the phone. Rachael Schwartz threatened to kill herself if forced to go home, but we all knew her parents wouldn't take this too seriously. They, like us, would be able to detect the throbbing note of delighted histrionics in her voice. Hannah Breckenridge defeated her nervous parents through sheer cold logic: There was no proof of foul play, after all, and it would be misguided for them to act on rumor and speculation.

In truth, we could not bear to think of leaving. Next year we would be too old to come to summer camp. We would be scouting out early-enrollment classes for high school. We would have crossed the threshold into the next stage of our lives. We would be teenagers.

Besides, we were busy with camp life. Sasha Rosen won the archery prize a record seven times in a row, and Mr. Benson told us that he would make a plaque for her, to put on the wall of the lobby and keep there forever. Hannah Breckenridge found a bird's nest, fallen to the ground, with all the tiny, sky-blue eggs smashed except for one. Having read about what to do in such a situation, she took to carrying this last intact egg around, tucked into her bra, even after Itsy-Bitsy had told her in a snotty sort of voice that the chick inside was certainly dead. Chaya Stein developed such a fierce crush on a boy in Cree Wesleyan that she swiped the headband he wore to play basketball and kept it doubled around her own wrist. We did not forget about Danielle—we often thought about her—but it was hard for us to sustain focus. We could not always whip up the panic necessary to continue our investigations.

Then, one balmy morning, something happened to bring the whole matter into sharper relief. We were wading into the lake for a swimming lesson, wincing as we stumbled on the rough stones. Itsy-Bitsy, clad as usual in a pinstriped bikini ("Flaunting it," Sasha Rosen murmured disgustedly), blew her whistle and gestured for us to get ready for a race. In the middle of the water floated a kind of raft. We were supposed to swim there and back as fast as we could; the winner would be awarded a peace feather. Rachael Schwartz was already starting to hyperventilate. Even more than the water itself, she was afraid of the raft, which was anchored to the ground by an algae-coated chain that trailed away into shifting clouds of sand. Something about that chain made her flesh crawl. Itsy-Bitsy, as impervious as ever, gave another blast on her whistle and lifted one white hand in the air.

Her shout was interrupted by a commotion on the beach. Two of the male counselors were struggling in the shallows, splashing around as their charges fled in terror. For a moment we could not tell if it was a real fight or if they were just wrestling in play.

"It's Danielle's boyfriend," Julia Goldblatt said suddenly. "It's Kyle."

We recognized the other counselor too: Joshua, from Chippewa Princeton, curly-haired and sunburned. Locked in a kind of painful embrace, both men staggered onto the beach, kicking up showers of sand. Then Kyle threw a punch. There was no mistaking it: He was out for blood. Joshua stepped back, his fingers to his mouth.

"Excellent," said Hannah Breckenridge, who had a ghoulish streak.

Joshua lunged forward. Kyle anticipated the move and dodged, both arms in the air. They fell into another bear hug, grimacing in anger, each trying to knock the other to the ground. Kyle kicked out sharply, and Joshua fell with a roar.

"—touch her," Kyle was screaming. We could hear him clearly from where we stood. "If you even laid a *hand* on her!"

Joshua, crouched with one knee in the sand, looked up and began to laugh. His impudent burble carried on the breeze.

"Dude," he cried. "Get *over* it already."

He climbed to his feet. Kyle aimed another punch, but his rage was getting the best of him. His movements were uncontrolled. He was almost growling. Joshua evaded the blow easily, leaned forward, and shoved Kyle away from him. Kyle stumbled and stood frozen for a moment. Then he darted toward the pier, reaching for his backpack, which lay in the sand.

A few of the smaller children had begun to sob in fright. Out in the lake, our group stood shoulder to shoulder. The water lapped quietly around our calves. Tal Klein, who was brainy, would say later that we had been the chorus in that little drama, witnessing the actions of the Greek gods on stage. Kyle knelt beside his backpack and began to fumble in the front pocket. Joshua wiped the blood from his split lip. The other counselors were already converging on the beach, appearing as though by magic from the woods. Soon the scene was obscured by a busy, chattering crowd. Joshua was led away to the nurse's station, still dabbing at his bloody mouth. A few counselors hurried out into the waves, wearing big false smiles, to round us all up.

"Everybody back to land," someone shouted. "Lunchtime!"

This triggered a general rush. Campers are always hungry, and our group was caught up helplessly in the pandemonium— squealing seven-year-olds, squabbles about towels, people falling over as they tried to get into their shorts. But Elisheva Levy kept her head. She stayed focused on Kyle's melancholy form and told us afterward what she had seen: One of his hands slipped into the pocket of his backpack, brought out a shining object, and turned it over thoughtfully.

"I couldn't *swear* it was a knife," she said later. "There was so much going on, and then Chaya stepped on my foot. But I'm pretty sure."

※

A week later, Naomi Cohen roused us from our bunks at four in the morning. She was the only one in our cabin who was ever brave enough—or motivated by enough urgency—to cope with the latrines at night. She had seen strange things in the darkness. Once she had told us about passing the picnic tables and observing several figures there in the gloom—counselors, AWOL from their cabins, handing around what looked like a cigarette. Naomi had watched the red tip glowing among the trees, the plume of rising smoke, and was convinced that what she had smelled was marijuana. "My parents are hippies," she had told us calmly, shrugging.

Now she moved between the bunks, poking us and tickling our feet. She shook Sasha awake and pulled on Julia Goldblatt's hair. Chaya Stein groaned and put her pillow over her head.

"Come on," Naomi was murmuring. "Get up, guys. You have to come with me. I don't want to turn on the light. I don't want to wake up Itsy-Bitsy."

Ten minutes later, shivering, we walked down the path together. The camp looked different in the dark—the pines were fizzy, unreal shapes, and between the trunks we could see the lake, as empty of light as a black hole. Tal Klein was trailing her entire sleeping bag over her shoulders, which led to a few catastrophes as the cloth snagged on branches and was stepped on by other girls. Above our heads, bats flickered and dived, the swoop of their wings just visible. Their cries echoed at the very edge of our hearing.

"This way," Naomi whispered.

"What exactly were you doing out of bed, anyway?" Julia asked.

"I had to go number two. Come on, over here."

"What the hell could be so important?" snarled Sasha, who was always rendered irascible by lack of sleep. Naomi refused to answer, merely pointing down the trail.

We heard Kyle's voice before we got close enough to see him. He was in the lobby of the mess hall, and from the sound of it he was either sobbing or laughing. Hannah Breckenridge flung out a hand to stop the rest of us before we barged past the bushes and onto the front lawn, where he might have glimpsed us. We caromed into one another, *sh*-ing desperately.

"There," Naomi breathed.

Kyle was seated on a bench, cell phone to his ear. He also held a bottle, from which he was drinking freely. One bulb glared above him, illuminating his cheekbones and the tufts of his dark hair.

"Are you still there?" he cried. "Hello?"

Rachael Schwartz jumped and squealed. Elisheva nudged her to be quiet as Kyle readjusted his grip on the phone.

"I'm trying to tell you what happened," he said. "No, I *won't* lower my voice. You're the one who— What?"

"Oh wow," Tal Klein said. "He's intoxicated."

"Drunk," Chaya corrected her. "He's *drunk*, Tal. Don't always talk like the dictionary."

"My father drinks," Elisheva said sourly. Several of us turned to look at her in surprise. Normally we would have been thrilled with this kind of salacious detail, but just now we had bigger things on our minds.

"—loved that girl," Kyle was saying. "I told you that, man. I was going to buy her a ring. Saving up. Listen, because I need you to understand—"

He gulped more of his beer. We could see the liquid dribble down his chin, staining his T-shirt.

"An accident," he said at last. "You get that, right? An *accident*."

"Oh God," Rachael moaned.

"*Zol zein shah!*" Sasha said. "Seriously. Be quiet."

Kyle shifted in the light, his glasses gleaming. He was listening urgently to the person on the other end of the phone. Suddenly he burst out laughing.

"Drunk dial?" he said. "I call you to pour my heart out, and you're telling me— You—"

He hung up with a savage gesture. The movement made us all jump. Rachael had a hand pressed over her own mouth to stop herself from screaming. As we watched, Kyle drank the last of his beer. The empty bottle seemed to interest him, and he turned it around, watching the light play on the glass. After a moment he held it up to one eye as though it were a telescope.

"Yo ho ho and a bottle of rum," he said.

With that, he clicked off the light. We waited in the shadows, hardly daring to breathe. The wind wafted down the hillside, carrying the vanilla smell of the pines. Kyle was still there—as our eyes adjusted to the darkness we could make out the turn of his shoulder, his head nestled against the screen. Perhaps he had fallen asleep.

"This is *mishugenah*," Hannah Breckenridge said at last. And it was.

꩜

The incident broke us into factions. Half of us were convinced that Kyle had murdered Danielle. He had spoken of an accident, which meant that the guilt was tearing him apart. He even had a weapon in his possession. He had called a friend to confess but had chosen to do so when drunk, and thus had not been believed.

The other half of us were less sure. We kind of liked Kyle, the way he threw himself wholeheartedly into the silly skits the counselors put on, the bright, cinnamon tone of his voice when he sang. Perhaps the "accident" had been a fight with Danielle, or even his very public brawl with Joshua on the beach. There was no way to be sure.

"I know what I know," Sasha Rosen said grimly.

"We don't *know* anything," Hannah Breckenridge argued testily.

Julia wanted to drop the whole thing. We were in our last week of camp; we should just try to have fun while we could. Elisheva wanted to ferret out the truth. We owed that much to Danielle. Naomi wasn't certain either way. She dithered, changing her mind midconversation. And Chaya Stein was the worst of all. "Innocent until proven guilty," she intoned, over and over, in a thoroughly self-righteous way—and so the argument went on, until Rachael Shwartz began to cry out of sheer frustration.

⁓

One muggy, sun-baked afternoon found us scattered around the tennis court, working halfheartedly to improve our serves. The courts were not shaded, and we were sweating profusely. Tal Klein kept stopping to check her shoulders for sunburn. We dragged ourselves across the grass to retrieve stray balls. Itsy-Bitsy, of course, was not walking among us as Danielle had always done, correcting our grips and cheering us on. Instead, she had settled herself on a boulder with two male counselors. They were ostentatiously sharing drags on a cigarette.

After a while, we glimpsed Sasha Rosen striding purposefully down the path toward us. She had absented herself earlier because her wrist was hurting and she wanted to stop by the nurse's station.

Now she was pushing a younger boy in front of her with the air of a prison guard marching a condemned man to the gallows. Her expression was triumphant.

Our play slowed down. Julia Goldblatt began to toss one of the balls to herself. Rachael Schwartz let her racket fall with a clatter.

Sasha, now steering the younger boy by the shoulder, approached Itsy-Bitsy and said politely, "Excuse me, Ilse. May I take the Apache Bryn Mawr girls over here for just a moment?"

Itsy-Bitsy, absorbed in tapping ash from her cigarette, waved her away without much interest.

"She's such a *tsatskele*," Hannah Breckenridge murmured. Naomi smothered a giggle behind her fingers.

We gathered under an elm tree, reveling in the shade. Most of us settled in a circle, cross-legged, though Chaya Stein flopped on her back on the grass. Sasha coaxed the small boy forward. We recognized him vaguely—a black-haired child who tended to flush crimson when spoken to. He had won the camp pudding-eating competition earlier in the summer.

"I met him in the nurse's station," Sasha said. "Go on. Tell them what you told me."

The boy looked at her.

"It's fine," Sasha said gently. "They're nice girls. I promise."

"Okay," the boy said. "Well, I'm in Navajo Harvard. Kyle is my counselor."

The attention around the circle sharpened at once. Hannah leaned forward, her chin on her fist. The boy turned red and began to rub at one cheek as though seeking to wipe away his blush.

"So one night," he went on, "I followed Kyle out of the cabin. I was scared of the ghost—it's stupid, I know. But I saw Kyle go out, and I didn't want to be there without him. I saw him meet up with that girl who disappeared."

"Danielle."

"Yeah, her. They swam out in the lake. Kyle had his backpack there. I saw them fight on the raft." He looked hopelessly around at us all, then said, "Anyway, she fell in the water. He jumped in after her. That's all."

There was a moment's silence.

"That's *it*?" Rachael asked, her voice high and impatient.

"No," Sasha said. "You're making him nervous. He's not telling it right. Here, act it out with me. Show them what you saw."

The boy squirmed a little as Sasha stepped into the center of our group. She mimed a square around her body, showing us where the raft would have been. Then she bent her knees as though about to dive into the water. The boy rushed up behind her and grabbed her around the midriff. Sasha struggled against him and fell forward with a cry.

"You said he kind of slashed her, didn't he?" Sasha asked the boy, who had turned pink right up to the tips of his ears.

"Yeah." Again he mimed grabbing Sasha's torso, this time whipping one hand across her stomach. "Like that."

"Good," Sasha said. "Thank you. Run away now."

The boy turned on his heel and bolted. There was an ecstatic expression on his face as he dashed down the path; it was enough to boost our confidence a little, that in his eyes, we were the coolest girls at Camp Reeds. His prestige would rise just because he had been in our presence.

"So you see," Sasha said impressively.

"I don't see," said Elisheva at once.

Sasha clicked her tongue impatiently. "He stabbed her. She drowned. The end."

"But dead bodies float, right?" Elisheva said. "They might sink for a bit, but they come back up. They get all—bloated."

"Ew," Rachael Schwartz said. "Stop it."

"Don't be a baby," Sasha said.

"How can we be sure he really cut her?" Naomi began thoughtfully. "Do you think he had the knife in his hand? That kid didn't say he saw it—"

At once a babble broke out.

"Of *course* he—"

"You have to admit it doesn't quite—"

"Innocent until proven—"

Hannah Breckenridge gasped, "Ahh."

Her chin was lifted, and her face wore an arrested look. We all paused and stared at her.

"What?" Sasha asked. "Are you cramping?"

"He *cut* her," Hannah said. "He *cut* her across the stomach."

"I just said that!" Sasha cried. "What's the matter with all of you?"

"No," Hannah said, leaning forward earnestly. "My dad's a cop. There was a case he told us about, and my mom got mad at him, because it was pretty gross. He said that if a body goes into the water—" She swallowed hard, looking faintly sick. "It will float back up. Because of the gases. But if you happen to cut its stomach, then it sinks. The gases just go into the water—"

She broke off. There was a moment of silence. In the distance, we heard the drone of a lawnmower starting up.

"I don't understand," Naomi broke in shrilly. "Why would he cut her? Why would he?"

"He said it was an accident."

"Are you saying Danielle is in the lake?" Chaya Stein said, turning pale. "Danielle is *still* in the lake?"

Rachael Schwartz made an odd little movement, as though shaking off cobwebs.

"I *knew* I was right!" she wailed. "I've *always* hated that water."

At the edge of the field, Itsy-Bitsy rose to her feet. In an unpleasant, singsong voice, she called, "Girls! Time to resume play, I think!"

&

That afternoon we broke away from the other campers and gathered in our cabin. We were so upset that some of us had begun to manifest symptoms of illness. Julia Goldblatt was too nauseated to participate in the kickball game, and Tal Klein was running a slight fever. Naomi Cohen, whose mother was a surgeon, explained in clinical terms what we were feeling. There was one little nodule in the brain that was responsible for both excitement and fear. Up until now, we had been chasing clues, putting together facts, essentially riding the crest of excitement—but now, faced with the awful truth, we had switched over. We lay on our bunks, clinging to stuffed animals for comfort. We turned helplessly to Sasha Rosen. This was her usual position in the group—the oldest of us all, levelheaded and authoritative.

She laid it out for us slowly. Sitting on the battered rug in the middle of the cabin, she gestured dreamily in the air. Danielle had been dating Kyle. But he had loved her, had wanted to marry her, and she had not felt the same way about him. For Danielle, Camp Reeds was a place of freedom, a loosening of the restrictions of daily life. Behind Kyle's back, she had fooled around with Joshua, who met her in a kind of easygoing unconcern. He might not have been the only other man she was seeing. Maybe Danielle had threatened to break it off with Kyle. Maybe Kyle had simply realized that she did not love him. One night they swam to the raft together, a romantic spot, a full moon. Kyle had brought his backpack, which contained snacks and a few beers for them to share—as well as his trusty knife. But they had argued. Kyle brandished the blade, maybe just to scare her, to show her how serious he was. Sasha painted the picture for us clearly. We could all see how Danielle had tried to flee, darting to the edge of the raft and preparing to dive off. She was a strong swimmer. Kyle had clutched at her—the knife cut across her stomach—the artery was severed. Her body had dropped into the black water.

"And so," Sasha finished.

Sprawled over our bunks, we avoided one another's eyes. Sasha's proud expression faded. We were all convinced. No one was naysaying anymore. Danielle's body must still be at the bottom of the lake—but it was deep and treacherous, with currents from the river that shifted the position of the shoals. The counselors had already dragged the shallows, holding hands in a long line, kicking their feet through the sand, their faces dourly expectant. The police had been there too, several uniformed figures scudding across the waves in a boat with its own siren and lights, shouting instructions by bullhorn and leaning over the side. The campers had collected on the shore to watch. But no one had thought to look in deeper water. We did not know what condition Danielle would be in by now. Was she still rotting away, being devoured by fish and snails? Had she been reduced to a bare skeleton?

Several of us began to speak and faltered. Our minds felt jammed. The sun trickled between the blinds as we huddled in the stuffy cabin. Sasha Rosen slipped almost unconsciously into the role of the teacher, allowing us to voice our thoughts one by one. Julia Goldblatt distributed chewable tablets of aspirin to the girls who were getting headaches from so much thinking. We could not agree on how to proceed. If we went to the police, they would likely not believe us—where was our proof? Hannah Breckenridge's father, the cop, was always complaining about prank calls. We could hardly dial 911 and explain the trajectory of our realization, from the evidence of the Ouija Board to the vague testimony of a ten-year-old pudding-eating champion.

Elisheva Levy wanted to call her mother. Sasha just rolled her eyes at that one. Our parents would listen with an exasperated expression—that look we knew so well, from the times we had thrown tantrums about curfews or homework. Our fathers would tell us we'd been watching too much television, that we *always* let ourselves get carried away. Our mothers would blame themselves for not having brought us home from camp earlier. They wouldn't really listen. We ourselves could barely believe that this time we weren't making it up. The whole thing felt perfectly in keeping with our gruesome games of Light as a Feather, Stiff as a Board. We had once played Bloody Mary too, repeating the evil name forty times in a row, and several of us got so worked up that we had really seen a nebulous face peering out of the mirror. It wasn't safe to talk about these things—not here, in the daylight, as though Danielle's murder belonged in the realm of sunlit reality. Perhaps all along we had been seeking to disprove, rather than to verify, that someone had done away with her. We felt as though we had unearthed her corpse from the depths of the lake, as though she lay among us now, glistening and terrible.

Our eyes met at last, black and frightened. Elisheva drew a shaky breath.

"Of course if there was anything real—" Naomi began, but she was overridden as in a rush, almost in unison, we began to backpedal.

"Someone else would have seen—"

"She probably just ran off—"

"We're being silly—"

Sasha Rosen's bell-clear voice carried over the rest. "Kyle wouldn't have *killed* someone," she said. "Right, you guys? Right?"

☙

Two days later we left for home. Camp ended on a rather anti-climactic note. Rain washed out our last jubilant bonfire, and it was still drizzling when our parents appeared, waving from inside their minivans, looking older than we remembered. The girls of Apache Bryn Mawr went through the motions; we clung to each other, sobbing, exchanging e-mail addresses, trading T-shirts and barrettes, those prized items that we had coveted from each other's duffel bags. But beneath it all ran a current of shame. During that summer, each of us had grown up. We had learned, none too gently, that life was not always fair, that sometimes love went unrequited and crime unpunished. We were not able to give voice to such ideas—not yet, anyway. But in the deep place, in the dark and secret core of our natures, we all understood these things. We had proven ourselves to be cowards. It was a relief to drive away, waving dismally to one another, knowing that we would not keep in touch. That was how the world worked. The realm of camp was an insulated bubble that did not sustain itself on contact with the rest of our lives.

It is strange how someone who vanishes can be etched so clearly on the brain. There were other counselors at Camp Reeds who we knew just as well, if not better, than Danielle. We had been their campers for multiple summers; we had sung with these women, rubbed suntan lotion on their backs, let them see us cry. And yet they did not linger in our memories. We knew they were alive, moving through the streets of their hometowns, changing jobs, falling in love, aging. Our minds were able to let them go. But

Danielle stayed with us; we could not shake her. Months afterward, we were still able to call up the freckle at the corner of her lip, the watery fall of bangs across her cheek. We remembered her voice, husky and dry. She came into our thoughts at odd moments. The slap of flip-flops on the street or the swish of a skirt passing through a revolving door would remind us of her. We were haunted by her—as the last and only keepers of her secret, as the campers who had loved her, as the ones who had, in the end, failed her.

~

Years later, several of us returned to Camp Reeds, now as counselors ourselves. Sasha Rosen worked with the eight-year-olds. Tal Klein took charge of Sioux Vassar. Naomi Cohen was the lifeguard, modestly dressed in a black one-piece. We were college girls by this time, dangerously sophisticated, sporting brash ponytails and bright red lipstick. It was both strange and delightful to find that the camp was almost entirely unaltered. We observed the same things that had held such magic for us when we were small—the face paint, the peace feathers, the crackling bonfire. We passed on the rituals and songs to our campers in the same way we might tell them about the tooth fairy, not believing it ourselves, but pleased by their acceptance. We took pleasure in strolling down the gravel paths. We made drip castles on the beach. We located the trees in which our initials were still awkwardly carved.

Around the bonfire on moonless nights, people would now tell a new ghost story—the love affair between two counselors that had ended with a body being dumped into the lake. According to the tale, this nameless woman was restless. You could hear her when the nights were still, pulling herself up out of the water, pacing around barefoot on the sand. Most of the campers had no idea that this fable might not be age-old. Shivering with excited dismay, they spoke of it as though it were written in stone somewhere on the grounds, as though it had always been the ghost story of Camp Reeds.

For us, the former girls of Apache Bryn Mawr, it was an oddly soothing tale. Danielle had often told us that the camp was her favorite spot, and it brought us a kind of peace to imagine that unquiet ghosts returned to the places they had loved, for their own comfort, and as a caution to the living.

# ISAIAH ON SUNDAY

H e wakes in a panic. It is Saturday morning—it is not yet time for work—the sky is still dark—something has startled him. Eventually his mind collects all of its straggling pieces. Someone is pounding at his front door.

Wrapped in a blanket, wiping the sleep out of his eyes, Isaiah lurches down the hallway. Through the window he glimpses that a steady downpour has begun; the panes are jeweled with moisture. The television screen flickers, bathing the walls in an unearthly glow. Isaiah likes to leave it on all night so he does not feel quite alone, with the volume low so as not to disturb his neighbor.

The hammering at the front door comes again. It sounds like cannon fire. Isaiah is fumbling with the bolt before he even thinks to look through the peephole. He steps back hastily as a dark figure bangs into the room.

His sister catapults into his arms. Frances is shuddering and dripping. She is drenched to the skin. Openmouthed, Isaiah stumbles backward as she wheels her bicycle past the hatstand and crashes it against the wall. Frances gleams like an apparition, her black hair in tangles, her skin beaded with wet. Her jacket is sodden; it takes a few tries for her to peel it from her shoulders. Then she grips Isaiah around the middle. She holds on, refusing to let go even as he negotiates their bodies like partners in a waltz so that he can close the front door.

Eventually he pries her loose.

"You're not seriously here," he says.

Frances begins to cry. "Don't call them," she says.

"What?"

"I'll sleep on the couch—I won't make any noise—" She looks up at him, her mouth working. One sharp fist lands against his chest.

"I *missed* you," she wails.

"You biked here?" Isaiah asks. "It's 2:00 AM."

"Three," Frances says. "They didn't notice. They never notice anything."

He stares at her, trying to gather his wits. With the onset of high school, his sister has begun to experiment with different styles. Today she has black mascara smeared around both eyes. Her T-shirt is decorated with a skull. The overall impression, as far as Isaiah can tell, is that of a vampire, pallid and moody. It does not sit well on the delicate bones of her face.

"Mom's going to kill you," he says finally.

Frances sneezes twice. She is trembling all over. Isaiah realizes that she is at the end of her tether; as a doctor's son he recognizes the signs of fatigue and mental strain. The next few minutes pass in a blur. He leads Frances to the couch, but she refuses to lie down and make a watermark on his cushions. He digs out a pair of sweatpants, and she changes in the bathroom, commenting loudly on the state of his towels. After every blink Isaiah is astonished again to see her there, wringing her hair out between her hands, rolling the cuffs so that his pants don't swallow up her feet.

At last she lies down, settling herself in the languid, boneless manner of a drowsing cat. Cautiously Isaiah sits on the armrest beside her.

"Frances," he says softly. "What—?"

Her eyes slip closed. Isaiah shakes her shoulder.

"*Frances.*"

"Too late," she says. "I'm sound sleep."

He waits, watching her. At first she is simply pretending to doze, but very soon her breath begins to come in a deep, regular rhythm. Isaiah tentatively touches her hair and her clenched fists. She is really here, in his apartment. Her laundry is piled in his hamper. Her bicycle leans awkwardly against his wall. It is not, after all, a dream. He can even smell her on the air—rain-soaked cotton and stale perfume. She has grown during his absence. She is lankier and paler than before.

As though to shield herself from his prying gaze, Frances rolls suddenly onto her side. For a moment Isaiah can see that the vampire look is just a brittle veneer laid over his sister. If he took a chisel to the right place, he could chip it away in shards, revealing the familiar girl within.

∾

The two of them were raised a world away, in Africa. Isaiah's father was a doctor, his mother a frenzied proponent of God. During Isaiah's early years, the family traveled the western half of the continent with such frequency that his memories run together in a rolling blur. The smell and taste of yam, pounded into pulp, folded into balls and served in soup. The beggars that lined the road, many of them children who had been maimed intentionally to garner sympathy and greater profits. The golden dust that rose and settled around his ankles. Frances as an infant, swaddled in a cloth sack that hung over his mother's shoulder.

In the desert, the sky looked as though it had been baked solid in a kiln. In the port towns, the clouds were the size of mountains. His mother bargained in the market for every single thing she bought; people seemed almost insulted if you did not argue, and cry that the price was far too much, and pretend to walk away, as though you were not going to buy after all, before making any purchase. Isaiah remembers a bird that woke him one night, screaming and beating its wings outside the door. He leapt out of bed, fumbling for the flashlight. The bird vanished into the darkness, and Isaiah turned, the beam of his light bobbing over the earthen floor, to see three scorpions frozen beneath the bed with their tails uplifted. His mother later told him the bird was sent by God to warn and protect him.

At a very young age, Isaiah understood that it was his father's job to heal people, his mother's to convert them. She often spoke of her triumphs. There was the woman dying of burns on her cot who, with her final breath, sang the hymn that says, "I must go anywhere with Jesus, no matter the roughness of the road." There was the witch doctor who gave up his wicked ways and set down his fetishes for good. One man walked four days to the hospital with two arrows protruding from his chest. He was a Fulani herdsman who had been shot during a dispute over his marriage to a third wife. Isaiah's father explained that one of the arrows had lodged inside the left atrium of the man's heart, the other in his right lung, and it had taken some doing to repair the sizable hole in the tissue while keeping the heart beating. But Isaiah's mother, her face set in a hard, fiery look, talked only of how the man had been converted right there on the operating table. She had held his hand while the bandages were removed, and they spoke together about the realm of heaven.

The first bus leaves at 5:00 AM. Isaiah is huddled outside the liquor store when it pulls up, rattling and steaming. The driver, who looks as though he has had a rough night too, nods wearily as Isaiah takes his seat. There is no one else on board. Through the scratched, smeared windows, Isaiah catches glimpses of the rising sun, tangled in the struts of the water tower.

He has left Frances slumbering on the couch. His sister is a champion sleeper; she has always been that way. When she rises, probably around noon, she will find his note, explaining that she should feel free to ransack his kitchen, he is sorry for the meager selection, and he has gone to work. The grocery store is located in a dozy neighborhood. Bungalows disappear under the ivy, bushes grow wild, and anything that lands in the lawn—a hubcap, a wading pool—becomes part of the scenery. Autumn leaves whirl in a stiff breeze. Isaiah cradles his cheek in his palm. Gradually he feels that he is waking up, the alertness filtering through his body like ink dropped in water. He climbs off the bus with a wave to the driver. The sun is higher now, washing the sky with light.

Saturday is his long shift. Isaiah stacks plastic bags so that elderly ladies can manage them, finds the bar codes on wobbly sacks of potatoes, and distinguishes between seemingly identical peaches with widely differing prices. His hands have become skilled; he can flick soup cans and boxes of crackers across the scanner with extraordinary dexterity. The customers tend to assume that he is stupid, which is fine with him: He feels like a fraud anyway, a pretend grownup, swathed in his stained apron, the ludicrous paper cap perched on his hair. He is only seventeen. This is not what his parents had planned for him, standing for hours at a cash register as his back hardens into stone. And yet his paychecks are nothing short of beautiful—embossed in black ink, with his own name printed there as large as life.

On his lunch break, Isaiah takes a sandwich out to the curb and watches a few kids playing football in the street. The boys dash between mailboxes and fire hydrants, hurling the ball back and forth; whenever someone shouts "Car!" they scatter like deer facing a rifle. Isaiah eats with meticulous slowness. His thoughts dwell on his sister—is Frances awake, has she caught cold? He tries to imagine her pedaling across town in the downpour, brushing her wet bangs from her face, negotiating the flooded gutters. Isaiah has not seen her for three months. It has been three months since he left his parents' house, and he has not spoken to anyone in the family since. His parents used to frequent this very grocery store, but when Isaiah took up shop here, they switched to the more expensive organic market on the other side of town. There was a screaming fight on the night he walked out, his mother sobbing, his father shaking his head in amazed disappointment. Isaiah does not like to think of it—though it crops up, frequently, in his dreams. The flash of his mother's hands. The bang of his father's fist on the tabletop. Frances rushing blindly from the room. His mother had shouted that he would be dead to her if he left.

He finishes his juice, listening to the scuff of footsteps, the jingle of coins dropping into the meters. A suspicion is growing in his mind. Someone has been calling him, in the morning and after work; Isaiah has grown accustomed to the brash, bright sound of the telephone dragging him from the shower, out of a nap. And yet the caller never says anything at all. A breathy silence. The number withheld. The clatter of the call being abruptly terminated. Isaiah has imagined it to be a nuisance, a telemarketer. But the caller is persistent, and for the first time he wonders whether it has been Frances, trying to memorize his schedule, trying to make contact. No doubt his parents have banned her from speaking to him. He has missed her more than he would care to admit. He even placed a framed photograph of her on his dresser—despite a prickle of embarrassment at indulging in such sentimental behavior—so that every now and then she would catch his eye, her familiar apple cheeks, the tousle of dark hair. In his shabby apartment, it is nice to have a spot of color.

ॐ

Even now, when Isaiah hears the word *home*, his mind goes back to the Nigerian delta. His adolescence was spent there; he grew from an undernourished and undersized child into a gawky young man. It was miraculous, after all his family's wanderings, to live so long in one place. He had the chance to make friends, real friends—to see the same faces every day. He had the chance to become used to his surroundings.

The delta was comprised of greens and grays: the frenzied burst of the plants, the pearly sheen of the sky, the buttery river. The villagers were always busy. There was fishing to be done, thatch to be woven, boats to be caulked. The town owned four canoes collectively, and one or more of the men was often seen maneuvering upstream with a net bundled in the back. The children played soccer, dashing around and hallooing to one another, and Isaiah and Frances ran with them, barefoot, their uncut hair swinging around their shoulders. The radio blared in the afternoons, and the women sang accompaniment. Isaiah learned to fry fish, how to tell when to turn the meat. Frances would mash fruit into paste with a stone. The delta was in a constant state of reclaiming stolen property; insects and fungus came to devour cloth and wood, and the rains washed away whatever was not nailed down. The floods would bury all that was left, covering stray bowls and shoes in layers of silt. During the rainy season, the place looked almost insubstantial. The river was the same color as the sky, so that the huts seemed to be painted on the air.

～

When he returns from work, exhausted, Isaiah finds that Frances has commandeered the couch, her purse in her lap, one hand rooting through its contents. She looks younger today—evidently she forgot her mascara when she fled the house. Her face is dewy, almost colorless, without those raccoon eyes.

Isaiah flops beside her on the sofa. He is unaccountably nervous. On the bus home, he expected—he almost hoped—that Frances would have changed her mind, vacating his apartment, carried off on the wind like the pungent smell of last night's rain. The television shows a lizard underwater. Its head is bulky, and it swims in a kind of slow-motion run, tugging away at the iridescent blue.

"It's a special on the Galapagos Islands," Frances informs him. "They were talking about the seals for a long time, but I like the lizards better, except for the mating, which is gross."

"I didn't know reptiles swam."

"These are the only ones. Except crocodiles, I guess. And turtles."

Together they gaze at the flickering screen. The lizard drops into an efficient dive, pawing at the rock to position itself. With a sideways nod it begins to pull away mouthfuls of trailing seaweed from the coral. Frances is still fishing through her purse. With an exasperated snort, she begins to remove item after item—a wad of Kleenex, a barrette, a glitter pen, and her cell phone, its sheath shining with stickers and fake gems—depositing each object unceremoniously in Isaiah's hands. He watches her idly, amused. Presently she emerges with a packet of cigarettes. Shooting him a significant look, she taps one into her palm.

"You're *smoking*?" Isaiah asks, louder than he meant to.

"I'm a teenager now," Frances says. "Have we met?"

"Don't do that in here."

"What, because your place is so nice?" She lights up, exhaling the ashy cloud like a professional.

"I mean it."

Frances makes a face at him, a mimicry of their mother's fierce scowl. Isaiah reaches over and plucks the cigarette from her grasp. She eyes him balefully as he carries it to the kitchen sink and washes it down the drain. It occurs to him that she waited until he arrived home to stage this little performance.

"Let's talk about why you ran away," he says firmly.

"So it's time to bond?" Frances laughs, then holds up the package of cigarettes. "Should I offer you one?"

"Just tell me."

She lifts one shoulder in a shrug.

"Come on, kid," he says. "You risked your life biking around in the middle of the night. You're going to have to tell me sometime, and meanwhile you're sleeping on my couch, and eating all my food—"

"It's nothing. Really."

He waits, and eventually she sighs.

"I'm not on drugs, Isaiah. I'm not knocked up. Nobody's been touching me in a bad way. I just—" She falters into silence. As he watches, she takes a lock of hair and begins twirling it.

"I'm not going back," she says at last. "That's all."

"Really?"

"Oh yeah," she whispers.

Isaiah open his mouth to argue, but on reflection he thinks better of it. Frances is as stubborn as a mule; she will dig in her heels for no other reason than she doesn't like to be pushed. Besides, as Isaiah witnesses the jut of her chin, her tensed shoulders, he has the sudden, fleeting impression that she is a little unsure—unable, perhaps, to articulate just what moved her to escape their parents' home. He may be asking her for reasons she cannot name.

"You know what?" he says. "We can talk about it later."

"Sure," she says quickly. "Fine. Whatever."

Isaiah approaches her gingerly, settling back onto the sofa cushions. Frances piles everything pell-mell into her purse, bobby pins and stray coins, breath mints and unmatched earrings. After a moment she slumps against him. She is tall for fourteen, her limbs dense and wiry. Isaiah can't see her face; she grinds her cheek against his collarbone. Her hair tickles where it meets his skin. They have never been much of a family for embraces—no crushing hugs, no shoulder rubs. He lays a hand tentatively on her back and pats the fragile knobs of her vertebrae. As Frances settles in, her body grows warmer and heavier. Last to relax are her hands, small and dimpled, the consistency of cream.

꙳

It was because of Isaiah that the family left Africa. One day, on the delta, he woke with a blinding headache. Soon he was shivering and weak. His back ached, his joints ached—he had never known the precise location of his hip, or his elbow, beneath the skin, until they began to throb. He lay on his mat, sometimes delirious, sometimes merely annoyed. His father tended him with the same brisk, cheerful warmth he exhibited with all his patients. He gave Isaiah foul-tasting tablets and tested his blood. Each time the bouts of fever and sweating recurred—once every forty-eight hours, as expected—his father cried out, "What? *Again!*" on a high, humorous note. He tried not to reveal how concerned he was.

But Isaiah was already familiar with malaria. It was the most dangerous to children. He had seen a young girl lapse into a coma; he had seen the brain-damaged cases, with their weird way of moving, their little backs warped and heads on one side. Isaiah knew his father was checking him for anemia, which could sap his growing brain of the minerals it needed. In the mornings he woke up sore and sweating, but also frightened. Would he know it if his mind were affected? He imagined a great shovel scooping out half his wit. He imagined his senses blunted, a mute, deformed boy staggering around the delta, unable to relish the warm curtains of rain.

He did recover—for a time. There were bright seasons in which he threw himself back into village life. His friends were pleased to see him up and about. Isaiah wheedled rides in the canoes. He ran between the huts with Frances and Musa, a younger boy who was missing a thumb. The three of them had invented a game called Smoke, a bit like Tag, except that your job was to allow the chaser to nearly touch you, and then to dodge with such deft rapidity that it seemed your body was not solid. Isaiah followed the women around, particularly Ladi, a gentle matron who taught him to fry plantains and prepare *isi-ewu*, spicy goat's head stew. Sometimes he tried to carry boxes on his head, the way the villagers did so easily—always ending, in his case, in disaster. He watched the older men standing calf-deep in the river, casting their nets. He watched the discontented young men playing pool on a table set up between the trees—its surface rumpled, pocked, and peeling, so that you could never predict which way the ball would go.

Then the malaria flared up again—and again. The headaches came back. Isaiah had convulsions. Sometimes he vomited. Sometimes the fever would not break, and his father was reluctant to leave him, sitting by his mat and bathing his forehead with a damp cloth. Once—he remembers it dimly—Joseph struck him across the face because he could not wake him. The slap brought Isaiah briefly into consciousness; he kicked his father angrily, and Joseph laughed in relief. There was a period when Isaiah was never really well. He felt cold, despite the sweltering heat. The headaches solidified into a constant presence, aggravated by bright light, soothed by darkness, but never gone entirely. The slightest thing could tire him out. Walking to the riverbank with his sister exhausted all of his reserves. Sitting up long enough to eat soup left him spent. His parents began to discuss him in low voices at night, when they thought he was sleeping. They began to argue. Listening, Isaiah understood the conclusion they were moving toward, inexorably, though not in perfect agreement.

∞

He does not work on Sunday. Regardless of the state of cold warfare existing between himself and his mother, he knows it would break her heart. Indeed, he himself would find it painful to defy the Sabbath—though his father often did, in days past, heading off to tend his patients as the rest of them laced their best shoes and slicked down their hair beneath his mother's beady gaze.

Isaiah once threw a tantrum, shouting that this was unfair. It was one of the few times he dared to openly defy his parents. Frances backed him up, thereby earning herself a portion of his punishment, which included a spanking, an extra helping of chores, and a lecture on the vital distinction between righteous and unrighteous labor.

In the morning, Isaiah rises late. He leaves Frances on her cell phone—perched on his kitchen counter, gobbling sweaty handfuls of dry cereal—and braves the long ride across town. He is going home at last.

The day is cloudy, saturated with a clammy glow. The bus smells of damp carpet. Isaiah is terrified. It is entirely possible that he will never return from this suicide mission; the house might grab him again, swinging its tentacles around him like a malevolent octopus, sucking him back into its hot, busy core. His parents' plans for him may come to fruition after all. Isaiah pushing trolleys down the sea-green walls of the hospital. Isaiah standing at attention beside his father, handing over sponges and surgical implements. Isaiah putting his wages into the house, mowing the lawn, sitting obediently beside his mother at church. Isaiah heading off on a missionary tour of his own.

For a long time he stands beside the old maple tree, willing himself to move up the front walk. The house is unchanged—an elaborate, falling-down affair, with two sagging porches, every screen broken and dirty. The lawn overflows with signs of children. A battered tricycle beside the stoop. A dangling tire swing. A stuffed animal hidden in the grass. There are pictures, rendered in finger paint, taped in the windows. There are dozens of initials carved into the porch steps. Isaiah takes a shuddering breath. The air is as thick as quicksand. He reminds himself that his mother will be at church, and this gives him the courage to knock.

With surprising speed, the door opens. A boy looks out warily. Isaiah doesn't recognize him—his face puffy and coffee-colored, his nose running freely. Evidently he has been keeping guard.

"What?" he says suspiciously.

"I'm Isaiah."

The boy's expression clears. He points into the living room.

"Not at church today?" Isaiah asks curiously.

"Got flu," the boy says, and slopes off into the kitchen.

Isaiah steps inside. The house, as usual, teeters on that fine edge between a joyful mess and total disaster. As a rule, his parents have between five and ten foster children of all ages living there, and the place looks like what it is—the combination of an orphanage and a school. The children are educated at home, as is Frances, and, once upon a time, Isaiah too. He picks his way across a maze of rubber boots. The cubbies his mother rescued from a Dumpster are crammed with mittens and hats. Backpacks slump in rows against the baseboard. The living room and dining room are now the learning areas. A blackboard stands firmly in front of the windows. The smell of chalk hangs in the air. There are no desks, just low tables of varying sizes, strewn with notebooks and erasers. The mantelpiece bristles with dozens of framed photographs; every face that has ever graced his parents' kitchen table is pictured there, smiling shyly, flashing bunny ears and gang signs. Frances and Isaiah are the only two children their parents achieved by birth.

"Dad?" Isaiah calls.

His father isn't hard to find. The small boy—who seems, disconcertingly, to have disappeared—pointed the way. Joseph is out cold in his recliner, his reading glasses askew on his brow. White hair rises like steam around his head.

"Hey there," Isaiah says, jogging his shoulder.

Joseph opens his eyes and blinks hopelessly. Isaiah is used to this—his father always comes out of sleep as though he has been beamed away by aliens, traveling among distant planets and solar systems. He gazes at Isaiah blankly for a while before displaying any spark of recognition.

"Well!" he says. "My famous son."

Isaiah kneels beside him and lays a hand on his chair.

"Sorry to wake you," he says. "But Mom's not around."

Joseph nods stupidly. "Is it cold in here?"

"No, it's fine."

"That woman and her thermostat. Well!" His father grins suddenly. "You've come back home. I *knew* you'd be back, if we just gave it time. That crackpot job at a grocery store—your mother always said—"

"I'm not back," Isaiah says quickly. "It's about Frances, actually. She biked to my house in the middle of the night. That's why she hasn't been around. Did you notice?"

Joseph rubs his eyes vigorously, then struggles to his feet.

"I just got in a few minutes ago," he says. "I didn't mean to pass out. There was a pileup on the freeway last night. Patients coming in at all hours. We've got this new batch of interns at the hospital, and I swear—"

"Dad," Isaiah snaps.

His father pauses in the kitchen doorway.

"Frances biked to my house in the middle of the night."

"I heard you." Joseph shuffles into the kitchen, calling over his shoulder, "Have you talked to your mother about this?"

"She's out," Isaiah reminds him.

His father mutters to himself, clanking around in the cabinets. When Isaiah enters the kitchen, he finds Joseph on his knees, digging a bag of coffee beans from the back of the refrigerator.

"No work today?" his father asks, frowning. "I hope you're not turning into a slacker now, on top of everything else."

"It's Sunday."

"Sunday? Oh, for heaven's sake. What time—?"

He dashes into the living room again. Isaiah watches him throwing together a pile of papers, digging his hat from under the couch cushions.

"I don't know what I was thinking," Joseph says. "I just popped home for a minute, and next thing you know—"

"Dad," Isaiah says. "*Dad.*"

"What?"

"Frances biked— She's a *kid*, Dad. Do you think you might want to call her? Or stop by to talk things over? I thought we could drive back over there together. I could show you my apartment. I'm sure Frances would like that." He pauses shyly. "I'd like it too."

His father goggles at him for a moment, then suddenly deflates, his arms falling to his sides.

"That's your mother's job," he says.

"It is not Mom's job. Jesus Christ."

"Lord's name in vain," his father says, all in one breath. "Don't worry, son. I'm sure it'll work out. It was good of you to drop by, anyway." He pauses, silhouetted in the doorway, his coat under one arm. "Do you see my reading glasses anywhere?"

Isaiah stares at him. His father's glasses are still perched on his forehead, glittering in the sunlight. He is the very picture of the Absentminded Professor, jovial and uncertain.

"No," Isaiah says spitefully. "Sorry."

Joseph waves to him and bangs out the door.

♋

Isaiah was thirteen when he arrived in America. For the first few weeks, the family wandered around in a daze, misinterpreting street signs and hovering at a loss in the supermarket, overwhelmed by the range of choices for simple things like toothpaste and toilet paper. Isaiah was still unwell. He looked odd: stooped and sallow. He stuck out like a sore thumb. At Sunday school, Frances got to her feet and introduced herself as "African American"—and was tactfully taken aside by an older girl. Neither Frances nor Isaiah could follow the slang of their peers, and as a result they remained blissfully unaware for several years that they had spent their initial months as pariahs, taunted and scorned by pretty much everyone.

But it was their parents who lost the most on that trip across the ocean. In Africa, Joseph and Hannah had been alive with purpose, missionaries for their God in a desolate land. Joseph in particular was a remarkable figure. Many women in Nigeria had had no access to health care at all. During prolonged labor, they would suffer ruptures in the rectum and bladder ("Fistulas," Joseph would say, his face set in grim lines), so that afterward they leaked stool and urine wherever they went. These women were outcasts. Their husbands and families drove them from their homes. Isaiah used to see them on the street, their heads bowed, people stepping around them as though they were lepers. And yet a minimal surgery could repair the damage completely. His father traveled the countryside on his motorcycle, visiting health centers and redeeming untouchables, all in a day's work. Isaiah would walk with him between the hospital beds, holding Joseph's hand as he asked his patients gently in Hausa, "*Yaya jiki?*"—how is your body? It was almost enough to make you believe in God, the way their faces would light up at the sight of him.

After returning to America, Joseph would often grumble that he was one doctor among thousands here, that his work felt less significant. But for Hannah, the reentry period was bumpier still. Overnight she became an ordinary housewife, a volunteer at book drives and bake sales. She spent her afternoons at homeless shelters and recycling centers. For a while, she kept her house in maniacal order, scrubbing the bathtub and sweeping the front stoop with feverish energy, as though any stray cobweb or patch of mold was the toehold of Satan's influence—as though by cleaning her home she could keep her soul burnished and blazing.

The first foster child had arrived out of the blue. Isaiah and Frances came dashing home from the park one day, late for dinner, to find a strange girl sitting on their front porch. She was wiping her nose on her sleeve and seemed startled when they spoke to her. Their mother was already home-schooling them; now there were three children in the classroom, the new girl learning arithmetic as Isaiah studied the Constitution and Frances taught herself to draw perspective out of books. Hannah told them to be kind. She told them to give the girl their old toys and T-shirts, which they did willingly, well versed in the notion of Christian charity.

It was only a few months later that the second girl appeared: tiny, frightened, and carrying a garbage bag that contained all her worldly goods. Then the first girl went back to her birth family— the second girl stayed—a third boy came. Isaiah rapidly began to lose track. Every day, it seemed, there was a new face beside the blackboard, a new bunk bed crammed into the rooms upstairs. Joseph brought home extra chests of drawers, sometimes going so far as to stack one on top of the other. Hannah collected used towels from the Salvation Army. In the bathroom there was a mug crammed with a dozen toothbrushes. The foster children came and went like ghosts, like cats, slipping in and out of Isaiah's life without warning. His mother was no help at all. She treated the presence of these strangers as she treated the changing of the seasons—inevitable, unpredictable, and wonderful beyond measure. She was happy at last. She might have lost her missionary work, but she had regained her purpose.

Over the years, Isaiah came to understand that because he and his sister were raised in a healthy, white, intact family, they were precluded from some part of their mother's love. His parents were not calibrated to give the full measure of their time and attention to privileged children. Not even their own.

∽

He does not return to his apartment. For a solid hour, driven by what feels like an engine churning in his chest, he paces the streets, working off his anxious energy. His parents' neighborhood is in a state of subtle alteration. Isaiah observes the *For Sale* signs, the lemonade stands, the elderly ladies shuffling after elderly dogs. The playground he and Frances used to frequent has been completely remade into an unwelcoming array of plastic equipment. Isaiah is chilled to the bone; the coat he brought is insufficient for the sharp, persistent wind. He is tempted, more than once, to turn tail and run. But he has come this far. He will face his mother. He can almost sense her presence; he is drawn into a dwindling orbit around her, circling the blocks in an ever-narrowing course. Red leaves whirl on the breeze, snagging in the windshield wipers of parked cars. Isaiah's cheeks are numb. But still he walks, passing hand-drawn hopscotch courses, the old baseball diamond with its ragged backstop, the place where Frances marked her fingerprints in wet cement.

Eventually he returns to his parents' front gate. His father's station wagon is gone, but his mother's battered minivan now lurks in the driveway. In the icy air, sounds carry and linger. Music drifts from somewhere behind the trees. A neighbor's lawnmower sputters and stalls. Hannah's voice is clearly audible through the living room windows, her singsong lilt as she leads the children in a discussion of the Bible. Their high-pitched tones answer her in a sunny chorus. From deeper inside the house, Isaiah catches the clatter of dishes. One of the older children is no doubt preparing lunch.

When he knocks at the door, the same coffee-colored boy appears, roaring over his shoulder, "It's Isaiah again!"—a pint-sized butler announcing a visitor to his mistress. Isaiah crosses the threshold with his hands stuffed nervously into his pockets. The boy looks him up and down.

"I'm Steve," he says proudly. "My flu is all done."

"Great," Isaiah says. "That's great."

His heart is pounding as he pokes his head into the living room. Hannah is seated cross-legged in front of the blackboard, her heavy gray hair knotted into a shining braid. She wears her usual outfit of shapeless brown linen. There is a trace of makeup—a vague nod to the rules of civilized living, perhaps. But her face is lined from wind and sunlight. Her hands are spotted as she waves her chalk like a baton. Four children are arranged in a circle in front of her, one scribbling on a notepad, one digging in his nose.

"And what do you think that meant?" Hannah asks.

"God was happy," a young girl lisps.

"Very good. Please continue reading on your own for just a moment."

This is her first acknowledgement of Isaiah's presence; she hasn't glanced at him once. He is acutely conscious of his physical person, his hulking form shadowing the doorway, his skin perfumed with the onion and flour of the grocery store, a stench that never seems to come off, no matter how much he showers. His mother rises to her feet in one surprisingly nimble bound. She approaches him with her eyes determinedly averted from his face.

"In here," she murmurs. "I don't want to disturb them."

"What?"

"Here." Hannah maneuvers him into the dimly lit nook beside the stairs. At last she lifts her gaze to his. Her eyes are ice-blue, flecked with brown, like earth held in glacier-water.

"Where is your sister?" she asks.

"At home. I thought—"

"You came here without her? That's what you're telling me?"

"I thought you could pick her up," Isaiah says helplessly. "She won't really talk about what she's doing there. I thought we could take your van over—"

"You'll bring her back. *You'll* bring her back. Do you understand?" His mother grips his arm. "I have work to do here. I can't go gallivanting off to fix your mess."

Isaiah takes a step backward. "*My* mess?"

"Of course." She draws herself up. "This is entirely your doing. You walked out that front door. You left us. Do you wonder that she was confused?"

"Jesus, Mom, I—"

"*Lord's name in vain,*" she hisses.

"I told you I would be leaving! You knew," he says, stung. "I told you when I got the job. I told you when I had my first month's rent. It's not like I ran off without any warning."

"You should have taken more time to consider all your options. You acted rashly, and this is the result!"

"I did take time," Isaiah cries, losing his temper. "It wasn't a surprise. For *weeks* I was packing, looking for the right apartment—" A sudden stillness from the other room indicates that he has an audience, albeit unseen. He lowers his voice and continues, "I never wanted to work at the hospital with Dad. And I'm no good with all these kids. I couldn't just stay here and raise—"

His mother has been gazing at him openmouthed, a glimmer of moisture brimming around her eyes. Now she snaps, "We're not discussing it. What's done is done. You have your apartment"—this last word spoken with withering disdain—"and I have my work here. But you will not keep your sister."

"I *can't* keep her," Isaiah says desperately. "That's why I came here. I need—"

"Then we're agreed. There's nothing more to say."

She turns on her heel and storms away, her braid bouncing behind her. Isaiah catches the flicker of one raised hand, wiping away her tears. Reeling, he leans against the cool wood, his face buried in the shadows. There is a rustle from the living room, and his mother's voice rings out again, louder and harsher than before. Isaiah closes his eyes and breathes steadily. A snuffle tells him that Steve has returned and is eyeing him quizzically, this mysterious, prodigal son of the house. Isaiah bites his lip, willing himself not to give way.

∽

In Africa, he believed in God. He knelt beside his mother and joined her in the hymns. He went house to house with his father, explaining that Kaza, a local fruit, was not a cure for HIV—that there was no cure for HIV, and people should not be deceived by hawkers selling Kaza in the market. Faith burned in his parents, though it manifested in them differently: his father through medicine, his mother through psalms. Isaiah remembers when he used to share this with them. He once felt as though God were present in the very air around him, moving in and out of his lungs, sustaining him as effortlessly as oxygen, as sunlight. There was a sense of boundless safety, of a world that was ordered into clear and comprehensible rules. The devil was named and put in his place, and even death held no surprises.

And yet, somewhere along the way, Isaiah's faith left him. He believes that it happened around the first time that he ever saw snow. He had studied the American climate, of course—he was not a complete dunce—but it was one thing to read the phrase "32° Fahrenheit" in a book, quite another to walk to the library in wind that seemed to be scraping the skin from his face. Snow made the air solid, a delicate latticework descending from the flat, gray clouds. The flakes landed on his cheeks and caught in his lashes. He tasted their juice on his tongue. The whole cityscape was transformed, buried beneath heaps of white, and oddly silent. Isaiah did not feel a childlike wonder at the sight. It only seemed as though a place that was already dying of lack of color finally gave up the ghost and expired.

God is a dream—that is what Isaiah thinks now. For most of his childhood he lived inside the dream of God, as his parents still do. Joseph and Hannah have grown and moved inside it, without ever pushing beyond its shimmering walls. They carry it with them like honey on the tongue. They strive to pass it on to everyone they meet, unable to keep such glory to themselves. It is a beautiful dream, rich and sweet, and there was a time Isaiah longed more than anything to return to that realm of belief, a state he remembers as a kind of paradise. But it is gone. He has left God in the same way that he deposits his dreams in his bed each morning—vivid, lyrical illusions, fading away quickly once his eyes are open.

This process of waking up has been a difficult one. It began with what felt like a hole in his chest, an ache, perhaps a question mark. The smaller, more delicate emotions were crushed beneath a kind of homesickness—for the delta, the bath of heat, his beloved friends, the misted river, and for God, too. Isaiah was afraid that his soul was on its way to the red flames of hellfire, so vividly described by his mother. This period felt a bit like the sensory overload that might be experienced by a newborn infant, in which every impression, however benign—a kiss, the smell of milk, a bird's call—seemed dangerous. After the soothing balm of the dream of God, the world itself seemed harsh and rough-edged; everything hurt. There were months in which Isaiah was simply numb. But gradually, almost without his noticing, the pain did lessen. His mind began to clear.

Nowadays, he scarcely feels that empty space in his chest; he probes it absently sometimes, as though testing the stump of a missing limb. It has taken him years to understand what it means to rub elbows with a raw world—to find beauty, and even significance, in chaos and confusion, the exquisite profusion of a thousand shades of gray. He has strange, upside-down moments now, in which everything he once thought reverses itself—what was grotesque seems lovely, what was wrong seems right. He has started to laugh again. Rather than shutting out new sensations, he has grown hungry for them. The slap of cold rain in the early morning. The tidal ebb and flow of dollars in his bank account. The reckless, pure loneliness of his own soul, without family, without friends, without God, entirely on his own.

❧

That evening, Isaiah watches from down the block as his sister walks away from him. Frances is wheeling her bike with one hand; her head is bowed. She knows he is there—he promised to wait at the bus stop until she was safely inside their parents' house—but she does not acknowledge him. In the waning light, her slim body seems ethereal, almost wraithlike. For a moment she stops, apparently gathering the strength to go on. Watching her, Isaiah holds his breath. Then, from somewhere inside the house, there comes a thin, high scream—and suddenly Frances is surrounded. Children of all sizes swarm around her, touching her, tugging at her coat, removing the bicycle from her grasp. Small hands push her up the walk. One girl actually tries to clamber onto her back. Frances laughs, brushing them away like flies. Somebody hands her a folded piece of paper, perhaps a welcome-home card, which Frances opens cheerfully. She allows herself to be led onward. On the stoop of the house, with one hand on the front door, she turns at last. The look she gives Isaiah is dark and smoldering. She glares for a long moment. Then she drops her gaze. She lets him go.

On the bus, on his way home, Isaiah feels light, almost weightless. It is not a good sensation; in a moment he might float up from the ground, unmoored. He stares out the window, watching the sky darken by degrees. A fat, wet moon is rising in the east. Shuddering and clanking, the bus turns onto the main road.

He has made his plan. He knows what he has to do. Isaiah will wait a few days, then head back to his parents' house on his lunch break. He will bring one of his old red scarves, which he will place in Frances's room—perhaps on her desk, on top of her books and calculator. She will be confused, he knows, when she finds it there. But a few days later he will return again, this time with a glass paperweight, the one from his dresser—a fragmented, kaleidoscopic bubble of glass, all swirls of blue and yellow—leaving it on Frances's bedside table. Over the weekend he will creep in with a tiny photograph of a wild-looking cat, its fur leaping out of its back, its eyes huge and staring. He will pin this on the wall just above her pillow.

Eventually his sister will figure out that he is the one leaving these bizarre offerings. She might find it funny; she might be moved. Either way, Isaiah will keep going. He runs his finger mentally through the list of potential objects to take from his apartment, his workplace. He will trail a bunch of grapes from the curtain rod that holds Frances's stiff blinds. He will set a stone frog in the middle of her floor. He will bring a cactus with one swollen flower rising off-center from its dome, which he will place on the windowsill, in the sun. He will come in at strange times, ignoring the curiosity of the foster children, avoiding his mother if at all possible. He will take the woven rug from his hallway, leaving it by Frances's wastebasket. Surely she will recognize it from her stint in his apartment. He will drape a necklace over her doorknob. He will slide a dried flower into her dresser drawer.

He will time his visits to be inscrutable, unpredictable; he wants Frances to step into her own bedroom each day in a state of awe, of expectation. He will leave talismans for her so that she won't be afraid she will be lost. He will leave her bright things she can touch like prayer. He will drop breadcrumbs to lead his sister out into the wide-awake world.

# IN THE SPIRIT ROOM

After the funeral, Jolene and I went back to our mother's house. We had grown up in these same rooms, though the place was somewhat altered now—our mother, who believed in plants the way other people believed in God, had turned our old playroom and study into greenhouses over the years. Jolene and I let ourselves in and stood for a few minutes on the threshold, unwilling to take off our coats and face the rest of the afternoon. The air was scented by orchids. The silence was absolute. Jolene, as the only daughter of the house, was the receptacle of family traditions, and in her old-fashioned way she had coped with our mother's death by covering all the mirrors and stopping the clocks. For two days we had lived like that, glancing above the bathroom sink to find a handkerchief staring back, startled by the blanket draped over a six-foot mirror in the corner. Now, with a sigh, my sister set about undoing the damage, folding up the sheets she had used, winding the grandfather clock again, returning the house to the realm of the living.

Eventually I slipped away and went upstairs. During Mom's illness, I had moved back into my old bedroom, now handsomely remade into a guest room—although my mother, not normally one for nostalgia, had kept the little sign that had hung on the door in my youth: *Maxwell*, carved into a wooden panel shaped like a train. I sat on the bed, still holding my jacket. Even here, Mom had kept plants. The very air in the house seemed rarified, freshened continually by so many open green leaves.

My mother's Alzheimer's had come on with astonishing rapidity. One day she was absolutely fine—the next I had given up my apartment to come and care for her—and at last Jolene had moved back from Texas, the three of us under one roof again. As the months passed, we had turned the house into a careful prison. Jolene brought in a locksmith to fix the doors so that Mom couldn't get out when we weren't looking. I took the knobs off the burners on the stove to keep her from starting fires. Once Jolene found her leaning out of a window on the second floor, waving to a startled child in the street; now the windows were nailed shut too. The fridge had been an issue. Jolene thought that it might be best to chain the handle, since Mom had a weakness for dairy products and tended to carry them around the house, abandoning her glasses of milk and dishes of yogurt in secret places, so that we could only locate them, several days too late, by the sour smell. But I did not like denying our mother her afternoon snack. In the end, we had to pick our battles.

Her death had come about as the result of a fall. It seemed such a mundane event, too small to claim a person's life; Mom simply lost her balance on the stairs. I was at work, Jolene catching a few hours' sleep in an upstairs bedroom. Mom had landed hard, and her head struck the banister, causing the subdural hematoma that proved fatal over the next few days. The mailman spotted her lying prone on the floor. I received a call at work and arrived home in time to meet the ambulance.

Jolene was inconsolable, her face buried in her arms. My mother, strapped onto the stretcher, had temporarily regained consciousness and seemed merely annoyed, as though the whole matter was a huge inconvenience. She put out a hand to me as I approached.

"What happened?" she asked.

"You fell," I said.

"And so?" she snapped. "People fall all over the world."

༄

The day after the funeral, compelled by forces beyond my control, I brought a sleeping bag with me to work. I did not mention this to Jolene. My sister was handling the situation by going into a kind of walking coma, subsisting on daytime television and cups of black tea. I patted her shoulder as I left, my satchel weighted down with enough food to see me through the evening. I was planning to spend the night in the museum.

The day was clear and cold, and as always I approached the Museum of Natural History from the front, striding up the sweeping marble steps like an ordinary visitor, eschewing the more private employee entrance at the side. It was autumn in Washington, D.C., the wind damp, the pavement speckled with dried leaves. Children raced each other down the stairs. An austere guard nodded to me as I passed through the doors. For twenty years I had worked there, in the rooms behind the scenes, cataloguing insects, now and then publishing a paper to commemorate a new species of *Carabus*. For most of my career, my mother and I had been colleagues, of a kind. Many people found it a hoot when they learned about us, a mother and son duo, slaving away together in the back rooms of the museum. I'm sure they imagined us working side by side as we catalogued our slides, looked up Latin names, and wrote our papers, destined to go unread by all but a select few.

The truth was that Mom and I never had much to do with each other. Her province had been the Botany Department. She was a legend in the field; at the time of her retirement, there were no less than fourteen species of plant named after her. My specialty, on the other hand, was beetles. I knew little about the day-to-day reality of Mom's work. She knew less about mine; she had always been squeamish about bugs. (I had once presented her with that pie chart—ubiquitous in biology classrooms—which showed all forms of animal life laid out by relative quantity. Beetles comprised one-fourth of the pie, by far the largest chunk, while mammals, human beings included, were relegated to a tiny golden slice, barely visible beside the invertebrates. Mom was unimpressed by my logic.) Now and then she and I would bump into each other in the hallways. We had made it a habit to go out for lunch once a week. Occasionally I would visit her office, or she would stop by mine, but we were both usually too busy, too engrossed in the task at hand, to welcome this sort of interruption. That much we did share—a passion for the work.

Today I took my time roaming past my favorite exhibits. The stuffed lion, its lips pulled back in a snarl. The dinosaur bones, guaranteed to awaken my inner ten-year-old boy. It never failed to give me a jolt of pride, stepping through the portal into the back rooms of the museum. The visitors could not penetrate this inner sanctum. I set my sleeping bag out of sight in the corner of my office and spent the afternoon trying to name a new species of beetle. The specimen was gorgeous, the size of my knuckle, with wings as burnished and bright as a fresh penny. Finding a new name was a pleasantly exhaustive business. *Carabus arvensis* was taken—I could not christen the beetle after the meadows it preferred to live in. *Carabus monilis*, too, had been used before—I could not name the beetle after the funny frill on its pronotum that so resembled a gentleman's collar. *Carabus mirabilis*—"the wonderful beetle"—was a possibility, but I thought I remembered seeing something similar in a list of species discovered by the Germans. This required a search among the ancient tomes of Latin names in the library. So the time passed. My peace was broken only by a few well-intentioned, if misguided, calls of consolation from my co-workers. The fact of my mother's death had apparently passed around the museum like wildfire.

Eventually the lights began to go out in the offices along the hallway. I heard footsteps in the corridor, and cheerful voices. The sky, through my office window, dimmed. The janitor knocked on my door and informed me in a mock-solemn voice that it was getting late.

"What?" I asked, with every appearance of surprise, gazing blearily over my glasses. "Is it that time already?"

He laughed and went away again, whistling. I turned off my lamp and unrolled the sleeping bag. There, on the hard tile floor, I spent the night. It was uncomfortable, and slightly ridiculous, but whatever compulsion had gripped me that morning had not yet lessened its hold, and I knew with terrible certainty that I was not ready to go back to my mother's house.

⟨◦⟩

I awoke with my brain already whirling. It was early, the smoky light filtering through the blinds. Jolene and I had planned to put Mom's house on the market and divide the spoils. My sister did not want any of the furniture, having a well-stocked home of her own in Houston, not to mention a husband with very particular taste. I wouldn't be able to take anything of Mom's either; as a poorly paid museum grunt, I tended to get by in tiny studio apartments as near as possible to the National Mall. Jolene was planning to hold a yard sale and just auction everything off. She had spoken of it with relish, not being of a sentimental turn of mind. But to me it called up a sinking feeling of nausea, of loss. I was more familiar with the house than Jolene was. Though we had spent our childhood there together, my sister's home was in Texas now, while I had lived with Mom for over a year, ever since she had succumbed to Alzheimer's—and even before that I had been a frequent visitor. I knew those auburn couches and clunky bookshelves well. The thought of them going away in the hands of strangers made me feel as though we were parceling off bits of our mother—her eye for color, her dislike of varnish, her addiction to Tiffany lamps. "What will we do with her plants?" I had asked, and even practical Jolene didn't have an answer for that one.

The morning was pale and golden. As I stood on the front steps of the Museum of Natural History, stretching in the light, it occurred to me that I did not have to go back to the house just yet. I had meant to shower, but I could get by another day without. I needed a change of clothes, but I had been planning to do a little shopping for months now. Perhaps I would buy a few shirts and keep them in my office, just in case. I would stock up on snacks, too. There was a great deal of work to be done, after all. I still had not named my beetle. (I had thought briefly of calling it after Mom, half in respect of her passing, half as a little inside joke, since she had treated most insects as something to be promptly flushed down the toilet. But since our surnames were the same, it would have looked like I was honoring myself instead—and in my field, you didn't do that. It showed far more humility to wait and let others name a new specimen after you, rather than to arrogantly do it yourself.) I set off up the hill, toward G Street, where I knew there were clothing stores.

When I returned to the office, laden with a few bags of shirts and underwear, there was a message on my machine. Jolene sounded half awake and gruffly affectionate.

"Sorry I missed you last night, doll. I fell asleep at the kitchen table, if you can believe it." She gave her wet, early-morning cough and continued, "We'll have that yard sale today. I hired some moving men to take all the furniture onto the lawn. As Mom was so fond of reminding us, we are middle-aged coots now—no point in giving ourselves a hernia. Just make sure you're home by four to help me. Okay?"

∾

My mother's Alzheimer's took away her ability to organize the world. First her words began to disappear. When I came by for dinner, she announced that there were four radios in the living room, and she didn't know how to use any of them. After a while I figured out that she was referring to the many remote controls, all speckled with incomprehensible buttons, that had proliferated as she purchased a cable box, a DVD player, and a new TV. Then she forgot the word for her calendar. She wanted me to buy her one of those things that showed the date and let her tear off a page each day.

"A calendar?" I asked warily.

"No, Max," she said, slapping me fondly on the arm. "Not *that*.

I mean those doodads that tell you what day it is. Jolene always knew where to buy them for me."

Presently time itself began to elude her. I stopped by to take her out for a walk, and she informed me that it might be Tuesday upstairs, but here, in the living room, it was definitely Wednesday. "What day is it out there?" she asked, waving vaguely at the window as I helped her with her coat. She forgot how time progressed. She forgot that each hour was a specific amount, measured and immutable, and that the time of day repeated, once in the morning, once in the evening. I reduced her to tears during a long and cyclical discussion about how she needed to take her medicine every twelve hours. At this point I thought it prudent to give up my studio apartment and move in with her for a while. She could no longer tell time, but she was fascinated by it, aware that it must be something profound. I would come in from work and find her on the sofa, a beady-eyed woman wrapped in a knitted shawl, eyeing the clock on the mantle as though it might explode.

Then there was the day I found policemen in the living room. There were two of them, a man and a woman, huddled beside the couch. I rushed past them, flinging my briefcase against the wall, agonized, already preparing for the worst—but Mom was perfectly all right. She was sitting on a stool in the kitchen, apparently in the process of giving a report to a third police officer, a young man holding a clipboard. The boy looked up at me in some relief. It transpired that Mom had found a few of her plants missing. Two orchids, a ficus, and a four-foot cactus had been stolen. Since no one had been in or out of the house except for me—whom, Mom insisted, she trusted completely—she was absolutely certain that ghosts had taken her plants. That was the substance of her police report: thieving ghosts.

I apologized and sent the policemen on their way. I went upstairs and verified that Mom's plants weren't missing, that she had
just moved them to another room and forgotten. Then I went into
my childhood bedroom and called Jolene in Texas.

As it turned out, I did not help with the yard sale. I didn't go home
at all. In fact, I spent the next four nights in the museum. I didn't
feel too guilty about this. The yard sale had been Jolene's idea.
She was the one with the head for numbers, and she had always
been better with people. She was the elder sibling, too, and there
existed between us an age-old dynamic: I was the golden boy, following proudly in our mother's footsteps, while Jolene was the
odd duck, shipping off to parts unknown, marrying a man Mom
had never liked. (Not that Mom ever particularly took to any of
my girlfriends, either. She could be a little possessive, believing
that no one was smart enough for me, or perhaps smart enough
for our family.) It was not the first time I had left Jolene stranded,
high and dry, with an unpleasant task to accomplish. I spent the
days advising on a specimen of larva that a colleague of mine had
discovered in Bolivia. Jolene left an irate message on my machine,
calling me a coward and a prick. But it was clear that she felt the
satisfaction of a job well done, watching Mom's new kitchen table
being carried down the street, our old bureaus and black-and-
white TV handed out as curiosities to the next generation.

On my fourth night in the office, I was plagued by insomnia.
It was a strange place to rest—the ceaseless rumble of cars in the
street, the unfamiliar rattle of the heater, the tap of branches
against the windowpane. At home I would have meandered down
and watched a little soporific television, or at the very least clicked

on the light and read for a while. But here I could not risk it. I was aware that what I was doing did not make a whole lot of sense—grown men did not curl up under a desk with a pile of dirty clothes for a pillow—but by some mysterious process, it was getting me through the dangerous aftermath of the funeral. If I were discovered, however, people would be concerned. I might be forced to take a leave of absence, to meet with a therapist. At the very least, I would have to go back to my mother's house, which I was not prepared to do. Fretful and uncomfortable, I tossed and turned. Mom's best cure for insomnia had always been to change position: She would urge me to spend the night on the couch or to flip the arrangement of my bed upside-down, so that my head lay where my feet used to be. Usually this worked. I hefted myself off the floor, rolling my sleeping bag under one arm.

The long hallways looked different in the gloom. I had never really explored the wings beyond Entomology. It was my tendency to stay focused on my own area of expertise; I was methodical ("a plodder," Jolene had always said, with a mixture of sympathy and exasperation). My work revolved around details. The plating of a beetle's thorax—the shape of the antennae—even the number of hairs on the leg might be the only distinction between separate species.

In the rooms behind the scenes at the museum, the world was strictly divided into categories: Zoology, Botany, Mineralogy. The exhibits for the public were not like this, of course; they were laid out in a kind of cheerful chaos, stuffed birds alongside monkeys alongside zebras, geodes beside flowers beside petrified bones. Each exhibit was created as much to entertain and excite as to educate. But the back rooms had another purpose. Here, our job was nothing less than to discover and label absolutely everything. To that end, there were elephant, trilobite, and robin experts, each shut away in his or her own office, peering at butterfly wings or fossils beneath a microscope. I had always enjoyed the idea of us researchers together, the fungus men, the soapstone women, the gnat specialists, carefully cataloguing the thousands of varieties in our particular disciplines that might be out there.

But I had never bothered to visit the rooms of these colleagues. Now, treading cautiously through the darkened hallways, I began my exploration. Many doors were locked, of course, and I moved quietly, trying not to scuff my feet. Paleontology was not far off. I knew by sight the people who worked there: the man with the snowy beard, the woman with the spattering of freckles, and that fellow who was terrifically handsome, the sort who might play one of us in a movie but seemed oddly out of place in real life. I found my way through a side door into a room of filing cabinets—ancient mahogany things, lovingly crafted. Inside there were bones. There were fossilized teeth, half sunk in sheets of limestone. There were vertebrae and tiny fingers. In the murkiness of the great office, the fossils seemed eerily portentous, colored in flickering gold by the streetlamp beyond the window. At last I took my sleeping bag into the corner and settled behind a bookcase, where my mother's advice was once again proven right. I fell asleep quite easily.

On the fifth night I found a room in the Zoology Department, one I knew of by hearsay but had never seen. Mom had referred to it as Get Pickled, though officially it was the Spirit Room, also known as the wet collections. Normally, to preserve living things indefinitely, you must dry them and treat them carefully with chemicals. In my mother's department, there were pressed plants kept under glass that might be several hundred years old. In Entomology we relied on naphtha, an effective if pungent solvent, to keep bacteria from getting at our beloved bugs. In the Spirit Room, however, the specimens were suspended in glass jars of alcohol or formaldehyde. On the shelves were a thousand gleaming containers, arranged importantly by kind: fish, amphibians, lizards, crustaceans. I moved in a daze among them. There were frogs, splayed in a half-human posture, their bulbous eyes frosted over by time. There were snakes whose coils echoed the curve of the jar. The chemicals bleached out all the colors, so that each mussel and anemone, goanna and flounder, was as pale, clammy, and luminous as an albino. It made the differences between them seem slighter—the wan monkfish appeared to be related to the ice-colored lobster several shelves away. It would have been a bizarre place even in the daytime, but at night it was positively otherworldly. Around each corner another ghostly oddity glared at me from within its glass cage. Feral lizards from Australia. Deep-sea fish with sabers for teeth. Miniature jellies ringed by feathery tentacles. I slept against the bank of windows, shielded beneath a table, and suffered from feverish dreams.

In the morning there was another message on my machine from Jolene. She sounded grumpy this time.

"I've spoken to your boss," she said. "He claims you've been at work, so apparently I can't file a Missing Persons Report." There was a pause—she might have sniffled. "And since there isn't such a thing as an Insane Little Brothers Report, I'm not really sure what options I have." She paused again. "Anyway, I've been on the hunt to sell Mom's house. I did find someone to take her plants—a local nursery. So that's good news. I've been meeting with real estate agents, and I think I found one I might actually trust, but— Look, Max, this is ridiculous. Just call me back, all right?"

～

Toward the end, Jolene had borne the brunt of our mother's care. This was in part because she had no job in D.C., as I did; in part because it was as much her nature to assume command as it was mine to relinquish it; and in part because they were both women. When Jolene and I discovered, for example, that our mother had been forgetting to bathe, there was no other recourse but for my sister to roll up her sleeves and dive in, while I discreetly retired with a book. I knew what it cost her. She had to abandon indefinitely her powerhouse career in a prestigious law firm—and her tetchy, nervous husband, whom she quietly adored—and come back to her hometown to be an underappreciated and unpaid nurse.

And yet it was lifesaving to have her there. There were days when Mom began singing to herself at the dinner table. There were days when the anti-psychotic medicine, which the doctors had prescribed to keep her from believing in ghosts, made her sick to her stomach, and she threw up every half an hour until it left her system. There were days when she was obsessed with milligrams. She would squint at her pill bottles, counting out how many milligrams there were in each, and then refuse to swallow them, insisting that 200 was all right, but 500 was just too many. In vain did we try to tell her that the concentrations were relative, that it was meaningless to compare each dose. There were days when Mom kept trying to make us understand that her legs were too big—no one could possibly understand how big her legs were. She complained that they were too big to fit into her bed, and Jolene and I would simply have to find her a larger mattress somewhere.

During these times it was essential to have another sane adult there in the room, someone to lock eyes with, someone to stay up late with, clinking your beer bottles together and laughing until you cried.

"You know, there's nothing as contagious as Alzheimer's," Jolene told me once.

"Hm?"

She made a grimace. "Mom and I spent the whole morning talking about the telephone. She had picked it up and dialed a few numbers, but the line was always busy. Finally I realized she was trying to figure out how to call some of her old friends. She couldn't remember their numbers. She had just been dialing her own number over and over, since we wrote it right there on the phone for her." Jolene passed a hand over her eyes. "So Mom went to take a nap, and after three hours with her, my brain wasn't working anymore. I sat up thinking, How *do* we find out what somebody's number is? How the hell *does* a telephone work?"

❧

Most men, during a midlife crisis, will try to return to the age of their greatest sexual potency. They buy sports cars, take trips to the wilderness, daydream about quitting their jobs. A colleague of mine explained that what triggers this behavior isn't usually the aging of the man, but the aging of his wife. Once he no longer has a fertile partner—once there's no chance, within his marriage, for him to pass on his genes to new offspring—he is biologically driven to try and attract a younger mate. This happens regardless of whether he has any conscious urge to stray. Suddenly he finds himself needing to flaunt his income and visit bars where young women congregate. Suddenly he's shopping around for toupees.

After two weeks of sleeping at the museum, to my great chagrin, I realized that I was undergoing a midlife crisis of my own. I still had not been back to my mother's house. I had not gone to meet with the real estate agents. I had not even found the nerve to return any of Jolene's increasingly frantic messages. Each night I brought my bedroll to a new room, a new wing. I was becoming expert at washing myself, section by section, in the sinks of the men's bathroom, changing into a brand-new starched shirt, noshing on trail mix and restaurant food. Perhaps because I had no wife, my midlife crisis had caused me to retrogress far beyond my sexual peak. Instead I seemed to have moved right back into my childhood.

When I was a boy, Mom had already begun her career at the Museum of Natural History. She did not want me going home after school to an empty house. (My father had died years before—I could barely remember him, a certain earthy smell, the feel of a bristly beard.) Jolene was old enough to be a latchkey kid, but not quite old enough to care for me. And so I came to the museum instead. Every afternoon I marched up the marble steps, stuffed my backpack into one of the lockers, and, in an important voice, told the woman at the information desk that she should let my mother know I had arrived. Usually Mom was too busy to leave just then. She had enjoyed a meteoric rise through the ranks, becoming in record time the Keeper of the Herbarium, a post she had always coveted. At meetings, she was referred to simply as the Keeper, a title that never failed to amuse and impress me; it evoked images of an Amazonian warrior, guarding the door to some hidden, coveted garden.

While I waited for her to be done, I would wander among the exhibits. Back then I had never gone behind the veil, into the rooms beyond. I knew that Mom did something with plants, but in truth I wasn't much interested. I loved the museum for itself. I loved the stuffed wild animals, posed so that you could catch a hint of how they had moved in life. I loved the gem room, the glittering Hope Diamond and the enormous crystal ball, larger than my head, that had been carved hundreds of years ago by unknown means. I discovered out-of-the way staircases. I counted the rings on the cross-section of a monstrous sequoia, which was mounted on the wall to chart the passage of time, its girth marked to show when major human events had occurred during its long life. I learned that there were bathrooms hidden at the end of the hallway of giant sloth and woolly mammoth bones. And without fail, I visited the insects, so firm and well-armored, mounted in rows like soldiers. Even the pins that stuck their bodies to the backing seemed wonderful to me.

When my mother finished with her work, she would bustle out between the glass cases, drawing on her coat—and when, invariably, she could not find me, she would page me. This was the most delicious moment of the afternoon. The loudspeaker would crackle, and Mom's warm voice would float through every hallway, every room: "Max, to the front. Max, to the front." The fact that the whole museum heard her calling me seemed like the most precious token of love.

༄

Jolene went back to Texas. She had settled on an asking price with a real estate agent, and there was nothing left to do but wait for a buyer. Her husband was pining for her. She herself was pining for her home and her career. I knew all this not because I spoke to Jolene, but because she left the information in a series of teary, half-crazed messages on my machine.

The first few were rather kind. "I know you're suffering over there, but give me a call—I have some numbers to throw at you." Or else, "Listen, let's meet for coffee. I can come to you. Just let me know where."

Presently, though, she began to lose her temper. "It's Jolene, your sister," she would shout. "I don't know if you remember me.

What the hell has gotten into you?" And once: "I came by the damn museum today. But guess what? They wouldn't let me in to see you. It's restricted."

Her final message was broken by sobs. She was calling from the airport, a last-ditch effort to reach me before leaving town. "Fine, fine," she wept. "I don't *have* a brother. When the house sells I'll just send you a check for half the money, and I'll never speak to you again."

I did not call her back. I did not find an apartment. I was frozen, no more, no less. It seemed that there was an initial stage of grieving, one that came before even denial and bargaining—a stage that kept me floating helplessly in space, unable to move forward. I kept returning to the Spirit Room on my nightly vigils, touching the glass of the captured specimens. I grew familiar with the grouchy faces of the fish, their plump lips invariably settled in a pout. I pored through a few of the books, reading up on the newt, the horned lizard, and the anaconda. (The latter hung in a massive glass container, captured in its full length, and even its ashy pallor could not diminish the power of those muscled curves.) While there, I discovered the existence of a species of crab that survived by digging holes in the rock. It then would systematically shut itself in, sealing off the aperture with secretions from its own body, until it had only a tiny window left and was trapped there forever, feeding on the plankton and scraps carried passively into its cave by the tide. Its view of the world was limited to whatever it could glimpse through the window it had made. I felt a certain kinship with this crab as I peered out at the street, between the blinds. A strong breeze from the river blew a torrent of leaves across the road. Tourists marched to and fro. Squirrels buried and unearthed their acorns. Once there was an ice storm, and in the nightly glow of the streetlamp the sidewalks glittered as though they had been transmuted into something other than simple concrete.

At last I got up enough courage to visit my mother's department. Entomology and Botany were separated by two floors and a veritable warren of corridors, and by the time I made my way there, I had slept almost everywhere else in the museum. I had probed the cabinets of Mineralogy, examining blocks of quartz infused with coils of a foreign crystal, as yet unidentified. I had looked through the drawers in Zoology, coming across bat teeth, rodent skulls, and leopard claws. I had laid out my bedroll beneath a table on which stood a variety of zebra heads, all of different sizes. I had found storage rooms in which a strange arrangement of leftovers could be found—old dinosaur exhibits, now outdated; a portrayal of human evolution that flirted with creationism; and a half-finished exhibit on the mating rituals of different species, apparently rejected as being too risqué for the younger set.

On my first night in the Botany Department, I broke into someone's office and camped out there, unwilling to brave the rooms that had been my mother's jurisdiction. Gradually, though, I grew more comfortable. I examined the pressed flower petals. The ferns had been Mom's favorite—so ancient!—each leaf and root precisely arranged to stand out crisply from the stem. Some of the labels had not yet been remade in the printed font that was now standard issue. Some of them were still handwritten in my mother's own curly script.

In the shaded halls over which she had presided, I understood what ought to have been obvious to me all along—that I had moved out of my mother's house as a young man only to live comfortably in her shadow at work. I had not resented it (as Jolene, I knew, always assumed I must). Rather, I had felt safe there. Mom certainly never treated it as strange. Other people might make jokes, but she appeared to accept without question that I would want to work in what she considered to be the best place in the world—even, perhaps, that I would want to work near her. Before my initial interview, she had put in a good word for me. Whenever she won an award for her scholarship, or had another species of plant named after her by an admiring colleague, or was promoted once again, we would go out together to celebrate. Sometimes I had the nagging sensation that she wished I were a bit more ambitious, more like her, or else more likely to reflect well on her. Sometimes I was certain that she rather enjoyed showing off for me, knowing that I would not mind it. I never got the feeling that she wanted me to move on, to move away, as Jolene had done, to complete the last stage of growing up, to become independent.

In her department, I came across the simple fact that time washed the color out of things. We might be able to preserve the shape and size, but the hue was invariably lessened. Only the insects seemed to be impervious. Butterflies, fire ants, cockroaches— pinned to the backing, they all blazed as brightly as they had done in life, their knobby shells and segmented wings invulnerable to the years. Elsewhere in the museum, however, I found each leaf and petal faded. Each bone was the same bland ivory as every other. Even the glossy pelts of the animals lost their luster.

My mother had been similarly diminished by her illness. She set aside her patterned clothes and allowed her hair to turn its natural silver, giving up the glamorous echo of youth. She left off her makeup, so that I was always surprised by the chapped pallor of her mouth. During the last few months of her life, she began to unravel completely. Dressed in habitual gray, her skin seemed as colorless as a snowflake, her features undistinguished and uncertain.

Our last conversation had taken place the day she died. After hitting her head, she was brought by ambulance to the hospital and sequestered in a private room. I met her there, feeling nothing but the calm delirium of shock as I sat beside the bed and watched her sleep. Mom moved in and out of consciousness. Her hands twitched on top of the quilt.

Jolene was out in the hall, haranguing one of the doctors, when my mother opened her eyes and looked at me.

"Where's Max?" she asked.

"Right here, Mom," I said.

She stared at me for a moment, then smiled, as though deciding I must be joking.

"No, no," she said. "The *other* Max. You know, my son."

☙

After three months, her house sold. Just like that, the spell was broken. For three months I had lived at the museum, creeping from room to room, never staying too long in one place, bathing in the bathrooms like a homeless man. There had been several near misses—once the janitor had banged open the door of the office in which I was nestled on the floor; perhaps he had heard me snoring, for he shone the beam of his flashlight around the room, frowning. The glow fell on my shoes, but he appeared to see nothing odd in a pair of old Oxfords beneath the desk, and he missed the rest of me, huddled in my sleeping bag behind the closet door. Another time I overslept, waking to the sound of voices. I was back in my mother's department then, stretched out beneath a table in the Herbarium. The room was ablaze with fluorescent light, and a few young women had come in and were collating slides. Slowly I crawled out from beneath the table, balling up my bedroll. They were intent on their work and paid no attention to me as I made my way to the door.

Then one day I received a copy of the housing contract, signed by the new owners. My sister had mailed it to me from Houston, without comment. Suddenly all things became possible again. Within the week I rented a furnished studio apartment, only a few blocks away from the museum. I threw away my sleeping bag, which had reached a rather alarming degree of filthiness. The drawers of my filing cabinet were crammed with dirty clothes—these, too, I had washed in the bathroom, inexpertly, and now I tossed them all in the bin. I even telephoned my sister, who evidently screened my call and did not return it. (It would be a few months before she would speak to me.) Finally I emerged from inside the museum, like a beetle larva rising out of water, ready for the next phase of its existence, blinking in the light.

It is a strange thing to lose a parent.

When, at the hospital, I told Jolene about Mom's last words to me—her wish to see her other son—my sister had rolled her eyes and muttered something that sounded like *Alzheimer-tastic.* But I wondered if Mom was trying to say something else. Her illness had taken from her the deepest core of her nature, her desire for discovery and order; it had taken away the place at which we came together, the part of us that was the same. Perhaps she was wishing for herself back. My mother would have hated to succumb to Alzheimer's, the vanishing of her renowned and formidable intellect. And yet, of course, she never really grasped that she was ill. Most sufferers of Alzheimer's are unaware, by and large, that they are suffering. Indeed—in strange, wild, illuminating moments—I had the odd sensation that her illness was a gift, rather than a burden. It allowed her to die unafraid. She had misplaced her awareness of time passing, of the possibility of loss. And perhaps it was a gift for Jolene and me as well. Our father had died sud-denly—he went to work one day, and the next day we buried him. With our mother, we had a long duration in which to understand that she was disappearing, to move into her house and care for her, to use the last months that were given to us.

∾

There are times when I still find her in my dreams. Through the back halls of the Museum of Natural History I follow her stocky, linen-clad form. My mother is young again—as young as she was when I was a boy, her hair tarnished by just a few locks of gray. Sometimes I catch her, grabbing her by the hand and earning myself an affectionate, if absent, pat on the head, but more often than not I never find her. She is always just ahead of me, the trail of her perfume leading me into the open, high-ceilinged rooms of the Botany Department, past Mineralogy and Entomology, through closets where discontinued exhibits of whale bones and gemstones gather dust. There are times, in these dreams, when I understand that the rooms of the museum are in fact the com-partments of my own mind—or perhaps the collective mind of the human race itself—cluttered up with all the lists of things we have insisted on learning. Here we have the carefully identified drawers, each animal consigned to its own species, each pebble categorized in bright, bold letters. Room upon room details our obsession to know and name everything, as though by labeling it we can come to own it, its nature no longer mysterious at all. And yet I am certain—for it brings me a steady rejoicing—that the task will never be finished, that we are up against nothing less than the full, chaotic measure of a limitless world.

# LANDSCAPING

I was carrying a son. I knew this because he would not rest, particularly at night, inside my stuffy bedroom. Eloise's snoring grated on him. He flipped and wriggled inside my womb. He was ravenous, and he drank me dry every night, so that I woke each morning with a parched mouth. I could picture my boy, the strange arrangement of him. He had only just shed his prehensile tail. Soft, fine hairs grew in patches on his skull, like moss on quartz. His skin was translucent, and brown fat was beginning to coalesce in pockets on his fishy body. My womb felt like a foreign sea, with his alien intelligence in the underwater darkness.

One night he would not stay still. His legs weren't strong enough to kick, but he beat his little body back and forth, sounding me like a drum. I knew what was bothering him. The boy hated to be indoors. I ran my hands over the skin of my belly to simulate the sound of wind.

He spoke to me. He said, "Dig a garden." His voice was earthy and wet, as though rising from the murk of an underground pool. It was not a dream, because Eloise moaned, rolled to blink at me, and said, "What? What?"

$\infty$

By the time he was born, it had become a rainforest. I planted stalks of grass, fibrous and razor-edged. I planted waxy jades that grew fat, bulbous leaves. I planted petunias and marigolds that bloomed like butterfly wings. I put down paving stones in the clay. I bought whole trees, nearly my height, from the local nursery, their roots bound up in burlap sacks. In the undergrowth these trees stood as tall as prophets, bobbing their bushy heads, as I knelt in my jeans, my hands streaked with mud, making room for wild ivy, crocus bulbs, and shivering ficuses.

I brought the baby into the garden, bundled in his basket. He twitched his skinny shoulders, and I tucked the blanket around him. His head lolled and his fingers curled and uncurled like anemones. I set him under a thicket of fierce grasses. The wind was very cold, and the sun came watery through the leaves of the maples and elms on the edge of our property. The garden burst from the ground. The ivy tumbled over the petunias, which had grown leggy themselves and were rambling beneath the jade. The paving stones were slimy with moss. A tiger lily I had not planted stood aloof by the wooden fence, and it was not the only flower that had arrived, mysteriously, on its own.

The baby made his high, tight cough. I took him into my lap and held him, tumbled in his blanket. He bumped his doughy feet on my thigh. He smelled of flour. I still had trouble differentiating our bodies, and I knew that for him there was no distinction at all between us. I looked at him, and his eyes said, "Bring me a river."

∾

Eloise, at the prow of the canoe, set a steady pace with her paddle. I sat at the stern and handled the steering and the allotment of sandwiches. My son, three years old, was settled in the middle with the sun in his hair. He had yet to begin talking, but he watched it all with his mouth open. He turned his head to follow each new sound. I could see only his profile, which resembled Eloise's in its sharpness. He was not, of course, related to her. It had made sense that I should carry the baby—Eloise had been able to keep her narrow flanks and something of her innocence; she had cooked for me and rubbed my feet, and watched with wonder as stretch marks darkened on my belly and my tush swelled, as my moods went wild and I crept outside to eat the earth in the garden.

The water was sluggish, thick and warm to the touch, and alive with glimmering dragonflies. Trees trailed their leaves in our faces. The flowers along the banks were so laden with pollen that they could not be bothered to flutter in the breeze. I saw the slender backs of river rats, the tremble of rabbit ears, and once, when I coughed explosively into my hand, something crashed away from us down the bank. Birds chattered in the branches, and fish leapt and gleamed. I saw mud detach from itself, hop along the bank, and belch a long froggy cry. There were turtles, too, kicking dreamily beneath the surface, brown and silent, stretching their long necks toward the air. An owl dropped suddenly from an overhanging elm and beat its huge white wings without a sound as it dived away from us above the water.

Eloise paddled in a steady rhythm, her neck sunburned, her bun a red tangle. With each turn of the oar, a dimple appeared in her right shoulder. She hummed a rowing song. My son slapped the flat of his palm on the surface of the stream. He shivered and ducked when mosquitoes sang near him. After a while he looked back at me. His eyes were happy and dissatisfied.

"What do you want?" I asked him. But it was clear what he wanted. Eloise laid the oar across her thighs, stretched both arms high over her head, and unwound her hair, letting it loose over her shoulders.

"What does he want?" she asked without turning.

"A mountain," I said. "Do you need another sandwich?"

"I'd love one." She kicked both feet over the edge of the canoe and sank her legs mid-calf into the river. She rolled her hands on her wrists. "Hey, kiddo," she said. "Say something, baby."

"A mountain," I repeated.

She picked up her paddle.

❧

We took him to the Rockies. My son was seven years old, small for his age, with a round, buttery face and a bit of the marionette in his walk. He smashed mushrooms beneath his boots and picked up spiky caterpillars. When we set up the tent, he would not stop circling its orange dome. My son was autistic— the doctors had stamped that term on him. It meant that he would never speak a word. If I laid a hand on the toy he wanted, he would shift my fingers without once glancing at me, as you might move a fallen leaf that had landed on the page of your book. He did not know my name. He did not know his own. My son lived in a realm of color and sound; his senses were so heightened that every breath was an awe-inspiring experience. Sometimes he had fits of ferocious anger, and I was marked with scratches down both my arms, my calves ringed with bruises. Storms of feeling moved across him. Earlier that month he had put his foot through a sliding glass door, and the doctors had recommended we find a home for him. But I would not. I brought him to the mountains instead.

Eloise laughed more in the high, clean air. She woke at dawn, when the sun made the vinyl walls of the tent echo with light. She had brought an elaborate rubber gizmo with tubes that she lowered into the stream to pump and purify the water. She had brought a walking stick. The sun turned her skin to copper, spattered with constellations of freckles. When we entered areas that were heavily wooded, Eloise did as the guidebooks had told her, whistling through her teeth and crying, "Hey, bear! Coming through, bear!" She dropped her pants and peed in the grass. She kissed me hard and bit my mouth in the tent. She tromped around in hiking boots and seemed almost pleased when an overhanging rock scraped her shin to bleeding.

One night I woke to the sound of an owl. The little pillow beside me was empty. I sat up and found my son standing against the tent screen, silhouetted, with the moon between his fingers. He leaned against the mesh, rolling his head in the fabric and pushing with both hands. His face wore its usual curious, detached expression. He was working methodically away, but he would never be able to push his way out.

‌

At home, from under the weight of dreams, Eloise knew she was dying and grabbed my arm. Her heart was near stopping. An aneurysm in her aorta had ruptured—I learned later on—and her heart suddenly swelled, full of blood and life, too big for her narrow ribs. I tossed the blanket off us both. She gripped my elbow.

"Get the kid," she said thickly.

I shook my head.

"I want to see him," she said. "Let me say goodbye to him."

"He won't understand," I said. The boy was nearly a teenager, tall and brawny, with Eloise's stillness and my unruly curls.

"He will this time," she said.

"He doesn't know you." I touched her face.

"The ice," she said. "Oh, God, the ice."

Her spirit did not leave easily. It took the shape of a bird and rattled around the room, banging off the windows and upsetting the lamp. It landed on Eloise's chest and screamed in agony, and then it cleaned its beak, forgetting it had ever been alive. It looked at me with inky eyes. I got up cautiously and opened the window. The bird flexed its wings and fanned the broad feathers of its back. I opened another window. The air smelled of rain. I opened all the windows in the bedroom, and the bird folded one scrawny foot beneath its torso and flapped onto the bureau. I heard the first patter of a drizzle outside, and then the sky opened suddenly, dropping a collision of water on the tender plants. The bird screamed again. It opened its wings and flew straight through me, its beak in my heart, its feathers tearing my chest open. It passed into the storm.

I woke on the carpet. I was sorry to wake. My son was standing over me, his chin lifted in the morning light.

∾

I cared for him until I died myself and was buried in the earth next to the body of Eloise. Then my son wanted the moon, and since I was not there to give it to him, he walked on his own, step by step, across the black and empty miles. The open space felt good on his bare feet. He tumbled onto the lunar surface, and his fall echoed against the spires of the mountains. The sky was always dark, and sometimes the ground was dark as well, and he walked in a dream without light, following the marbled disc of the rising earth. The moon smelled of pepper and ash. My son crossed over the knife-sharp mountains and into vast, gray seas, littered with salt deposits and drifts of shale. He passed through bony deserts, where the humped surface shone like snow. He felt the icy wind from the cliffs and heard the splash of stars. The moon matched him in his silence. My son lived his life clean of love, troubled only occasionally by the distant flight of a small, white bird; and that was me.

# FIRE BLIGHT

After midnight, Cosmo found himself in the baby's room. The crib was half assembled, missing its front panel and the carved headboard. A mobile of paper flowers hung from the ceiling. The diaper pail was already in place, gleaming beneath the bare bulb. Cosmo had brought a trash bag. He set about gathering up the stuffed animals and tossing them into the depths. His instructions had been specific—everything was to be thrown out, none of it given to friends or donated to charity. His wife wanted these things removed from existence; she did not want to think of the sturdy cardboard books and Earth-friendly pacifiers she had shopped for so carefully being used out in the world somewhere, treated as though they were ordinary, handled until they broke or were discarded. Cosmo would strip and repaint the walls, which had been papered on two sides with ducks and bunnies. He would take down the yellow curtains his wife had hemmed. Elaine had been firm.

She had asked this of him as he had helped her down the walkway from the hospital to the car. She was out of danger then, but still weak, her face shadowy and wan. Her hands had trembled where they gripped his shoulder.

"It'll take a few days to get all that done," Cosmo had said.

"Fine," Elaine said at once. "I'll go away while you're working."

But he could not manage it—not tonight, anyway. After a while he headed down to the garden. The wind was cold, and Cosmo zipped up his coat as he waded among the zinnias, searching for any hint of slugs. He had been waging war against these creatures for several months now. First he had placed beer cans around the flowerbeds—an odd little trick he had read about in a magazine— but though some of the slugs had been drawn to the smell, fallen in, and drowned, it had ultimately done more harm than good. The cans blew over in the wind and got knocked down by inquisitive birds, so that the whole yard stank like a pool hall for a while. Then Cosmo had tried to achieve détente. He knew that slugs were essentially a mini-recycling center, and he had gone so far as to put edible flowers in his garden, off behind a bush where Elaine did not have to see them sitting there sadly riddled with holes. But the slugs were not satisfied. They were encroaching again. In the moonlight, the silvery network of their slime trails showed up clearly on the leaves.

∾

In the redwood forest, Elaine woke to the sound of an owl. Her first thought was for her physical person. Was her lower back aching? Did she have pressure or pain? It took her a moment to get her bearings. The tent was rustling in the wind. Indeed, the cacophony of unfamiliar noises around her seemed loud enough that it ought to have woken her long ago. Tree branches creaked far overhead. In the distance, a bonfire was crackling. There were crickets and frogs, their disparate songs meshing in a staccato, high-pitched chorus. Elaine lay still. She was perfectly well. Mentally she ran a finger down the list of possible symptoms, ticking them off one by one. She had not been suffering from nausea or dizziness. The infection had passed over without trace, and her surgery had left few visible scars. There was, perhaps, a little soreness, but that could easily be all in her head. It was tempting, she knew, to prolong the somatic side of things, fixating on any small twinge and even calling up phantom pains in order to have something concrete with which to cope—something that could be managed with a few pills—something that would heal in an orderly, measurable way.

Elaine remembered the look her husband had given her as she had stood on the front stoop, her suitcase in one hand. She had unearthed the old tent from her college years. She still had a few sick days left at work; they would not expect her back yet. Cosmo had offered to come away with her—he spouted a few facts about the redwood trees, looking excited—but Elaine shot him down. Even in the moment of parting, she had stood away from him, unwilling to let him touch her.

"You will come back?" he had asked at last.

"Yes," Elaine said. And then, annoyed by his naive hopefulness, unable to stop herself, she added spitefully, "I'm sure the redwoods will make everything better. I'm sure I'll come home cured."

But her husband had nodded, as though satisfied.

❧

The phone rang just before dawn. Cosmo was flipping through a gardening magazine, avoiding his wife's empty side of the bed. He was pricing out copper edging, which, if used to line the flower-beds, would keep the slugs away entirely—they could not cross it without receiving a small electric shock. When his cell phone rang, Cosmo glared at it. It was not hard to guess who might be calling. He ran a gardening hotline, and his more obsessed clients tended to seek his advice at all hours. They phoned in the early morning, before heading off to work, to ask him how to get rid of snapdragon rust. They called while driving down the highway to describe in detail the waterfall they were thinking of buying. They called after midnight, having spotted something that could be a shrew hole among the marigolds.

Cosmo hefted himself up and took his time fishing a T-shirt from the closet. He caught up the phone and shuffled down the stairs.

"Cosmo? It's Art," said a man's deep voice.

"Ah, yes. Morning, morning."

Art was one of his regulars, a sweet-tempered neurotic who called on an almost daily basis—and whose garden Cosmo could now picture intimately, from the weathered paving stones to the pear and quince trees by the fence.

"Listen," Art said. "I'm about to leave for the office, but I've just stepped outside to take a look at the orchard. There's something *really* obscene going on over there."

"I see," Cosmo said. "How upsetting."

"I don't know exactly how to describe it. At first I thought it might be aphids. I have to tell you, that would be bad enough."

Art went on, rattling through a list of possible dangers. Cosmo reached the kitchen, and his mood soured. There was no warm smell of coffee. Elaine—who typically rose even earlier than he did—usually brewed a pot before heading out to the city, and he was accustomed to being greeted by that friendly scent, the sense of being cared for. The kitchen was silent, too. His wife usually left the radio on, quite accidentally, so engrossed in NPR's morning report that she forgot to switch it off before stepping out the door.

"—looks like it's been *burned*," Art said at last, coming to the point, and Cosmo snapped to attention.

"Did you say burned?"

"Well," Art said, "I noticed it on a couple of the pear tree branches. At first I thought some kids had actually come in and, you know, torched them. But then I looked closer. There are sores on the wood. Oozing sores. And there are dark streaks on the trunk, too, different from the bark. But mostly they just look—"

"Burned," Cosmo said. "Your trees have fire blight. Art, this is very serious."

He did not bother to chastise the man for letting his orchard pass unnoticed during the bloom, when the disease could be spotted in its early stages and stopped with a simple spray of bleach solution. The spring in Santa Clara had been wet and balmy, ideal conditions to spark a plague, and Art was not the first to call the hotline asking whether his trees could possibly have been set on fire, the branches and leaves blackened and withered. Cosmo explained how to scrape away the cankers to check for reddish flecking. Any sign of pink tissue was bad news.

"And this is urgent, right?" Art asked. "I mean, the trees might die?"

"It depends on how far gone they are."

"Oh, hell. This is the *last* thing I need just now."

"I understand," Cosmo said gently. But there was a clatter on the other end of the phone, and Art hung up with a bang.

The hotline rang all morning. Cosmo fielded calls as he made coffee, fed the cats, and tinkered with the sprinkler system. He had no time to brood about his wife. His clients called with descriptions of wilted leaves and larvae they had found. They called to ask about soil solarization. They wanted to know how to create a butterfly garden—whether to plant dill or hollyhocks, milkweed or asters. Cosmo was sometimes amazed that people would choose to spend their money (the hotline was cheap, but not toll-free) on an hour-and-a-half discussion about the pros and cons of planting coleus or the best kind of lily to choose for their ponds. These were rich Californians, amateur gardeners with time to spare. There was something soothing for them in the simple, immediate fact of a human voice on the line.

Cosmo had learned about plants as a child. His boyhood had been "rocky"—Elaine's term—with an alcoholic father and a milquetoast of a mother who could not stand up to her husband. The only good times Cosmo remembered had revolved around the garden. His mother would suit up with her apron and trowel. As Cosmo knelt in the crumbling earth, she would guide his fingers over the plants, muttering instruction. She had taught him to tell the difference between a sun-loving vine and one that required shade. She had taught him to recognize the mix of gum, frass, and sawdust left by a peach tree borer, the white tint of fruit infected by a mosaic virus, and the yellowing of leaves that could indicate chlorosis, the floral version of anemia. There was nothing about plants that she did not know.

This intelligence had been passed down the matrilineal line, mother to daughter, and if Cosmo's father had been normal (the kind of man to drag his son out from among the flowers and off to the baseball diamond or a Boy Scout meeting), the knowledge would have been lost when she died. Instead she had passed it along to him. Sometimes, as Cosmo answered calls on the hotline, he heard her dreamy voice echoing beneath his own. In another period of history, they might have burned her as a witch, and her son along with her.

৵

Elaine tramped along the trails of the redwood forest, drinking in the silence. The massive orange trees looked like something from another world. Some were large enough that it would have taken twenty men to span their girth, standing fingertip to fingertip. One or two trunks were actually split, and the trail dipped neatly between them, like a road passing through a tunnel in the mountains. Armed with a walking stick she had bought at the gift shop, Elaine hiked until her legs began to cramp. She stared up at the frothy, distant canopy, which admitted a watery light, ghostly and golden. The smell of the trees was overpowering. One of Elaine's friends—a true California hippie, complete with swinging braids and hand-woven sandals—had said that the redwoods were possessed of an overwhelming *chi*, a pulsing life force that could be felt by gurus and their more gifted disciples. Elaine stood for a while with her hands pressed to the trunk, but apparently she didn't have the right stuff. She felt nothing except rough, mossy wood.

At last she reached the crest of a hill and gazed back down the trail, which wound beneath the shrubbery and disappeared around a bend. She was quite alone. Few of the tourists managed to come this far; they tended to peter out in the valley. A brook rushed and sputtered between the trees. Elaine took off her shoes and sat on a dusty stone, kicking her feet in the water. A dragonfly buzzed over a stagnant pool. This was as good a place as any.

With a lump in her throat, Elaine took the canister from the pouch at her waist. It was shaped like a hip flask—small, metallic, and carefully sealed. In the hospital, she had asked specifically that the remains be cremated for her. She had been in a delirium, sweat-soaked and aching. The faces had swum before her—impassive doctors, genial nurses, and Cosmo, omnipresent, baffled and helpless. Phrases had caught her ear: *episodes of absent breathing, neonatal respiratory distress, unusually inactive.* The infection in her womb had taken away her rationality, her clear head. She had wept and tugged at the blankets. She had tried to stand up and was eventually restrained. There was blood everywhere, on the sheets, on her gown, on the fuzzy socks she had brought from home. The pain was a constant thing, like a musical note struck on a tuning fork, high and unending. Cosmo himself had seen the baby—the not-yet-a-baby—being carried off, hairless, the skin transparent, the wrinkled hands bobbing. It was born too soon, only twenty-one weeks in. It had no chance.

Normally, Elaine knew, the tiny body would have simply disappeared. The hospital took care of that side of things. But she had insisted that she be given the ashes—she had cried and begged—the nurses had tried to soothe her—and at last poor Cosmo had stepped in, not understanding at all, but shouting on her behalf anyway. Then Elaine had slept. She had slept for days, buried beneath her fever. The surgery had taken place without her knowledge or consent. Cosmo had signed the papers that would save her life and seal off her fertile organs permanently.

Slowly she uncapped the canister. The ashes drifted on a slight breeze, coating the wings of a white moth, dappling the surface of the water. Elaine waited, expecting to cry. A bird began to sing in the far distance, and the redwood leaves surged overhead. Perhaps she did not have any tears left.

❧

In the afternoon, Cosmo worked on the baby's room. He carried the wooden dresser out to the Dumpster. He stripped the wallpaper, leaving ragged curls on the soft yellow rug. The crib fell apart in his hands, and he wound up having to wrestle it down the stairs in several trips, spar by spar, the screws and brads raining onto the landing and frightening the cats. He was pretending—as much as he could—that Elaine was just on a business trip. She had a job as a district manager for a clothing boutique, and she was often required to travel up and down the coast. It was normal for her to be gone for a few days, even a week.

They had planned for Cosmo to be the stay-at-home dad, answering calls as he changed the baby's diaper and prepared lunches of strained peas. Elaine had stocked up on parenting books, advising him on the best schedule for naps, worrying about the pros and cons of breast-feeding. Cosmo was less scientific. Now and then a bright image would unfold in his mind. Himself with the baby in his lap, flipping through a picture book. Teaching the boy (or girl) to kick a soccer ball. Walking the child unsteadily through the garden. The pastel-themed bedroom now seemed a bit like one of these daydreams—foolishly optimistic, shining there at the top of the stairs for just a few sanguine months. They had waited until Elaine passed the crucial benchmark of the first trimester before upending what had once been a storage room and packing it with bibs and booties.

Presently Cosmo unearthed the rattle his mother had shipped to him specially. He sat holding it in both hands for a while— painted wood, intricately carved with his and Elaine's initials. This seemed like a good indication that it was time to take a rest. When the telephone rang, he answered it with every semblance of calm. He was settled in a lounge chair, a glass of iced tea at his elbow. One of the cats was on the patio beside him, hissing and spitting as it stalked honeybees.

"I'm sorry to bother you," Art said earnestly, and Cosmo sighed to himself—the man was, after all, paying for the privilege. "But I *really* need your help. I went out to look at the fire blight one more time, and I found it in the quince trees too. The *quince* trees, for God's sake!"

"Oh, dear," Cosmo said.

"This is all my fault," Art said, and he launched into an apologetic tale about his ineptitude in the garden. Cosmo smiled wearily. Over time, he had formed a mental image of Art, and of all his regulars. There were more than a few lonely hearts who called often enough to be on a first-name basis—Janice, the dog lady; Kyle, the hypochondriac; and Art, the flaming homosexual. From time to time they would drop tidbits about their lives, which Cosmo had gathered up into an incomplete but interesting collage. Art was one of his favorites. He had a math-related job—a teacher, an accountant?—that required a large chunk of his time. He was obsessively neat. Cosmo suspected that he had a steady partner, since Art made the occasional reference to a significant *him*, as in, "He said he'd fix the gate yesterday, but of course he didn't." Once, in the middle of a monologue about birdhouses, Art had said breathlessly, "Oh, that's *him* on the other line!" and hung up.

"You're sure this is a bacteria?" Art cried now. "It looks like the whole damn place has been set on fire. It looks like arson!"

"Remember the sores," Cosmo said. "It's definitely a bacteria."

"Oh *God*," Art said. "I can't handle this right now. These aren't even my trees! They're not—" He broke off on a high note, with what sounded like a sob.

Cosmo waited curiously. There was a pause, and then Art said in a husky voice, "I'm sorry, you must think I'm a nut. It's just that planting these trees was *not* my idea. And now I'm in charge of making the place nice to sell it. I can't have dying trees. That's a real estate no-no."

"You're selling your place?" Cosmo asked, stunned.

"Well—" Art took a shaky breath. "Yes, I have to. And you know how much work I've put into it. *You* know better than anyone."

"Yes, of course."

The very thought sent a shiver up Cosmo's spine. He knew his own house so well—the layout of his yard was printed into his brain. He had arranged the patio himself, tended the tiger lilies, stocked the koi pond with goggle-eyed carp. The place was a work of art, years in the making.

"Anyway," Art said, pulling himself together. "This has to be done quickly. I'm no good with trees, but I'm a competent gardener." He sniffed dramatically. "I have a *lot* of skills, in fact. A lot of skills."

"You know," Cosmo said carefully, "if the blight is as bad as that—if it's spreading to your other trees—it might be time to call in a professional."

"There's no *time,*" Art wailed. "I've got people coming in to see the house. It's got to be done now!"

"All right," Cosmo said. "All right."

They went through the process, step by step. The sick branches would have to be pruned. It was unpleasant, sometimes, to cut so far into the healthy tissue of a weak and ailing plant, but there was no other way to stop the fire blight. Cosmo was surprised by Art's depth of feeling. He had known the man to be peevish, excitable, and occasionally paranoid. Art was the type of gardener who saw invasion everywhere. A half-chewed leaf meant earwigs. A stray mound of earth meant gophers. Cosmo had talked him down from many ledges—from spraying everywhere with caustic pesticides, from throwing out an entire rosebush that showed only the slightest sign of wilt. Art's voice trembled dangerously through the rest of their conversation, and Cosmo soothed and murmured. He attempted again to raise the idea of a professional gardener; he did not like the idea of his tearful client wielding a saw. The last thing Art would need just now was to lose a few fingers.

"I've got it," Art said finally. "I'm ready."

"Fine," Cosmo said. "But please call me later to tell me how it's going. And can I suggest again—"

"I've got it," Art said firmly. He hung up, and Cosmo sat for a moment clutching the phone.

❧

In the evening, Elaine lit a fire and stewed pasta in a billycan. These were skills she remembered from years ago; she was surprised at how the details came back, the fact that the kindling should be stacked in a tripod, the right way to hammer the tent stakes into the ground, in case of wind. The redwood forest looked spooky in the failing light. The sunset was broken, uncertain, and the birds called from so high up that they seemed to be miles away. She knew nothing about these trees except what Cosmo had told her—thousands of years old, among the largest living things on the planet. Elaine shivered as she huddled beside the flames. The scar from her surgery was definitely burning now, but she had elected to tough it out, eschewing pain medicine. In a way, the ache felt good.

She had suffered through four miscarriages before this final one. She and Cosmo knew the routine by now. For some reason it had often begun at night. There would be a bit of dull cramping, which Elaine would steadfastly ignore, flipping through her magazine as Cosmo glowered at his *New York Times* crossword puzzle.

The bedroom windows were usually open, the blinds billowing in a breeze. One of the cats might climb drowsily over her feet. The pain would begin to worsen, eventually shifting from her belly to her lower back. She might feel a tensing in her buttocks. And then there would be wetness, pooling around her thighs.

"Cosmo—?" she would say. He would glance up absently, the pencil still poised in midair. Elaine would watch his expression change as he registered her anxiety, the slight contortion of her posture.

The rest of the evening would pass in trips to the bathroom and pads tucked into her underwear. She would call the doctor, and they would discuss exactly what kind of blood flow she was seeing, whether there were any clots or bits of tissue. Cosmo would hover around, asking whether she wanted any tea, if he should get her a heating pad, until Elaine was ready to scream. The doctor would be kind. He would be soothing, unwilling to commit himself to any particular diagnosis. They had run so many tests. Elaine's womb was normal, no growths, no fibroids. She was not suffering from any underlying illnesses like diabetes or lupus. Her immune system was not attacking the fetus. There was simply no medical reason why she and Cosmo could not conceive naturally. The doctor would be calm and reassuring as he reminded her of all these things. But Elaine would know. She could feel it happening inside her, a solid structure beginning to crumble, like clay in running water.

Over time, she had found ways to cope with the terrible aftermath. She would close her ears to the well-meaning friends who told her it might be all for the best. She would throw herself back into her career. There, at least, there was no sympathy to suffer through, no one to squeeze her hands and glare meaningfully into her eyes. At home, she and Cosmo would bear up well enough.

The doctor had warned her that the psychological fallout could be severe, that many happy marriages had been destroyed by a lack of communication. Elaine had listened politely. Cosmo, she knew, would cope in his way, puttering around the garden, chatting ad nauseam with his clients about millipedes and green tomatoes and who knew what else.

Elaine had learned to manage the sadness on her own, counting to ten and waiting for the crest of the wave to pass over her. She had learned to control the urges that sometimes struck when she passed a playground and glimpsed a little girl in the sandbox, her entire attention absorbed in burying her doll, or a towheaded boy toddling after a ball. She had learned not to speak of the dreams that plagued her. Baby powder and milk. Pink bellies and downy heads.

♄

Cosmo spent the evening in a state of mounting concern. The telephone shrilled, and he leapt to answer it, hoping to hear Art's voice. Instead he was inveigled in a long discussion about whether to pollard a difficult willow tree. He got a few of those odd calls he used to savor, as they had made Elaine laugh—sometimes people rang the hotline with issues so strange they clearly had no idea whom else to ask. A woman called to inquire how many snails her daughter would have to eat before it was time to head to the emergency room. A man with a gruff voice wanted to know how deep he should bury his dog's body. (Elaine's favorite, years ago, had been a young woman, who—sounding mortified but determined—asked if it would be all right for her to poop in the backyard while the plumbing in her house was being fixed.) The sky darkened outside, and a light rain began to fall.

When Art finally called again, Cosmo was seated in his favorite armchair, the cat a warm puddle of fur in his lap. The clock had just struck nine.

"It's done," Art said.

"Ah, yes?" Cosmo let out a long breath. "Glad to hear it."

"The trees are gone."

"Beg pardon?"

"*Gone*," Art said. "I tried to do what you told me, I really did. I got the saw. I went to the sickest tree, and I cut wherever I saw the sores. There were branches all over the ground. I dropped a big one on my foot. But I kept finding more of the sores. I kept cutting. And by then, the tree was—" He paused. "It just looked so sad, only one branch left sticking up, and raw places cut all over the trunk. So I sawed it down. Put it out of its misery."

Cosmo shifted involuntarily, and the cat let out a yowl, dislodged from its sleeping place.

"Then I went to the next tree. But it was the same thing. It looked like a person with leprosy, you know, everywhere you look there's another little patch of blisters. I kept thinking I was done, but then I'd see a twig I had missed, black and charred—" He paused again. "So I cut that one down, too."

"And the quince trees?" Cosmo asked, finding his voice.

"Oh," Art said. "They were the sickest of all. I think the fire blight must have started there. They were goners. I sawed and sawed, but the tissue was pink all the way through. No healthy bark left."

"I see," Cosmo said.

"I carried all the branches out to the alley," Art said. "I'm dead on my feet. I'm a mess, really, my hands are all torn up. But I think it will look okay. I mean, right now it's just stumps, and a lot of sawdust, but—" He took a heavy breath, and then he began to cry in earnest. Cosmo listened, aghast, as the man broke down. The cat, disliking the noise, sprinted from the room.

"Art," Cosmo said softly. But there was no stopping him. Art let out a sniffle and then almost screamed in anguish. Not knowing what else to do, Cosmo got to his feet, the phone crooked under his ear.

"Can I—" he began. "Is there someone I could—?"

Art moaned, and Cosmo heard him blowing his nose.

"I'm so sorry," Art said. "This is ridiculous. Honestly."

Another sob escaped him, and for a moment he was overcome. Cosmo stood in the living room, his mouth open. The rain picked up, and a burst of spray misted through the screens.

"You see, he left," Art said at last. "I was living with— Well, I'm sure you know I'm gay. We'd been together for nine years. And then one day I walked in, and there was a note on the table."

"A note," Cosmo echoed.

"Yes, a little *Dear John* letter. Nine years ended by a slip of paper. I felt like I'd been fired." He laughed wildly. "And Steven was gone."

Cosmo grunted.

"For a while," Art continued, "I thought I'd live in the house anyway, you know, just buy out his half. But God, Cosmo, here I am, the only *faggot* on the block. I've got the dog—Steven left his *dog*—and it's not even a pretty dog. It looks like a hyena. So I walk his damn mutt, and I work on my garden. The neighborhood kids are scared of me. I'm the creepy guy who lives alone in the big house. I'm Boo Radley!"

He burst into tears again, and for a time his words were lost. Cosmo tugged open the door to the garden. The rain had dwindled. The air was hung with damp curtains of chill. He kicked on his boots and stepped into the soaked grass. Art wept, and Cosmo moved quietly among the plants. Heavy leaves, bowed under the weight of moisture, brushed against his legs.

He was aware that he ought to confide in return. That would be the normal thing to do—the polite, friendly response. Cosmo ought to share some part of what he himself was suffering. But he could not manage it. The words were stuck in his throat. He could scarcely breathe.

"My wife—" he began. "Elaine—"

"Hm?"

Cosmo faltered. A cool wind blew up around him, and there was a moment's pause, during which Art blew his nose. From the distance came the chuff of a train. At last, somewhat feebly, Art said, "Anyway, I did want to ask—would you recommend that I put some stones over the poor little stumps? You know, some big boulders? Just so it doesn't look like there was a natural disaster back there."

"That would be nice," Cosmo said. "But make sure you wash them before you put them in the garden. Sometimes rocks will bring in lichen or pests you don't need."

Art sighed. "It's perfect in a way. Those were Steven's trees. His one contribution. And when he left, they just withered away to nothing."

Cosmo moved deeper into the yard, sniffing the air.

"Well," Art said, now sounding mortified. "I suppose I ought to go."

"Mm." Cosmo was steeling himself. If he did not speak up now, he never would. If he did not speak up now, Art would not call the hotline again, and God only knew what the net loss of income would be.

"My wife," Cosmo said loudly. "She lost the baby."

"What's that?" Art gasped.

And then it was easy. Once the dam had broken, a veritable tide of words came tumbling across Cosmo's tongue. He told Art about Elaine's surgery. He told Art that he had not really talked about it, not to anyone; if he did not verbalize it, the knowledge tended to stay somewhere else, on a back burner of his mind, like a bad dream. He told Art that he could not imagine his wife out in the wilderness; she was a city girl, unaccustomed to sleeping under the stars. Elaine had been gone nearly a week, and in an odd way he was having trouble calling up an accurate picture of what she looked like. During the pregnancy, she had been swollen and blossoming, almost fey in her giddiness. She had not moved with the usual languid weight of a gravid woman, but seemed buoyed up, drifting as though through water.

The miscarriage had come on so suddenly. The two of them were walking back from the ice cream store when Elaine had doubled over. Ten minutes later Cosmo was screaming for an ambulance. He told Art that he barely remembered the hours in the hospital, doctors bustling, doors slamming, Elaine groaning. There had been a terrible moment, after they had carried off the remains of the baby, in which Elaine had wailed that she wished she were dead too. She had shouted it for everyone to hear. He tried to hold her, but she slapped him away.

As he spoke, Cosmo's senses were abuzz. He could smell the wet coals of someone's outdoor barbecue, releasing, after the downpour, the scent of yesterday's meal. He could hear the flutter of a moth, the lonely, faraway whistle of a train. Art was soothing and kind. Cosmo murmured that he was afraid Elaine might never return. He paced the wet grass, listening as Art poured himself a glass of lemonade and fussed with his icemaker. The sky was filled with the eerie calls of bats, the swish of swallow's wings. The moon rose between the leaves.

Gradually the talk turned to boulders, and real estate agents, and the best neighborhoods in which to invest. But Cosmo's thoughts were elsewhere. It seemed as though some doorway in his mind, hitherto shut tight, even to himself, had suddenly opened. Inside that private room was a mess of conflicting emotions. He was angry with Elaine. She had treated this tragedy as her private sorrow, as though Cosmo, too, had not lost a child—as though he had not lost his chance of ever having children. He had been so busy caring for Elaine that his own heartbreak had been steamrolled over.

Cosmo had wanted to be a father, a good father, unlike his own. He had wanted to see his gray eyes and Elaine's snub nose duplicated in a small, soft face. He had been ready for parenthood, and it felt now as though some part of him had died. Some part of him had been sliced down, toppled, and excised from him—a stone rolled over the place where it had stood. Those last moments in the hospital would haunt him forever. The baby had just looked so lifelike as it had been carried away, its tiny hands reaching for the air.

∽

When Elaine returned home, two days later, she was struck first by the stillness. Standing in the front hall, she set her suitcase down uneasily. She had learned over the years how to discern where her husband—naturally more silent than other men—might be hiding; she could tell, like a spider seated in its web, one leg poised on each strand, how to go to him unerringly. Today, however, the house felt abandoned. An odd smell hung in the air, earthy and damp.

There was dirt on the living room floor. Cosmo had evidently left a mess for her to clean up. With her nose wrinkled, Elaine followed the muddy trail to the staircase. There were footprints on the steps. There were twigs and leaves caught in the banister. Cosmo had apparently gone to pieces in her absence. The hallway was strewn with pebbles and clay, leading into the baby's room. Elaine sucked in a brave breath, turned the corner—and stopped in her tracks.

A tree stood in the center of the room. Cosmo had piled a waist-high mountain of crumbling black soil upon the clean wooden floor. Buried in the heap, listing slightly toward the window, was a five-foot sapling. The thing looked brand-spanking-new, as though Cosmo had picked it up at a nursery and transported it directly here. Its fronds were pale green, the bark a glossy copper. A few roots poked out of the dirt. The cats had made merry with their new plaything; there were inky footprints on the floorboards. Not quite trusting her senses, Elaine stepped forward, her hand outstretched, and let her fingers close around the wood.

The rest of the room was absolutely bare. Cosmo had repainted the walls and spirited away the crib and baby clothes. The framed pictures of lambs had been taken down. There were no more packages of diapers. The mobile had been tugged out of the ceiling, and even the holes left by a nail or two had been carefully spackled over, all evidence of their hope removed. The pile of earth was the only thing left, with silt and loam scattered right into the corners. A breeze wafted through the window, and the sapling trembled. Its limbs were delicately sculpted. A few fragile flowers gleamed among the twigs. Elaine gazed for a while with her mouth open. Then she buried her hands in the branches, the bright, cold leaves against her skin. She ought to have been upset, she knew. She ought to have been furious, or at least concerned, but the first emotion that came to her was a kind of wrenching elation, as she took in the wild, blooming layout of her husband's creation, this strange, new living thing.

# THE LAST ANIMAL

The two women burst through the doors of the Mexican hotel lobby together. At first glance they were indistinguishable, two gray-haired sixty-somethings in bright print dresses, trailing the scent of perfume and mothballs. Their bodies showed the marks of arthritis and fatigue. They might have been sisters, twins, with their airport-disheveled hair and anxious eyes. They wheeled their luggage inexpertly into doorjambs and coffee tables on the way to the front desk; their bags were stuffed almost to bursting, since they had brought a change of clothes for every conceivable weather condition, even snow. It was Marge, the bolder of the two, who approached the concierge, and in her usual way with non-Americans, she pitched her voice a little higher than normal and spoke with exaggerated slowness.

"We have a room reserved," she boomed. "Look it up under Markby. That's her." She hooked a thumb at her companion.

Here, for the first time, if you had been watching—which no one was—you would have seen the two women separate for a moment into distinct beings with widely different personalities. Marge negotiated the payment of the room, mistrustfully and at top volume, but Delilah stood back, and in her dark squirrel's eyes there flickered a hint of naughty amusement. This was her vacation. She had been planning it forever, saving up, researching hotels, making lists of local attractions, and trying in vain to learn Spanish from books on tape. From the first, she had been certain she wanted to bring a traveling companion, and in the absence of a suitable man—the upright, competent sort who would carry bags and cope with panhandlers—she had asked Marge, of all her wide acquaintanceship, to travel with her for five full weeks.

Her children had been appalled. Though Jenny and Chris were both grown now, well into their thirties, they remembered strident, inappropriate Marge from their childhood. Marge gave offense to nearly everyone she met, but she was too narcissistic to notice it. (In all their years of friendship, Delilah had never once seen the woman embarrassed, and had finally learned not to burn with vicarious shame or attempt a hissed apology, but rather to just sit back and enjoy the ride.) Marge loved to travel, despite the fact that she was suspicious of anything unfamiliar. Her stomach could not tolerate spices, and she coped with her diarrhea by updating Delilah on the state of her bowel movements through the hotel bathroom door. She lived in fear of one of her cats sickening and dying in her absence and insisted on calling the poor cat-sitter at least three times a day. At the beach she shielded every inch of her skin with a covering of some sort—hats, glasses, towels, and shawls—and then groused that she never got tan. But Delilah had her own reasons for wanting

Marge with her, not least of which that Marge was a source of constant, if unintentional, hilarity.

The payment of the room at last concluded, Marge gathered up the keys with a threatening glare at the concierge and took Delilah's arm.

"Come along, my dear," she said. "You look about half done in. He *claims* the beds are firm, but we'll see."

Not until that evening did Delilah have the room to herself. After testing the mattresses, faucets, and ceiling fan, and failing to reach her cat-sitter by phone, Marge marched off to examine the hotel pool. Delilah watched through a crack in the blinds until her friend's broad, swimsuited back had disappeared. Then she hauled her suitcase up on the bed, fumbled beneath a layer of shirts, and brought out a battered envelope, yellowed at the corners. For a moment she sat on the bed, biting her lip and eyeing the envelope warily. Then, her face resigned, she drew out a single sheet of paper, which she traced dreamily with her hands, as though reading Braille.

*My love,*

*Have landed in a town called Playa del Carmen in the Yucatan Peninsula. Hired for a week's work at the local hotel, translating the signs into English for the American guests, of all things. High school Spanish lessons continue to pay off.*

*Know I won't be home to see you again. Know you won't understand why. I do love you, little one. Am missing your funny ways every day. Missing the kid, too, though you won't believe that. Think of her constantly. Wonder what the new boy will look like.* (Here Delilah, reading, laid a hand on her belly.) *Maybe when he's born you will send me a photograph. If you ever forgive me, that is, which you won't. Have slept with a local prostitute every night this week.* (Delilah's eyes bounced, by habit, to the next paragraph, where a new subject was introduced. But that would not do. It was her last moment with this letter; she must read it all. She dragged her gaze back to the treacherous lines.) *Skinny and hungry girl, not pretty like you. I take her out on the beaches to do it, for the humiliation. Anybody could walk by. Looks at the sky while I'm on top of her. Face empty. Yesterday watched her walk away, so little and tired, counting the bills. She tripped over a bucket some kid left in the sand.*

*Need your love still, always, but I've got it, you're so true and loyal, I've got your love in my pocket with the cigarettes. Right here. But I need this too, hurting that dumb, skinny kid. Like a broken bird. That's what I know you'll never understand. Could say it's because of that old Korean war, and it's true, but I know it's no excuse. It is true. I wasn't like this before. Tried not to be like this for so long after I came back. Worried about what I would do. Kept thinking about hurting you. Kept thinking the worst things. It's no excuse, of course. Lots of guys came back just as messed up as me, and they're still good husbands and dads somehow. But I'm gone. Won't be here more than a week. I'll keep moving, until I fall off the world, which will happen one of these days. Hope these letters aren't messing you up too much. Think of you always. Always.*

*Lew*

Delilah sat for a minute with her head bowed. The letter fell over her, its weight rendering the air porridge-thick and hard to breathe. After a moment she sighed, kicked her feet into flip-flops, and slipped out the front door, clutching the letter in both hands. The Mexican night was as warm as bathwater.

The sky was the rich purple she recognized from Lew's descriptions, scattered with stars and wet clouds. She made her careful way down the path to the beach (and spared a moment's fond irritation for Marge. Here they were, paying a small fortune for a hotel bungalow in walking distance of the Gulf of Mexico, and Marge would spend the week doing laps in a ten-by-twenty chlorine pool). The beach was empty of people. Delilah stood irresolute for a moment on the cold, pale sand. Crickets (or cicadas, or geckos—she could not be sure) chimed in the palm trees around her. Waves crested as they came in and laid their long black tongues upon the sand. To Delilah's uncertain eyes, it seemed that ivory pillars rolled across the water, rather than curls of foam. She took the letter from her pocket. She took a pack of matches from her bag.

The flame lapped over Lew's handwriting, his curly *w*'s and sharp erect *t*'s, the spelling mistakes he had made and blacked out, the tiny drawing of a tree he had done unconsciously in the margin. Delilah sat down in the sand. When she had burned Lew's first letter, back at the beginning of her trip, her heart had thumped so wildly that she'd actually been afraid she might have a coronary. Each time, however, had grown progressively easier. She had watched four letters go up in smoke now; she was familiar with the way it progressed, the ache in her chest, the ensuing emptiness. Now, as she watched her husband's final note crumbling into windblown ash, she felt something more—light and airy, as though wings were beating somewhere about her person.

Lew had disappeared thirty years before in a manner that was both spectacular and mundane. On a Tuesday morning, he had driven

Delilah to the doctor. She had been well into her second trimester then, eager to see her obstetrician. It was a rainy afternoon in Seattle, the clouds low and dark, the streets bright with damp. Lew had dropped her outside the clinic, at the lobby entrance, rolling down the window to shout that he would park down the block and be right back. Delilah had watched him turn the corner, watched the car until it was out of sight.

He never returned. That final image, the back of his head framed in the rear window, was the last glimpse of him she ever got. Delilah had waited for him in the uncomfortable plastic chairs at the doctor's office. She waited for him afterward, standing on the sidewalk for over an hour, squinting against the drizzle and trying not to cry. Lew did not come back to collect her. He did not pick their daughter up from a playdate that evening, as planned. He did not turn up at his office the following morning. It seemed that he had driven around that corner and vanished outright, popping like a soap bubble.

For three days, Delilah had no news at all. She called his friends— his co-workers—the police. She filed a Missing Persons Report. She did not sleep, guzzling coffee and holding her bewildered daughter in her lap. For three days, she imagined the worst things. Mugging. Car bomb. Dead in a ditch.

Then, on the fourth day, she was startled by a persistent ringing at her doorbell. Two uniformed officers stood there. Delilah came onto the porch to meet them, her bare feet cold against the boards. Her hands were trembling as she smoothed her hair out of her face. In the background, from inside the house, floated the sound of Jenny's morning cartoons. The officers had been brisk as they reported their news.

The car had been found. It had turned up in the long-term parking section at the airport. It appeared that Lew had driven straight from the doctor's office to the international terminal. He had booked himself a flight to Mexico City. The policemen explained these things to Delilah in low, official tones. They did not add that Lew was gone forever, leaving his family in the rearview mirror—but then, they did not need to. After all, he had climbed aboard with no luggage and no return ticket.

∿

The next day, Delilah and Marge took a guided tour of the hotel compound. They passed the beach, where the sand was littered with broiling tourists. They visited Marge's pool, where a pale young woman cut slow strokes through the water. In the dining area, only a few places were occupied, though a harassed-looking nanny was shepherding ten or twelve children who rampaged everywhere, spilling water on the tablecloths and barreling between the chairs. The first aid area was just another bungalow, painted white, with a red cross on the door. No doctor was in evidence—only a man with a bloody, bandaged foot, feverishly dreaming on his cot. A mess of young boys tumbled about in the nearby grass, chasing a soccer ball and cursing cheerfully in Spanish. The field bordered a cliff, about which they seemed amazingly unconcerned. A goat tethered to a rope was their halfway mark.

As the tour wound through the heart of the hotel, Marge was in her element, making notes in a little pad. The guide described all the activities that would be offered during their weeklong stay, and Marge scribbled them down: *cooking class, marimba concert, glass-bottomed boat tour.* Delilah stayed quiet. Marge would, she knew, take pleasure, as the days passed, in ticking off each activity as it was completed. She would throw herself wholeheartedly into a lecture about the local sea life or a demonstration of salsa dancing;

she would take pictures of each event, which would eventually be pasted into a scrapbook, so that every aspect of her trip could be shared with her unwilling circle of friends, captured in chronological order and exhaustive detail.

But Delilah was less enthusiastic. In truth, she found herself at a bit of a loss. Kayaking, sunbathing—none of that was why she had come here. Playa del Carmen was the last stop on her vacation. She had chosen this spot for one reason only: to burn Lew's final letter here, on the sand, in the same place where he had written it and mailed it to her. Now that she had done so, the ostensible purpose of her trip had been achieved. She was left at a loose end.

She had never told anyone about Lew's letters, not even her children. Jenny and Chris had been thrilled by her wish to travel, but could not fathom why she felt the need to cling so relentlessly to the coastline of the Yucatan Peninsula. Delilah could not explain that she had been planning for three decades to travel Lew's route and eradicate his last remnants, letting go of him finally. Part of her maternal duty was to protect her kids from the reality of their father's insanity and the extent of the damage he had wreaked in her own heart. She had managed to pretend that this trip was a vacation and nothing more, a chance to see a little beauty before she died. Marge had thought it was a great idea. Yet her children had been undaunted in their efforts to widen the scope of her travels. Jenny, who voyaged the Caribbean yearly with her doctor husband, had discovered real tourist gems in the Bahamas and Bermuda that Delilah simply *had* to try. Chris, who was younger and more inclined to fly off on a moment's notice, sleeping in flea-riddled hostels with a group of friends, was effusive in his praise of the music, ambiance, and top-rate ganja of Jamaica.

Delilah had ignored their advice. Her route was predetermined and could not be changed: Campeche, Progreso, Rio Lagartos,

Cancun, and now Playa del Carmen, in that order and no other. That was the path Lew had traveled; one letter had come to her from each location. She did not want someone with her who might gaily suggest they bop over to Mexico City or take a boat trip to a nearby island. She needed something very specific on this journey: She needed Marge. Marge, who was wary of every stranger but incurious about her loved ones, would never notice if Delilah seemed upset, if she slipped away for an unexplained hour or two, if she lit small fires on the local beaches. Marge's rough-hewn frame and sour disposition were as familiar as breathing. Baffled by maps and a stickler for rules, she clung to Delilah's schedule as if it were written in stone.

Lew had sent five letters in all. In the days and weeks after his disappearance, Delilah had been in a fog. She scarcely remembered that period now, though it had been a busy one. With a toddler on one hip, a demanding and unsympathetic boss, and a severe case of morning sickness, she had moved through her days in a blur. She could not remember how she had come up with the right day care center for little Jenny. She had no recollection of the inevitable conversation with her obstetrician, in which she had explained that the father would not, after all, be there for the birth—that he would not be there, ever again. She had vague impressions of her friends' well-meant but unhelpful sympathy. Her mother's scarcely veiled I-told-you-so smirk. As the days had passed, one slipping into the next, there had been a general impression of dreaming. It felt as though nothing in the world was solid or constant. Nothing could be relied on. She could not even trust her own senses.

What she remembered was the letters.

Those pages, marked in her husband's writing, stood out in her mind with all the hot glow of a streetlamp on a hazy evening. Even now, she could have recited each one by heart. Lew's mental state seemed to have fluctuated. Some of the letters had been coherent, almost cheerful; others had been downright unhinged. His desire to harm others had spiraled, occasionally, into an urge to harm himself. He had spoken often and with longing of falling off the edge of the world. One note had been little more than a poem about the old, sea-battered rowboats kept by the hostel where he was staying in Progreso:

*Just can't get over them. Old tubs almost. Gaps between the boards. Wood warped. Been at sea so long they don't look like wood anymore. Really worried somebody might throw them out. Keep coming back to check on them. Been sketching them too. Might send you a doodle.*

Delilah had read between the lines, and when his letters stopped—stopped forever—she knew what he had done. She had even dreamed about it: Lew in a rowboat on a great green swell, gazing into the deeps, and then the final, fatal splash.

ॐ

It was early morning when Delilah first saw the man. She and Marge were in the hotel gift shop at the time, examining a rack of leather bracelets. Marge was a sucker for this kind of tourist trap. Back home, in Seattle, her apartment was decorated with odds and ends that she had picked up while on vacation in Costa Rica, Canada, Italy. Nothing was too touristy or too cliché for her. Half of the fun of traveling was bringing things back and hanging them on the wall. Now Marge wandered tirelessly among the shelves, fondling sand dollars and necklaces made of shark teeth. She was captivated by a row of wooden flutes. Idly, Delilah picked up a carved frog, painted with garish splotches of yellow. Turning it over, she saw *Made in the USA* stamped on the bottom. Smiling to herself, she replaced it on the shelves.

It took her a while to realize that she was being watched. In the corner, dressed in a Hawaiian shirt and a straw hat, a man was hovering. Delilah had the impression that he had been there for some time. She gave him the once-over. Pudgy. Genial. A human teddy bear. There was an awkward moment when their eyes met, and then he turned, pushing through the front door with a jingling of bells.

But that was not the end of it. She saw him again at lunch. As Marge cornered the cook to ask how the meat had been prepared, Delilah noticed the man in the straw hat sitting at a nearby table, reading the paper. She saw him again at the first aid station, where she and Marge stopped to see if there was any Dramamine in stock. (Marge had brought her own supply, of course, but it had dipped a bit low, and it would not do to run out.) Delilah, weary from the heat, was leaning against the wall, staring out at the water, when she caught a glimpse of the man moving away, down a nearby path. She recognized the tilt of his hat.

She saw him again in the afternoon, when she allowed herself to be dragged down to the pool. Marge swam laps, grunting and sputtering, and Delilah settled on a lounge chair, a book unopened at her side, her mind wandering freely over her lost husband, and her children, and the workplace from which she had so recently retired—slaving away as a paralegal in a midsize law firm. She had never loved her job; she had been grateful to walk out the door for good. Now, as she sprawled in the ferocious sunlight, the office where she had spent so many years—the fabric-covered cubicles, the genteel *burr* of the phones—seemed impossibly far away. On the other side of the horizon, behind the sky. Delilah was halfway into sleep when a shadow fell across her. She opened her eyes. The man was standing over her, blocking the light. He had shed his Hawaiian shirt and straw hat. He was wearing nothing but a red bathing suit. He gazed down at her for a moment, then wheeled with surprising speed and leapt into the pool.

That evening, Marge's usual complaint flared up. Her stomach could not cope with the fried bread and flavor of the Mexican cuisine. She decided to eschew dinner completely, give her system a chance to clear itself out—and besides, she wanted to get her cat-sitter on the phone and have a serious chat.

Delilah walked down to the dining hall alone. She spent the meal pretending that she was not looking for the man in the straw hat. A band, set up beside the palm trees, was playing a complex, fruity tune. A few young couples were dancing. Delilah craned her neck at the sight of a Hawaiian shirt bobbing among the tables. She turned sharply when someone called *Hi!* to another woman.

But he was not there. As this fact sank in, Delilah summoned the waiter over to order a glass of wine. She was beginning to feel ashamed of herself. In truth, she had little dating experience. Since Lew's disappearance, she had done the right thing: Over the years, she had given it a shot, most recently with the help of the Internet. Jenny had aided her in setting up an online pro-file, complete with an outdated photo and a trite list of interests. Delilah had gamely put on perfume, had her hair done, gone to movies and the theatre. She had enjoyed the whirl of dating—nice clothes, new people, interesting activities. But somehow, nothing had ever come of it. She remembered one suitor, black-haired and svelte, who had leaned in for a kiss at the end of a long evening of ballet. As their lips met, Delilah had found herself thinking, with remarkable detachment, that she felt nothing. No butterflies in her stomach. No ache in her loins. It was like kissing the wall or the back of her own hand.

This was, of course, the fault of her husband. So many things could be traced back to Lew. Perhaps there could be no recovery from a blow like the one he had dealt her. Perhaps she had shut up her heart like a house in winter. She was not sure what she hoped for anymore. These days, she did not envy her married friends. She would see them at dinner parties, sharing bites of dessert and sniping at one another good-humoredly, with just a touch of malice. She did not want what they had—not really. Only now and again had she ever experienced true jealousy. The situation was always the same: Delilah would find herself staring at an elderly couple, in their eighties or nineties, sitting together in a stillness that was pristine and unbroken. They might be settled on a park bench; they might be waiting for the bus. The man would examine his fingernails. The woman would fiddle with her bracelet. Not a word would pass between them as the wind blew across their figures, ruffling their clothes. In those moments, Delilah would be overcome by a surge of melancholy, as powerful as an ebbing tide. It was the silence that she envied—a bond that had deepened past speech, past touch, past eye contact. The closest she had ever come to that kind of thing was her friendship with Marge.

Now she sipped her wine, her gaze fixed firmly on her plate, so that she would not continue to make a fool of herself by scanning among the tables. There was nothing special about the man in the straw hat. He was not handsome; he was, in fact, almost aggressively nondescript. Delilah was sure, based on the garishness of the shirt he had been wearing all day, that he was an American, like herself. He was her same age, or thereabouts—but that was all he had going for him. Besides, he was almost certainly not interested in her. The hotel compound was small. It was silly to think he had been following her. Indeed, he had probably been as surprised as she was to see her popping up every time he turned around. Delilah felt her cheeks flush. Hopefully he would not think that *she* had been pursuing *him*.

It was late by the time she returned to her bungalow. The sun hung just above the horizon, a watery pulp, staining the high clouds pink with light. As she moved up the walkway, she found the door blocked by a square, bathrobed figure, arms folded. Marge had evidently been waiting for her.

"How are you feeling now?" Delilah asked politely. Marge did not move aside to let her come in, so she leaned wearily against the doorjamb.

"Someone stopped by for you," Marge said. "A *man*."

Delilah's hand flew to her mouth. "What? Who was it?"

"No idea. Shifty sort of fellow. He didn't leave a name." Marge squinted keenly. "You look tired," she said with decision, and motioned Delilah inside at last.

The room was brightly lit. The hotel maids had swept and made the beds, leaving a lingering hint of perfume.

"This man," Delilah said. "What did he look like?"

"Straw hat." Marge clicked her tongue. "Hawaiian shirt. Red sunglasses."

"And did he—" Delilah began, but Marge was pursuing her own train of thought.

"I just called home," she said. "Blackie is fine, but Pugslie still has that funny sneeze. I told the girl to bring him to the vet tomorrow morning. Better safe than sorry."

"Did he ask for me specifically?" Delilah said.

"Who?"

"The *man*. He wasn't just going room to room trying to dig up a date?"

"Oh, yes, he asked for you. By name," Marge said, sitting on her bed with a squealing of springs. "He asked to take you *kayaking* tomorrow, of all things. Said he'd stop by in the morning."

She yawned and shook out her mop of gray hair. Her gaze strayed toward the phone. Delilah knew she had already moved on in her mind, back inexorably to her housebound cats and the plight of their imperiled stomachs and throats.

"Marge," she said quickly. "How did he know where I was staying? Did he say?"

Marge's face clouded over.

"Oh, yes. He said all right. He told me he *followed* you, just as bold as brass. One evening, he followed you back from the beach. Can you imagine the cheek? He told me that outright, as if it weren't strange at all."

☙

That night, Delilah dreamed about Lew. This was not unexpected. Her subconscious had been busy in the thirty years since his disappearance. The dream was chaotic, a jumble. Two piercing brown eyes, as bright as copper. A hot, shuddering embrace. Delilah moaned a little—and at once, Lew let her go. She saw him gliding away, moving with unnatural smoothness. She followed him—she always followed him—but could not catch him. Through an unknown landscape, down cobblestone pathways, up marble staircases, she chased her husband, the echo of his footsteps leading her helplessly forward.

It took her a while to wake. She was twisted in the sheet, her nightgown damp with sweat. The air was filled with the rush of wind. On the other side of the room, in her own bed, Marge was snoring genially. After a moment, Delilah hefted herself upright. She slipped into the bathroom.

She had never told anyone about these dreams, or the fact that they had come, like clockwork, every week for three decades. It was not the sort of thing she could share with her friends—or, God forbid, her children. It was embarrassing. Now she examined her reflection in the mirror. A thin, pale mouth. A thatch of white hair. In truth, she did not remember her husband—not really—not anymore. He had been gone too long. He had been absent longer than he had ever been present. She did not remember whether he had been kind. Whether he had smoked. Whether he had paid his bills on time. She was not sure if their lovemaking had been tender, or earth-shattering, or lackluster. She was not certain what foods he had liked. She could not remember if he had danced well. She had no recollections at all of Lew holding little Jenny in his lap, playing with her, reading to her. What she was left with was pain, rather than memory. Lew had ripped himself out of her life so violently that the wound of his leaving obscured all that had come before.

Even in her dreams, he was less a man than a phantom. His features were always uncertain; his figure often changed shape before her eyes, now slender, now bulky, shifting like smoke. He had become, in the truest sense, a ghost: vacant and insubstantial, characterized by emptiness.

Delilah knew that she was not the only one to be haunted this way. She remembered a night, more than twenty years ago, when she had woken to the sound of screams. Her son Chris, in his bedroom, was howling bloody murder. Delilah had flown down the hall, breathless, flinging a robe around her shoulders. Outside Chris's room, she had collided with Jenny, in her bunny pajamas, white with fear.

Chris had been nearly out of his mind. He had pawed at her shoulder, gulping and gasping. He had been shaking from head to foot. It took him a while to make himself understood. A nightmare. A man. A shadow figure had been there, in his room. The man had tried to take him away.

At the time, Chris had been seven or eight; he had not had the language to articulate what he really meant. Delilah had rocked and soothed as he soaked her nightgown with tears. It was one of countless instances when she had been ludicrously aware of her own inadequacy. To be a single parent was to be always somewhere on the spectrum of failure. The math simply did not add up. One could not take the place of two. She stroked her son's hair. She knew what his dream had been about, even if he did not. The faceless figure might have been his father—or the specter of death—or a symbol of the human potential for misadventure and loss. All these possibilities would be equally terrifying to a small boy. It had been Jenny who finally got her brother back to sleep that night. She had sung to him, a private composition Delilah did not recognize, a tune the children had created together while she was at work. Chris had hummed along until his eyes slipped closed.

In the morning, Delilah did not go to breakfast, and neither did Marge. Without discussing why, they lazed around the bungalow for hours. Delilah had her game face ready: Mount Rushmore, the ice queen, the same haughty, disdainful mood she had mustered in days past when Chris had been in trouble at school again and the inevitable conference with his teacher drew near. Marge flipped through magazines and scrutinized her mottled nails. Delilah straightened picture frames and checked surfaces for dust. Marge unpacked all the clothes in her suitcase and folded them again with exquisite care. Delilah took a shower, and, unconvinced that her hair was really clean, took another. They left the screen door open, and the noise of the hotel filled the little room: children pounding by in the dust, the echoing clamor of the beach, a maid warbling some Mayan tune in the next room over, and beneath everything, the low, energetic boom of the sea, as omnipresent as a heartbeat.

The man did not come until lunchtime, when Delilah had all but given up and Marge was beginning to make smacking noises to indicate hunger and annoyance. Then a knock sounded at the screen door. A shadow fell into the room, but retreated politely back from the stoop. Delilah and Marge, marooned on their separate beds, exchanged a quick glance; then Delilah got gracefully to her feet. She had dressed carefully (earrings, white kerchief, soft sandals) but not so nicely that Marge might notice any special effort and feel compelled to comment. In the seconds it took her to cross the room, her trepidation rose in a rough wave. She flung open the screen door and was immediately blinded by sunlight.

Someone was there. Delilah shielded her eyes and perceived a hazy form standing along the walkway.

"Hello," said a man's voice. "I'm Adam."

His figure clarified slowly, like the shape of an undersea stone emerging through the broken surface of water. He was wearing the same Hawaiian shirt as before. Delilah found herself wondering if it was the only shirt he owned—or if, perhaps, he had several of them, all identical.

"Adam Connolly," he said, and he lunged at her, one arm extended. Delilah shook his hand.

"Hi. Hello."

"I wanted to take you kayaking," he said. "Maybe this afternoon, when it cools off a little?"

"Fine. That will be fine."

He smiled, a rather gooney grin. A silence fell between them.

From inside the house, Marge cleared her throat pointedly.

"Oh, yes," Delilah said. "I wanted— My friend—" She faltered, pointing back into the bungalow, where Marge was no doubt straining to hear every word. "My friend told me you came for me yesterday, and that you knew my name. I must say, I was surprised by that. Do we know each other?"

He stepped closer.

"I did a little recon," he said. "I saw you around. I asked at the concierge's desk. They're pretty informal here."

"Oh," Delilah said faintly.

"I don't know anyone else at the hotel. You seemed nice. I'd ask your friend to come along too, but"—he dropped his voice conspiratorially—"she's a little scary."

In no time at all, he was gone. Delilah had shaken his hand, not once, but twice. She had agreed to meet him at the marina at four. She came back into the bungalow feeling rather dazed, as though touched by heat stroke.

As the afternoon passed, Marge tried every tactic in her considerable repertoire to prevent Delilah from going. At first it was stony silence, but Delilah had years of practice with that one and was simply immune. Marge dragged herself tragically around the room and sighed a great deal, but Delilah did not ask what was wrong, and so Marge was forced to step out onto the stoop to check the weather and announce, to no one in particular, that it looked treacherous, very changeable; there might be a typhoon any moment. Delilah slipped into the bathroom to change into her bathing suit, examine her body in the mirror, and cover herself with a sundress she did not plan to remove even if the kayak capsized. When she came out, Marge was sitting on her bed and glaring into the middle distance.

"What will I do," Marge inquired in a high, fractious tone, "if my traveling companion is murdered at sea? I suppose I'll manage *somehow*, which is more than can be said for her children. But at least I'll be there to help them with the funeral arrangements."

Delilah laughed, knelt down, and gathered up her friend's cold hands in hers.

"I won't be murdered," she said. "I've got to do this. It'll take my mind off things. Do you understand?"

Marge did not, but she was overwhelmed by the simple human gesture, and when Delilah headed off in the direction of the marina, she only watched from the doorway in anxious silence and did not say a word.

∾

The sea was bright, calm, and scattered with blue coins. Delilah made out the shapes of reefs, minnows, and glowing bubbles that could be jellyfish. The kayak was an odd, plastic contraption, with an open top, so that the sunlight brushed her feet and knees. She sat at the prow, with Adam behind her. He was wearing the same hat and Hawaiian shirt, along with reddish sunglasses. These emblems obscured, somewhat, the nature of his features and physique. Delilah found it difficult to get a sense of what he looked like, as though he were a generic paper doll, rendered unique only by his garb. His oar-stroke was strong and rhythmic, which was good, because she had copped out after the first fifteen minutes. Her paddle lay abandoned across her thighs, and she massaged her arthritic shoulder. She was annoyed with him for being so quiet, though she could not think of anything to say either. The first few topics of conversation she had dredged up—the weather, the length of their respective stays—had died between them after a few sentences.

She was not afraid of him. He seemed a modest, meek fellow,

the sort you might pass on the street without noticing. He paddled in a steady beat, humming a little under his breath. The marina was long gone, and they had passed the familiar beaches. Delilah had not realized how close together everything was in the resort once you got a little distance on it. The kayak was only fifty feet from shore, but she could already see how the coastline cohered into a distinct shape: a sandy, rolling dragon's back, studded with hotel compounds and clumps of lush vegetation. Mysterious smoke rose here and there. Sailboats skimmed along, as brisk and light as windborne dragonflies. Delilah took off her flip-flops and sank her feet in the sea.

"Do you usually talk this little?" she asked over her shoulder.

The rhythm of the paddle paused, then resumed its even stroke.

"Yes," Adam said.

"And do you always follow women around?"

"No."

He laughed, and to her surprise, he threaded his hand through the curtain of her hair and cupped the back of her neck. She closed her eyes. The pressure felt good, and his hand burned like a coal.

Something nosed her foot beneath the surface of the water. A tremor passed through her as she imagined a silvery fish. Then something nosed her again. She opened her eyes and yanked her feet back into the boat, which rocked so wildly she thought it would capsize. There was something in the water where her foot had been. It was a monstrous dark shape, as broad as the kayak itself. For a moment she thought a dead elephant calf had floated over from Africa.

"Don't scream again," said Adam, behind her.

The creature raised a fat head from the water. It was gray all over, as puffy as a child's toy, with tiny black button eyes sunk into the flesh. Its expression was bemused and benign, so much so that Delilah was nearly tempted to touch it, before remembering the terrible stories Marge had spun about hidden teeth on gentle-looking animals. Its nose was broad and whiskery, and two nostrils flared, exhaling a breath of air like a tire bursting. It smelled of something she could not place, earthy and rotten. She squinted into the water, trying to understand its shape, and saw two flat flippers against its chest, just like misshapen hands, and a rotund body that trailed to a strong curved fin at the back. It had breasts. She tried to make them into the flares of a bulky ribcage, but they were unmistakably lobes of flesh that hung separate from the torso and bobbed in the water when it moved.

"What is it?" she breathed.

"That's a manatee," Adam said.

"Does it eat people?"

He scratched his chin unconcernedly, as though he wandered past a few manatees daily in his bathtub.

"Seaweed, mostly," he said. "Pet it."

"Are you nuts?"

He reached past her and scratched the animal behind a feathery hole that might have been its ear. The manatee blinked sleepily, then closed its eyes and exhaled a long sputtering breath. Delilah put her hands over her mouth.

"Stop," she said desperately. "What if it climbs into the kayak?"

Adam grabbed her wrist and forced her to touch the animal's shoulder. She felt warm skin, like the side of a pig that had rolled in the mud. For a moment, she found herself carried right back to her childhood. A field trip to a farm. The bland, dozy face of a sow behind her fence. The manatee blinked lazily and opened its soggy mouth. It seemed to be enjoying the attention. Delilah could not understand how it maneuvered underwater when it was so fat. The skin was rough, layered, like the sole of her foot when she'd been walking without shoes in the summertime.

"I'm not comfortable with this," she said quietly, but she kept touching the creature's side, and Adam gave no sign that he had heard her.

⁓

In the evening, Marge celebrated her relief at Delilah's survival by laying out guilt trips of prize-worthy caliber. Delilah accepted this as her due, but she still managed to manipulate the situation until Marge agreed to head down to the hotel bar for a calming drink. The bar was on the beach, only ten minutes' walk from their room, but Marge balked at the prospect of crossing the sand in the semi-darkness. She had read in a guidebook that the homeless slept there for warmth and in hope of easy tourist prey, and she insisted on rustling up a flashlight and a whistle to blow in case of attack before they could set out. Delilah waited as Marge laboriously stored all her valuables in a pouch beneath her clothes, having read in another guidebook that many Mexican locals were accomplished pickpockets. By the time they were out on the sand, the moon was high—but even that was a source of concern.

"The wild dogs around here go crazy at the moon," Marge said dolefully as they followed the bobbing flashlight beam. "We'll just have to hope it isn't full enough to set them off."

Delilah, who was torn between her usual mixture of frustration and perverse delight, only smiled and said, "Wild dogs? Really?"

"Yes, they roam in packs around the beaches at night," Marge explained. Reading Delilah's silence correctly, she added in a frosty voice, "It's a known phenomenon. I've read about it on more than one website, you know."

The bar was a beacon of red-gold light, spilling a cheerful glow over the sand. Music jangled beneath a roof of stars. The place was clearly made to be dismantled during the day, and Delilah liked its ramshackle aspect: bottles scattered in no particular order on the shelves, heavy countertops broken into segments for easy removal. Three young barmen, as similar as brothers, darted beneath the uncertain light with rags and glasses in their hands. Marge had been particularly scornful about the people that would frequent this place—as though drunk twenty-year-olds had no business at a *bar*, for heaven's sake—but the younger generation seemed to have congregated away from the lights, out on the shadowed sand, where a speaker was hung to broadcast the beat and there was room to dance. Even so, Marge and Delilah had at least fifteen years on anyone else seated on the high stools. The bartenders seemed genuinely, if humorously, delighted to find senior citizens at their watering hole.

"That's the better part of the Latin man, I suppose," Marge roared for all to hear, sipping her martini. "The respect for the mother figure. If we were forty years younger, we'd see the other side all right."

"*You* might," Delilah said roguishly. "I was never as pretty as you."

Marge blushed. The drink was taking effect. "Did you have a good time in the kayak today?" she asked, almost kindly.

"Yes, the weather was lovely, and I saw some funny animals." Delilah was determined to avoid the word *we* at all cost. She had dressed up—white pedal pushers, glittery sandals—just in case Adam might be there.

"Oh?" Marge said. "The sea life around here is fascinating, of course. All of it quite, quite dangerous."

"I saw a manatee, if you can believe that."

"No, no. A shark, perhaps. Waiter?" Marge clicked her fingers for another drink, and a young man rushed over to refill her glass. Delilah was finding the bartenders increasingly difficult to tell apart, clad as they were in identical white aprons, their hair slicked back, their smiles mocking and pleasant.

"Adam *said* it was a manatee," she insisted.

"Adam," Marge sniffed.

"He seemed very sure. It was a big fat thing, like a toy."

"Don't be silly," Marge said. "Manatees are rare in these parts— *extremely* rare. Finding one here would be like winning the lottery. I expect this gentleman friend of yours was just trying to impress you. Making things up."

"It was a manatee," Delilah said stubbornly. "I know it was."

"A porpoise, maybe. Or a fish."

"It had breasts," Delilah said, lowering her voice decorously.

"Did it?" Marge set her drink on the countertop with a bang. "Now *that's* something. Well, I never. It must have had a baby nearby. You just didn't see it. They breast-feed, you know. Like humans." She drummed her fingers on the bar. "I've read about this. Manatees were probably the root of the myth of the mermaid, in the old days."

"You read that?" Delilah murmured, thinking of the packs of wild dogs. "It didn't *look* very human."

"Well, no," Marge said irritably. "But you aren't a sailor who hasn't seen a woman for sixty days at sea." She picked up her drink again, and her face darkened as she observed that a great portion of the liquor had spilled. "Waiter?" she called, snapping her fingers, and a different young man swept over, beaming, to wipe up the spill.

"Ladies okay?" he asked in a thick accent, and Delilah nodded fervently, hearing the words "Can't even *talk* properly" drifting out of Marge's brain as clearly as though they had been spoken. Out on the beach, the music picked up a notch, and the shadowed forms began to gyrate with greater urgency. The black sea shifted ominously, as though it would tolerate all this noise only to a point.

"Will you be seeing that Andy fellow again?" Marge asked.

"Adam? Yes, he's taking me snorkeling tomorrow."

"Huh," Marge said, and it was a measure of the alcohol's effect that she stopped herself there.

Delilah fell silent too. Her thoughts drifted back over the course of the afternoon. Animals had never been her forte. House pets, as a rule, left her cold. She was always the guest at the dinner party who winced when the family dog came barging over, all slobber and grin. Despite her children's earnest entreaties, she had not allowed them to have so much as a gerbil; it was one of the few parental arenas where she had never had trouble holding her ground. The worst, however, had been her occasional encounters with wildlife in its natural habitat. Snakes in the bushes, deer in the park, manatees in the ocean—Delilah would be unsettled for days by such incidents. It had something to do with the unpredictability, the unfamiliarity. These creatures existed on another plane. Their movements were disconcerting, their minds impenetrable. You could stare all day into their dark eyes and never know what they were thinking.

Even now, her stomach turned over at the proximity she had endured to that alien creature. She could still feel the bristle of the manatee's whiskers beneath her hands.

∽

At dawn, the sea was glass-clear. Adam wore red swim trunks and a great quantity of soft fur over his chest and belly. On the sand, a few parents led their small children to the water's edge. The sun had just crested the horizon. It was a blinding coin, a lemon slice, a melting cup of light.

Adam pulled a mask and snorkel from his bag. Delilah spent a few giggly minutes trying to get the rubbery mouth to fit between her teeth. Over her bathing suit, she wore a floppy T-shirt that said *Seattle!* in sparkling letters, so that she would not burn once the sun was high. She felt shy about the pale and doughy aspect of her thighs and restrained herself from making snide comments about her own appearance; she remembered dimly that this was not the best way to earn a man's approval. Adam was as quiet as ever. The few comments he made were all business, explaining that they should wait to put on their flippers until they were actually in the water. Otherwise they would have to do the comic dance of trying to walk on a beach with monstrous feet that caught in the turf and kicked up showers of sand.

Delilah waded with him into the shallows. The water was warm, murky, and somehow jubilant; she had the impression that the ocean was slightly sentient, and that the shallows were proud, even spoiled, because they basked in the sun all day long. She picked her way over rolls of cloudy seaweed, and Adam held out a hand to steady her. A thousand tiny fish gleamed and darted around her feet.

"You all right after yesterday?" he asked.

"Yes," she said, wondering if he meant the manatee or her hangover.

They swam out together. Immediately a black forest of seaweed loomed up, and Delilah was surprised to see that it was rooted—but of course, the plant could not survive by drifting lamely about on the tide. She was fascinated by the fish, orange and yellow, that flitted about like deer in a copse of trees. She forgot to swim on, hovering above a particularly unruly tangle of plants in which an evil minnow lived. This was the sort of wildlife she could cope with: miniaturized and innocuous, like the contents of a snow globe.

Soon Adam tapped her shoulder and beckoned her forward. The bottom began to yawn away with surprising speed. It was ridged like the roof of a mouth. Bigger fish flickered through a fog of rocking sand. Delilah saw a stingray rippling over the sea floor, nearly camouflaged. Fan-like plants waved majestically to her. She had reached the oceanic version of a valley, and the water cleared: less sandy, more open, perhaps forty feet deep. Adam was leading her toward a high plateau, capped with a coral reef.

Then her back began to tingle. It was an odd sensation, as though someone was watching her. Slowly she rotated to look out into the deeper water, remembering what Marge had said about sharks being able to see the electrical impulses that were generated by muscles in motion.

Something was there. Delilah perceived a shadow, far away but massive, hovering near the surface. She squinted, her heart starting up an undisciplined clatter. The creature was not a shark; it looked instead like a shark that had been stepped on. Something bumped her elbow and she almost screamed, but it was only Adam, drifting near. She clung to him. Perhaps the thing would eat him first. He gestured at the animal, as though she had not noticed it—as though she were not paralyzed by the very sight of it. It was as wide as a ship, as thin as a surfboard, and very much alive. She wondered if a boat had run it over. Its wings lifted and fell, like an airplane in a low current, keeping it in place.

Adam, beside her, did not seem frightened. In fact, he nudged her and made his hands into a camera shape. She almost hit him. The creature dipped slightly, and she saw that it was a ray, but a humongous one. It had to be twenty feet across, at least. The wings were chunky, like slabs of plaster, rather than silky and billowing. There was a gash in its front that could have been a mouth. Its back was splashed with black and white. It beat its mammoth wings and dipped toward the bottom. Delilah cried out into her mouthpiece as the ray swept toward her.

But then it rose, like a kite in strong wind. She saw its belly, white and vast. It had halved the distance to her, but it was vertical now and clearly did not plan to come closer. There were pock-marks and shadows on its gut, a great wealth of muscle. It flapped its wings again. The pulse of water carried her hair off her shoulders. Delilah wondered if it could possibly be intending to leave the sea—to jump, as whales did in documentaries? It did not slow its pace; in fact it seemed to be accelerating as it swept toward the sparkling underside of the waves.

Before her eyes, the ray ripped the surface of the sea apart and vanished. Shards of sunlight ricocheted around the sandy floor. Delilah yanked her torso out of the water, kicking wildly to stay afloat, and tore her mask off. The creature was airborne now, printed as big as a pterodactyl against the sky. The sun shimmered on its back. She saw the whippy tail and the deep, painful-looking fissures where its wings separated from its body. It leveled out, making itself horizontal. She would not have been surprised to see it flap its wings again and lift into the air. Instead it was falling.

Adam surfaced next to her and jerked his mask up to his hairline. He was beaming all over his face. She felt his hand grab hers under the water. The ray was about to belly flop. Delilah thought it would smash like a snowball dropped on a flat of ice. She thought it would raise a tidal wave and drown them both.

"Adam," she breathed. He clapped his hands over her ears. The creature landed like thunder.

∽

Afterwards she napped. This time, she did not dream of Lew. Instead, it was the manatee that loomed up in front of her as she swam. Warm water. A salty tang in the throat. Delilah tried to wake; she was not happy there, floating in the briny blue, with that creature hovering so near, nudging her with its snout. The waves jiggled her to and fro. The sun was blinding. The manatee scraped her shoulder with its whiskers. Delilah was not exactly frightened; instead, to her surprise, she found herself merely annoyed. There was something she had to do, and if the manatee would only leave her alone, she would be able to remember what it was. Something about a pack of matches. Something about a letter. She kicked her feet. She attempted to launch into the breaststroke. But the manatee moved to block her, glaring into her eyes.

When she woke, in the fuddled state between clarity and dreaming, it suddenly seemed quite extraordinary that she should have encountered both a manatee and a manta ray—two such rare and wild animals—during her brief time in Playa del Carmen. These were the sort of beasts usually relegated to shows that specialized in vanishing species; they were not to be found each time a know-nothing tourist paddled out from the pier of a glitzy hotel. Days ago, on her welcome-to-the-resort tour, the guide had actually warned her about this. Marge had been present as well, scribbling in her notebook. As the guide had led them past the marina, he had pointed out the canoes and snorkeling gear, then explained that the ocean was very clear, very nice, but he did not want them to be disappointed by what they might encounter out there. Clownfish, yes. Anemones, yes. But not blue whales, he had said, with a light laugh. Sometimes the tourists, especially Americans, expected to see giant squid or great white sharks. They came to the hotel wanting miracles. But such things were just not possible.

Delilah, of course, had been pleased to hear this. Now she turned her pillow to the cooler side. Her senses came into focus slowly, returning piece by piece from the synesthetic jumble of sleep, where smells were tumbled into colors, into sounds.

In the evening she called her children. Marge had gone out to swim laps in the pool. Delilah settled herself by the window in a wicker armchair. She had a glass of lemonade at her elbow, and the warm air poured over her chest and throat. She tried Chris first, but of course she only got his voice-mail, one of his endless incomprehensible messages, his baritone speaking in muffled, intermittent bursts over a stumbling beat and eerie tune. She supposed this was the "electronic music" he had begun to create lately, to her dismay. Next she dialed Jenny, who answered on the fifth ring, sounding breathless and elated.

"*Ma*," she said. "I was wondering if you were still alive. How are things?"

"Good, really good," Delilah said, feeling a little tearful, as she always did when it had been a long time since she spoke with her children. "You wouldn't *believe* this weather."

"Is old Marge giving you any trouble?"

"No, she's been fine," Delilah said, glancing at Marge's pristine bedspread. In fact, Marge had fallen in with a crew of lunatic bird-watchers, Americans who had come to Mexico for the sake of the pelicans and herons. They had spent the day traipsing about with binoculars and a collection of reference books; Marge had come home with thrilling tales of seafowl glimpsed at sixty yards.

On the other end of the line there was a burst of static. Delilah was used to this. Her daughter was too restless to sit quietly during conversations, but had to walk, shift position, and periodically drop the phone on the floor.

"Well," Jenny said, "you tell her that this is your first vacation ever, and if she ruins it, I'll kill her." There was another eruption of static. "Have you got a tan? Are you drinking every night? Have you met any guys?"

"I went kayaking," Delilah said, sipping her lemonade. "That was yesterday, and I saw a manatee. Today I went snorkeling and saw a manta ray. I'm sure it was a manta ray. I looked it up."

Jenny roared with laughter. "Oh, perfect, Ma, beautiful. Of *course* you did. But seriously, have you been near the water at all? You really ought to try it, you know. Just once, anyway. It's very warm in that part of the world."

∾

The sun had barely risen when Adam knocked on the door of the bungalow. Delilah came coolly to meet him, pleased that she was already showered and dressed. He explained politely that he would like to take her out again, but that it would be a longer trip this time, because he wanted her to try parasailing. This, evidently, was an activity that involved being suspended in the air and dragged after a boat; he wanted her to experience it before they parted. Delilah began to explain, equally politely, that her system had already been overloaded by what she had experienced during her stay in Playa del Carmen. She needed a bit of time to recover. She was reluctant, too, to leave Marge alone for another day. Marge had asked her to accompany the bird-watching party that afternoon, and she felt that it would be politic to accept.

But then she changed her mind. She remembered Marge's incredulous expression when she had heard about the manatee; she remembered Jenny's light, unbelieving laughter. Setting her jaw, Delilah gathered up her purse, hat, and flip-flops, and closed the door firmly behind her.

An hour later, in a roaring tide of wind, she clutched her sunhat to her head as the speedboat shuddered beneath her. Adam stood with his elbows on the railing. On the boat with them was a duo Delilah found hilarious: a rich businessman and his topless trophy wife. The deck was shabby, with slabs of flooring that had come up and been nailed inexpertly back down. A few chairs, bolted to the floor, swiveled as the boat moved. The prow was manned by two Mexican boys who looked like members of some glittering mafia—gold chains, black sunglasses, and amber tans.

Delilah's eyes watered in the wind. She glanced occasionally at the black harnesses on the deck beside her—a flat of wood, like the seat of a swing, attached to a complex web of rigging. Her thoughts drifted back to Marge, who was no doubt standing comfortably on dry land, peering at the ocean from a safe distance, through binoculars. The boat nosed to the left, and Delilah staggered against Adam. The topless lady, a dishwater blond with no chin, imitated the crewmen's speech in a murmur—"*Está bien*; I can do that, *bueno*." Her husband ignored her altogether, gazing out at the expanse of sea as though appraising its possibilities.

"I feel like I'm on a movie set," Delilah hissed to Adam. "I think I'm too old to have topless women on my boat."

"Why do you think they're so happy?" Adam indicated the two crewmen, who were now sharing a cigarette in silence, too cool to speak even to each other.

"I'm not going up in the air, you know. I've made up my mind."

"Sure," he said. "You can watch me and wave."

The boat ground to a halt. The blond stumbled against the railing, and her hand rose instinctively to protect her flying cleavage. The two crewmen strode to the aft deck, their faces blank behind their sunglasses. Delilah gasped as one of them gripped her shoulders and began buckling her into a harness. She found herself unceremoniously hoisted up on the bulwark, still clutching her hat. The crewman grabbed her waist and nuzzled her buttocks onto the plank of wood.

"Wait a minute," Delilah cried, as the boat rumbled into life. "Just hang on!"

A wave swept under the hull, and her stomach lurched. Adam was crammed in beside her on the swing. Delilah grabbed the rope desperately as the speedboat, along with the whole blue curtain of the ocean, fell away beneath her. The glide was so smooth she did not seem to be moving at all; the boat got smaller, and the world rocked away from her on its axis, but she stayed where she was on the plank of wood with Adam at her side.

The gauzy parachute filled with sunlight. One flip-flop swung off her toes and then fell, landing with a delicate splash. They were still climbing. The boat was a pale triangle. The golden coastline of Mexico was now dwarfed by the red expanse of the continent behind it. The sea swept unbroken to the edge of the horizon. A windsurfer fell in slow motion, tipped by the breeze, and his sail flapped open across the water like a butterfly wing.

Far below, the speedboat cut to the left, and the rope arced lazily after it. The swing sank slightly until the slack caught, and then the wind increased wildly around them. Adam took Delilah's hand.

The boat was heading into deeper water. From this height, the sea was a gauzy skin over vast blue depths; Delilah could see where the rocky ground began its underwater decline, the coastal plateau giving way to an inky void. Fish flashed like jewels, and she realized they must be large fish indeed to be visible at this height. She shivered. The water broke, foamy and clouded, against islands of coral and reef. The wind was cool, flower-scented.

"Look there," Adam said, pointing.

Delilah followed his finger to a round rock, perfectly oval, like a coin. She squinted in confusion—it appeared to be moving above the blue slabs beneath it. It was certainly moving. She could see now what she'd mistaken for darting fish: the vast flippers and reaching head of a sea turtle. At this distance it looked like a pet in a bathtub, but she was not fooled. The thing was bigger than she was.

The speedboat whined at the end of its trailing leash. The turtle was far enough from the boat that Delilah wondered if it would be visible to the people on board. Probably not. Once again, it appeared that she would be the sole witness to something extraordinary. A distant bell rang at the back of her mind. It seemed odd to her that no one else, in all of Mexico—in the whole world—could verify what she and Adam had experienced over the past few days. Nobody else had petted the manatee. Nobody else had swum with the manta ray. Delilah bit her lip, frowning. But she had no time, just now, to contemplate the matter. There was too much to take in. The turtle broke the surface. Its head came out of the water, ancient and dark. She caught a glimpse of charcoal eyes. Waves lapped around the moving island of its shell.

Then the boat cut its motor beneath them. The rope went limp, and they began to drift rapidly downward.

"This is normal," Adam said quickly. "They dip you—just your feet. They'll start the engine up again as soon as we touch the water."

Delilah nodded. She was falling, the wind lifting her dress around her knees. The turtle swelled like a sponge in a sink. It exhaled a glittering mist with a hoarse old man's cough. Her shadow pooled over its back, dappling the swirls of blue and yellow. As she sank toward it, the turtle swam beneath her, as eager as a dog kicking out toward a thrown stick. The eyes were full of sleepy underwater thinking. The shell was plated like glass, as luminous as mother-of-pearl. The sea swept up toward Delilah's feet, and she twisted around to see the turtle's sinewy neck and the sagging skin of its shoulders. It coughed a booming spray and dived. Two waves collided, closing over it, and suddenly it was a rock again, a monstrous oval stone with a dream of legs and arms. It passed directly beneath her as her feet touched the sea.

Afterward, she would find herself unable to say just what possessed her in that moment. The instinct came over her with all the force of an edict from heaven. She had the impression of a signal, of something she had been waiting for—waiting, perhaps, over months and years. Without pause, Delilah undid the buckles on her harness and fell out of the swing.

The ocean received her like an open mouth. Her ears were full of the smack of her own descent, and her hands stung where she had tried to catch herself on the water's surface. She opened her eyes, burning against the salt, and saw the blue-green shell of the turtle looming under her like the back of a car. She struck out with both feet and kicked its hide, stunned by the solidity of it; she budged it no more than a puppy running full-tilt into the legs of its owner. The turtle moved with astonishing speed. Its flippers were visible on either side, churning water.

Delilah reached toward its luminous back. Her dress fanned out around her, and coils of her own hair drifted before her eyes. Beneath her scrabbling fingers, the shell felt like cold cobblestone, the crusted hull of a sailboat. Her hands slipped. She clawed frantically to keep her hold, but the turtle rolled beneath her. The wash of its flippers lifted her up. She could not breathe.

She let go. The turtle plunged away from her. Her lungs were bursting, and Marge's face appeared in her mind, clucking her tongue in resigned shame. Delilah kicked with aching legs until the open air broke against her face.

"Over there!" someone screamed. Adam was paddling toward her, one arm slung over the wood plank. The silken parachute had fainted into the ocean. Delilah peered into the blue depths, shaking now, appalled by what she had done. The turtle had vanished, a blur against deeper blue. Adam's sunglasses were askew, his shirt soaked. His expression was unfathomable as held out a hand for her. The speedboat was grinding toward them, none too quickly. One of the crewmen leaned lazily over the prow, smoking a cigarette and shaking his head. Delilah clutched at the slippery wood and felt Adam grab her around the waist, steadying her. She was chilled to the bone. Her arthritis was on fire. She buried her face in Adam's shoulder and did not look up, even when strong hands gripped her torso and hoisted her into the air.

☙

He said he would come for her that evening and take her out to dinner—but he never turned up. Delilah mooned around the bungalow until nightfall, as heartsick and hopeful as a teenager. In the morning she feigned a stomachache to justify a few more hours' anxious waiting. Marge went shopping with her new bird-watching buddies, returning gleefully with a dozen wispy, identical scarves and a life-size wooden parrot. Delilah spent the day flipping through channels on the snowy television screen, unable to follow the plot of any of the familiar American shows, dubbed now into Spanish. She went to bed under a black cloud.

By the following morning, to her own chagrin, she was forced to admit that she had been rejected. Adam appeared to have vanished into thin air. It stung more than it should have, their acquaintance being so brief. Over the years, Delilah had learned that men could be maddeningly inscrutable. Throughout her unsatisfactory forays into the dating scene, she had discovered that much. Some men were married but claimed to be single; some were divorced but claimed to still love their ex-wives. Some hung around interminably after being tactfully rejected, and some—like Adam—disappeared without warning. This time, however, she was plagued by echoes, a welter of old feelings. In Adam's company, she had, however momentarily, been able to forget what had brought her to Mexico in the first place. She had not thought about Lew's letters, about what it meant that she had burned them all finally, ceremoniously, removing them forever from the world. For a few bright, shining days, she had shaken off the sensation of loss that had characterized most of her adult life.

As she trailed dourly down to the marina—Marge had booked them on a glass-bottomed boat tour of the local reefs—Delilah tried to convince herself that there was a certain relief in Adam's desertion, a sense of returning to the land of the living: a sane and sunlit realm, without manatees, giant turtles, or men in Hawaiian shirts. Marge chattered about the coral reef they would likely encounter, and something about a green flash; the boat was meant to stay on the water all day, treating the passengers to an emerald sunset. Delilah paid no attention. She permitted herself the luxury of replaying every memory of Adam she could dredge up. The gray glint of his hair in the light. The gravelly rumble of his laugh. The strange look of triumph on his face when she had thrown herself into the sea.

The trip offered little to awaken her from her stupor. At her side, Marge was dressed in a hilarious plethora of safety gear, everything from a life vest to a special kind of watch, which sent out an electronic signal that was meant to deter sharks from attacking. This was the only way she would allow herself to venture away from the security of the shore. In her usual frenzy, she took pictures of absolutely everything: passing seagulls, Delilah's feet, eight thousand snaps of blue water with some distant shape that might have been a fish. The guide gestured expansively as he pointed out areas of interest. The ship was laden with tourists, *ooh*ing at the hull of a sunken rowboat, a flounder poking its funny head through the sand, a bundle of kelp bobbing on the current. The boat did indeed have a glass bottom. Delilah passed the time by squinting

THE LAST ANIMAL

into the sea. For a while there were bright reefs to observe, but soon the water was deep enough that she could see nothing but swirling blue.

By sunset, the tour had reached waves so big that they almost didn't register, drifting beneath the boat like mountainsides. Mexico was a black stain on the horizon. The guide dropped his voice to an impressive whisper, explaining that these were ideal conditions for observing the green flash, a phenomenon that only occurred on the ocean. Marge regaled everyone with a long explanation of light waves and atmospheric inversions. The sun hung weak and dreamlike in the western sky. Soon it would set, with no clouds to block the view, a supernova of red and gold, and some sort of green flare in the middle. Delilah couldn't quite picture it.

Marge got the camera ready. The couples on the tour snuggled closer together. The guide held up an expectant finger. Delilah glanced down and noticed that her purse had fallen into the puddle of water sloshing around in the bottom of the boat. Aggrieved, she picked it up, and through the glass window in the hull she saw a dark flicker on the sea.

No one else was paying attention. Delilah held her breath, scarcely able to believe her eyes. A black shape—massive, far larger than the boat itself—was passing beneath them. She caught the outline of a giant fin, and understood that it must be a whale, perhaps a blue whale, the variety her daughter Jenny had once claimed to see from an airplane.

The other passengers on the boat began to clamor and exclaim, pointing at the horizon line.

"Keep your eyes on that sunset!" the guide announced. "Any minute now—"

The whale kept moving. Its body seemed endless. As Delilah's eyes adjusted to the gloom, she made out the crease of the enormous spine. The boat lifted up on a swell, and she realized that the whale must be doing it, its bulk large enough to displace the sea around it. There were white scars cut into the flesh. The animal's back glided smoothly into a bottleneck, and the tail appeared, as broad as the sail of a ship. The whale seemed to be angling itself in the water, preparing to dive into the abyss below.

"There!" the guide shouted. "The green flash."

Delilah cried out. A second shape was present in the water—she was almost certain. It looked like a human form, clinging to the last rim of the tail. Delilah barely had time to comprehend what she was seeing when the whale plunged with remarkable speed. The man's figure, still clutching the tail's edge, trailed away like smoke. He went down into the darkness and did not rise.

"Well!" Marge said triumphantly, setting her camera down with a thump. "*That* was certainly something to see."

For a moment, Delilah sat stunned. Then she turned to her friend, one hand reaching. There was still a chance for her to get verification. Even now, Marge might be able to catch a glimpse of the silhouettes against the sea. This time, Delilah could confirm what she had seen—an objective witness at last.

She opened her mouth to ask, then closed it again. Slowly, she laid her hands back in her lap. On the whole, she preferred to remain in the realm of mystery and miracles. In the end, she preferred not to know.

## ACKNOWLEDGMENTS

This collection would not have been possible without many, many people—friends, teachers, well-wishers, and colleagues. Thanks to Scott, my one and only. Thanks to my parents, who have always set the standard when it comes to unconditional love. Thanks to my wise and wonderful agent, Laura Langlie. Thanks to my terrific editor, Dan Smetanka, and all the amazing folks at Counterpoint Press. Thanks to my generous grandfather, my brilliant brother, and my loving and supportive in-laws. Thanks to Patsy, who lent me her view, and Alexis, my long-distance lifeline. Thanks to my family, both the one I was born into and the one I have acquired along the way.

# ABOUT THE AUTHOR

ABBY GENI is a graduate of Oberlin College and the Iowa Writers' Workshop, as well as the recipient of an Iowa Fellowship. "Captivity" won first place in the *Glimmer Train* Fiction Open and was listed as a distinguished story in *The Best American Short Stories* in 2010; it was also selected for inclusion in *New Stories from the Midwest*, published by Ohio University Press. "Silence" won first place in the Chautauqua Contest and was published by that literary journal. "Dharma at the Gate" has been published in *Glimmer Train*; "Landscaping" has been published in *Confrontation*; and "Terror Birds" has been published by the *Indiana Review*. "Fire Blight" appeared in *The Fourth River*, and "The Girls of Apache Bryn Mawr" was published by *Camera Obscura*. "Isaiah on Sunday" was published by *Iron Horse Literary Review*, and "In the Spirit Room" was published by *Crab Orchard Review*. Her stories have also received honorable mentions in the Kate Braverman Short Story Prize and in *Glimmer Train*'s Very Short Fiction Competition. She lives in Chicago, where she is at work on a novel.